CW01468122

A
MAN
WHO
SEEMED
REAL

A story of love, lies, fear and kindness

Elizabeth Tebby Germaine

This paperback edition published in 2023

The right of Elizabeth Tebby Germaine to be identified
as the Author of the Work has been asserted by her in
accordance with the Copyright, Designs and Patents Act
1988

All rights reserved. No part of this publication may be
reproduced, stored in a retrieval system, or transmitted by
any form, by any means, without the prior written
permission of the publisher, nor be otherwise circulated
in any form of binding or cover other than that in which
it is published and without a similar condition being
imposed on the subsequent purchaser.

A CIP catalogue record for this title is available from the
British Library

ISBN: 978-1-7384225-0-0

Imprint   E J Lewis

This is my simple religion. There is no need for temples; no need for complicated philosophy. Our own brain, our own heart is our temple; the philosophy is kindness.

Tenzin Gyatso 14th Dalai Lama

CONTENTS

1 JULY

At Jonathan's house

Jonathan turned the car into the short drive where uneven shrubs straggled over worn bumpy gravel and patches of brown grass, and parked in front of the old family home, a handsome, detached Victorian villa in an old-fashioned tree lined street with pretentious steps up to the front door and a porch with stained glass windows. His mother was dead and the house was his. But he was never free of disturbing memories of his recent life, during the weeks of guilt and confusion about leaving the priesthood he had met a young girl with striking psychic abilities, and he wanted her desperately. But after a brief time together she had left him, confused after hearing about his activities in the village and probably reading misleading newspaper reports.

Now the house was something solid, tangible, here he could have a rest and he was pleased with his powerful new car. When he had turned off the motorway and was approaching the town there was the odd thought that he could just have kept driving, following an unknown road to some entirely new and unspecified destination. Was there anywhere he could get relief from this mental turmoil?

He couldn't believe that Pam had gone, it didn't make sense, they belonged together. He believed she felt that too, but she was haunted by the fact that he had once spoken with the homeless man who had ended up attacking and killing her brother on the common. What was going to happen now? Where had she gone? If she did want to get in touch how would she find him? All he could do was write letters to her family house in Greybrothers Road and keep hoping that one day she would come back and find them. Perhaps the tenants would have an email address?

Now everything he had in the world had been reduced to a carload of bags and boxes and suitcases. He began dragging them out of the car, walking to and fro to the front door and dumping them on the grubby driveway. Then he put the key in the lock.

He stood in the porch and was shocked see the inner door was open and he heard a radio on in the kitchen. By the bookcase in the hall there were two pairs of untidy shoes next to several empty wine bottles and a small bag of rubbish, and a jacket had been flung across the banisters.

'Jonathan!'

'Jeremy!'

The cousins stared at each other across the large hall. Similar high foreheads and pale brown hair, Jonathan tall and slim and Jeremy shorter and heavier.

'What on earth are you doing here Jeremy?'

'Well – I thought you knew. I wrote you a letter. Aunt Angelica gave me a key months ago – she said…'

'No, I got no letter. But I've been moving about. Are you here for the funeral?'

'She gave me a key, I'm living here.'

'*Living here*? No not – not possible. I'm probably going to sell it.'

'I… er… went to see her a few times in the nursing home. You knew that didn't you. You hardly went to see her.'

Jonathan turned away and began bringing in boxes and bags and piling them up in the hall. He glanced at his cousin. 'I had my reasons – I don't need to explain them to you.'

'She was sad, she missed you.'

'Oh no – she hasn't put a sensible sentence together for months and you know it.'

'Oh but that's where you're wrong Jonathan. She was kind to me…. after the accident.'

'Yes, well of course I'm very, very sorry about the accident and Pauline and Petra's deaths of course I'm terribly sorry about it. By the way I would have come to their funerals if I'd known about them.'

'I wasn't functioning really, I'm still not well, I didn't really stay in touch with anyone. Natasha's gone, I don't know where. She got in with a tricky crowd and stopped talking to me much. And for that matter, going back to last year, I would have come to Annabelle's funeral if you'd asked me.'

Jonathan went outside again and brought in more cases and bags. A box broke open and books spilled out onto the floor and he bent down and arranged them in a pile glancing at their titles.

'So, you've left that village then Jonathan? Too ashamed to stay I presume?'

Jonathan sat down on the stairs still holding a book in his hand and stretched out his long legs between piles of cases and bags. 'I will not be drawn into this Jeremy. I came here to clear up and sell the house. To look calmly at my early life, to take a bit of time – to recuperate.'

'Well - I need to be here and I'm…'

'Don't be ridiculous. *You do not need to be here!* You have a house of your own to live in. Your precious aunt has gone now.'

'Don't call her that. And I don't.'

'Don't?'

'Don't have a house of my own.'

'What?'

'Had to sell. Things went downhill you see. Not my fault. Since the accident Jonathan I… you must understand, I couldn't cope, I …'

'Of course it was a shock, terrible, terrible. Of course.'

'You don't understand …I've lost everything. Natasha

went off somewhere …'

They stared at each other.

'Look Jeremy, I know… I know what that guilt can be like. When Annabelle got ill so suddenly I…'

'No, you don't!' Jeremy shouted. 'You and your bloody religious claptrap… Take it on, believe it all, a priest one minute and then – ok – now we don't believe after all, let's leave it all behind, never mind who gets trampled on in the way, never mind who…'

'Stop this.' Jonathan spoke quietly. 'You have no right, you have no idea what this has been. Stop making shallow judgements.'

'Oh. I see. Exclusive rights to the moral high ground as well. I know what I read in the papers. And what about the will, huh! Bet you don't know about that.'

'Whatever it is, it doesn't mean you can live here. You need to sort things out. Of course I'm very sorry for your terrible loss.'

'Hmm!'

Jonathan stood up. 'Jeremy I'm not getting drawn into this. You must have known I'd be back. Her funeral's on Friday, after that you need to be gone from here.' He placed a book on top of a pile and made his way through the boxes and suitcases and opened the front door. It was a heavy, hot afternoon, he would go for a bit of a walk into town, it would be good to stretch his legs after the long drive. Things felt odd and confusing, and he stood with his hand on the door handle.

'Jeremy, I'll say this once,' he began, 'I'm not going to be drawn into any silly squabble you want to invent. I am not going to defend my recent behaviour in the village or anywhere else. I am not going to tell you my plans, I have had reasons for everything I've done and a great deal of thinking has gone into my recent very painful decisions. If I tried to explain them to you no doubt you would take further opportunities to mock or insult me. As for losing Pauline and Petra in the car accident, well of course it was the most awful thing, and I can't possibly know how you feel and…'

4

'You're damn right about that!'

'And obviously you have guilt mixed in with it all. You survived without a scratch, and Natasha too. I am deeply sorry about all this, but it doesn't alter the fact that I have a right to live peacefully in my own house, and decide things in my own time …'

'It's not your own house!'

Jonathan hesitated. 'It's best if I don't comment on this right now.'

'Hmm!'

'I'm asking you politely to stop all this. It doesn't achieve anything. There are things in the past…'

'You bet there are!'

'… unresolved family things … your mind is made up and I haven't got the energy to try and talk some sense into you.'

'Cheek! You pompous bastard.'

Jonathan let himself out of the front door and closed it quietly.

When he returned an hour later the garage was open and empty apart from pots of paint and brushes and various tools on the shelves. Jeremy must have been parking his car in here. This was mildly irritating. But if he was out Jonathan would have some precious moments of peace and quiet and he let himself into the house.

He stood in the untidy hall. This was the moment he had felt robbed of earlier and he listened to the echoes in his mind and felt the pain from all those childhood years - but it was mild and hazy. A sad, neglected house with its threadbare carpets and grubby curtains where a closer look would reveal tasteless reproduction furniture, bookshelves full of detective novels, cookery books and travel brochures and faded, nondescript paintings on the walls. He saw his mother sitting on the sofa or standing at the kitchen sink, or quietly polishing a table, or hoovering. She was always just turning her head to look at him. And what was in that look, irritation, disapproval, impatience, disappointment? He wandered through the silent rooms choosing not to listen to what she was saying. Upstairs at the back of the landing in the room where Jeremy had been sleeping the door was open and the bed unmade, with piles of clothes and shoes lying on every surface.

He came down to the kitchen and looked around and made sandwiches and tea and carried a tray out into the sunbaked garden. There were some old garden chairs and on the grubby table were a couple of detective novels, an unwashed dinner plate and several empty wine bottles.

He dozed in the heat. Come back Pamela, please come back. I need you, we belong together. You know that too. He sat remembering the first time he had seen her, she had fallen asleep on his sofa at the vicarage, having collapsed at his front door, exhausted after a broken night and the shock of being told her brother had been found dead on the common. He remembered how she looked at him when he had to tell her he had previously met and spoken with the man who had done this. She had turned away, puzzled. He relived the moment when they had stood together and looked at the flowers and cards propped up against the tree where it had happened - the feel of her slim hand in his. He held her in his heart, she was safe in there. Always. Pamela, please come back to me. You must.

He opened his eyes. The large garden was neglected, the grass was long and ugly weeds had taken hold. Tangles of rose bushes still heavy with pink and yellow flowers stood amongst overgrown shrubs. Suddenly he jumped up and rushed over to the garden shed and wrenched open the door. He pulled out a garden fork and a pile of tools clattered to the ground. He ran to the rose bushes. He thrust the metal down into the hard dry earth. While he hacked at the soil and tugged at the stems odd words from the bible mocked in his mind. *Some seed fell among thistles and the thistles grew up and choked it.* Back in the shed he found thick gloves to protect his hands - his mother's gloves. He was well below the roots now and the bush toppled to one side. Petals flew off the flowers and scattered. He smashed at them with the fork. *Others have only parables, so that they may look but see nothing, hear but understand nothing.* He dug again. He fetched a garden spade. He grabbed tendrils of greenery and pulled them free. Large patches of a vivid, green, flat, spiky plant intruded everywhere, its roots like brown worms, curling, bullying their way. Some shrubs had shallow roots and he piled them upon each other, throwing them down. *Blessed are you who are who are in need, the kingdom of God is yours.* The kingdom of God is in Syria. The kingdom of God is in Aleppo. *Blessed are you who now go hungry, blessed are you who weep, blessed are you when men hate you.*

He took hold of endless clumps of clematis that had climbed in all directions, over the fence and the evergreen bushes and branches of the apple tree. Where did they begin and where did they end? This plant was a monster, its unforgiving, tangled stems intertwined themselves around everything in their path. *Do not be afraid, from now on you will be catchers of men. Do not be afraid!... They wanted to hurl him over the edge, they took him to the brow of the hill, meaning to hurl him over the edge. But Jesus walked free and went away.*

He bent to the rockery and clutched heavy ornamental stones and flung them into the pile of plants. *John said that God can make children for Abraham out of these stones here... Already the axe is laid to the roots of the trees, and every tree that fails to produce good fruit is cut down and thrown on the fire.*

He started on the flowers in the border, pulling and clutching the stalks, smelling the sap and the sweet fragrance, some stems broke off leaving roots behind. He dug and dug and piled up the earth. He approached the apple tree and began to beat the branches with the spade. Some fruit fell on the paving stones, some on the grass. A branch snapped and hung crookedly. *Take care how you listen. For the man who has will be given more, and the man who has not will forfeit even what he thinks he has.* There will be no seeds in this garden, no plants, no roses, no wallflowers. No rockeries and borders and fruit trees. It will be a desert, a barren place with no life in it, no purpose, no meaning. Jonathan went on striking the fruit that remained on the tree, the branches shook and apples fell heavily onto the overgrown grass.

Jeremy came back into the house carrying bags of carefully selected groceries, he put them on the floor in the hall and closed the front door. He came into the kitchen and glanced out of the window at the back of the house. Jonathan was hacking at an ornamental tree with a pickaxe, there were piles of plants and bushes and soil everywhere and he was shouting something.

Jeremy rushed outside. 'Jonathan!'

Jonathan paused for a moment and then attacked the slender trunk with renewed energy. It broke in two. He took the upper branches and snapped one in his hands and flung it on a pile of bushes.

'Jonathan what are you doing!'

Jonathan paused again, picked up an apple, took aim and threw it straight at Jeremy.

'Jonathan, what the …'

More apples were coming, raining on him, hitting his face. 'Stop! Stop it. You are insane!'

'Oh no Jeremy, oh no. Never more sane I assure you. Take that!'

'Ouch! Look Jonathan, let's…'

'I never had a snowball fight in this garden. I never had a water fight. I never had an apple fight. But how about this?' He bent again. 'Now you – that's a different matter huh! Darling Jeremy and his cute Aunty Angelica. Oh, so happy you two were.'

'Stop it! You're doing me an injury, stop it! Ouch!'

'Go on then! Join in!' Jonathan picked up the garden spade and started beating the tree again. Apples thudded on the ground. 'Just doing some gardening Jeremy. Something you've obviously neglected since you've been living here. Living here! Don't make me laugh. Living! Crawling in your

alcoholic slime more like. Don't know a weed from a fruit tree eh! Well, you don't need to know, there won't be any.'
    'For Christ's sake, what's the bloody point of...'
    'Absolutely! My thoughts entirely dear boy. What's the point of weeding, pruning, mowing, tidying up, collecting fruit, planting bloody flowers and all that! No need. All gone.' Jonathan kicked at the untidy pile of bushes and threw down the garden spade. He came up to his cousin and stared down at his face. 'No need to worry dear boy, not your problem. Got a bruise on your face? I'm so sorry. I'm so, so sorry! But darling Aunty Angelica won't notice. Thank God the funeral is soon. Lay her to rest. Rest in Peace. Let's hope we can all REST IN PEACE. Ha ha! After that you can pack your bags. Now leave me alone!' He pushed past, staggered into the house and slammed the back door.

2   SEPTEMBER
Belinda

It was a small bare room in the psychiatric hospital and the sun shone through the clean, faded, floral curtains at the windows. Belinda sat up on the bed. She was wearing a loose gown and a jug of water, and a plastic cup stood on the locker which was empty inside. She stumbled to the door. It was locked. She hammered on it.
    'My rucksack! Give me my rucksack! Help!' She shouted and shouted. After a few minutes the door was unlocked and a nurse came in. 'Hello. It's Belinda isn't it? How are you feeling?'
    'How do you know my name! You're not sending me back home are you? I won't go, I won't go, I'll fight you. Where have you taken my rucksack, I need it back, I need it.'
    'No, we aren't sending you back home. You're in ... a hospital for a little while. Till you feel a bit better.'
    'Where's my rucksack! I need to see it, it mustn't get lost. My name is on the scroll of the living, I'm not going to die, I deserve to live.'

The nurse took hold of both her arms. 'It's alright, Belinda, it's alright. We've got all your stuff in your bag. It's all safe.'

'Well give it back to me! You have no right to take it away.'

'We want you to be safe Belinda, so we've got it safe for you.'

'I need to write some more, give it back to me.' Belinda sobbed, 'I need to... understand... I'm not what you think I am, I'm not! He was following me.'

'Who was? You can tell me.' The nurse spoke gently and led Belinda to the chair by the bed and sat her down and perched on the edge of the bed.

'The angel of wrath. He was coming to get me because I can't be forgiven. He was going to pour the plagues on to me and I would die and there was no place for me, I was not a chosen one. Oh it's all such a muddle. I was running away from him and there were these trees and I wanted to fly up into their branches, and then he wouldn't see me, but he kept on following me and he saw me going under the bridge and he waited until I fell asleep and then ...'

'What happened then Belinda?'

'He was a thief in the night and he stole my money. But it wasn't my money I stole it too.'

'But he didn't steal your ... your diaries?'

'No, I... but who are you? Where am I? Why did you lock me in? Am I being punished now?'

'No, not punished. We're trying ...'

'You are punishing me!' Belinda jumped out of the chair and ran to the door and pushed it open. She went out into the corridor and leaned on the wall. 'Which way?' she sobbed, 'Which way to go. There's no one to show me the way. Is he here, waiting to follow me again? But he's got my money. He can't have my notebooks, he can't have my story. That belongs to me. It's mine. Where's my rucksack, give it back!'

The nurse came up behind her. 'Belinda, my name is Gabrielle. I'm here to get to know you a bit.'

'So you are an angel too!' Belinda shrieked, 'Why can't you leave me alone! You're pretending to be a good angel, I've heard about you. You come and tell Mary a story, but she was a simple girl, a simple country girl and she believed you, but what you told her was fantastic and unbelievable. UNBELIEVABLE!' she screamed, 'Go away and leave me be! I don't want your lies.' She started to walk shakily down the corridor but another nurse appeared and with Gabrielle they took both her arms and she nearly fell.

'I'm not an angel,' said Gabrielle, 'I'm a nurse and I'm here to help you till you feel better. Now come back in here and have a bit of a rest.'

'No!' Belinda struggled but they were strong and they almost lifted her back into the room and laid her on the bed. Gabrielle held her down while the other one fetched a trolley and came back and gave her an injection in her thigh. Then she pulled the hospital gown down again in a business-like way. Belinda went on screaming. 'You have no right to do this! Give me my things back. Stop telling me lies and let me go. Stop… all lies, he's… following… leave me alone and give me my rucksack, I need to have it….' She became drowsy as the nurses watched. 'That'll teach her,' said the second one, arranging her equipment on the trolley, 'Accusing us of lying indeed. What have you been saying to her Gabe?'

'I was just trying to get through, make a start,' said Gabrielle, 'There's no need to be so unpleasant. We could have tried talking a bit longer.'

'Waste of time. There are other people to see, so get on with it.'

As Belinda fell into a drugged sleep, they wheeled the trolley out of the door and locked it behind them.

3 SEPTEMBER
The good angel

'No! I won't look at him, I won't talk to him!' Belinda shielded her face and Nurse Gabrielle sat beside her and put her hand on her arm. 'You don't have to Belinda, just talk to me. You remember me don't you?'

'You're the good angel. But you went away and then they took me into hell. It's the terrible sights and sounds of hell. I always wondered what it was like. And they're watching and waiting until I sin again, they've been talking with him. And he's been talking with him, planning.'

'Who's *he* Belinda?'

'The man over there. Talking with the angel who was following me. He's tall with ordinary clothes on, but that doesn't fool me. I told you. He's caught up with me now and he's hiding here but he's talking with everyone, and they all know about me, and he thinks I don't know he's here and he's been talking to him ...'

The psychiatrist was sitting at a table, making notes. When there was a pause he gave Gabrielle an encouraging nod.

'And how are you feeling now Belinda? We had to move you because someone else needed your room. But you can spend some time with other people who can ...'

'No, no, no ...no. I can't. You don't understand. It's not safe! They've got the mark of the beast on them, oh I know, they try to hide it, they're very clever at that. But their names aren't written on the scroll of the living. They're in hell already. Why have you put me in hell?'

'And what does the mark of the beast look like Belinda?'

'Oh no, no...I won't look at him, I won't speak to him, I'll just talk to you. Tell him I can't answer that question.' She lowered her voice to a whisper and leant closer to Gabrielle, 'He's been planning what to do with me, he's writing it down on the list.'

'You don't have to speak to him Belinda, just go on talking to me, do you remember I came into your room ... I talked to you, do you remember that?'

'Yes, I think so. You told me... when was it, was it yesterday, I can't remember... you told me, you were being kind, you said.'

'It was about trying to stay calm, do you remember?'

'Oh yes, and how I mustn't attack people. But I have, I have. I have stayed calm for most of the time, except for that time which ...it was so horrible being locked up, no one would put up with it would they? But I've been good and now you make me sleep in a room with all these people who've been planning with the angel... they pretend they're mad, they say crazy things and fight with each other and throw their food on the floor, but I know it's just to pretend they haven't been planning with the angel what to do with me... It's so noisy, and it's never quiet and... they are going to attack me. It's terrifying, it's absolutely terrifying. Do you understand?'

'Do you remember what happened before you came in here? Can you try and remember?' said the psychiatrist.

'Why does he talk to me when I can't look at him, why does he ask me this?'

'He wants to help Belinda, we both want to help you. We are both wondering if you can remember what happened before you came in here.'

'I... was running. I'm good at running, I'm very fast, but my rucksack was heavy. And so many words chasing each other around, they get tangled up and then they go backwards and confuse me, they are like a road where I don't know the houses, which was my house, where has it gone? He locked me out then he changed the lock and ...he was laughing at me when I ran down the road, and I wished I could fly into the trees and hide in the branches, but he laughed at me and I fell down. I tried to remember the words, I did try, but it was all about the bowl of wrath and the beasts and the sword coming out of his mouth, and I didn't understand, and then I thought it was nonsense and I'll be punished for thinking that... you are punishing me now but you pretend you are trying to help me... No, don't say anything. I found this little place to rest,

13

and I listened to the water in the stream and the sun was shining on the water and the trains were going by, and when I woke up he'd been there and stole the money and he'd gone off to make plans with the others.'

'Tell us some more Belinda.'

'So I sat there and I said sorry to God, but it's not enough, and now I'm in hell and God won't listen to me because I thought it was nonsense, and he knows my thoughts, I don't even need to speak them out loud, but I won't listen because he's been talking to the angel.' She lowered her voice again, 'He might pretend he's trying to help me but I know he's been talking to the angel. And you're going to make me go back in there with them and it's not safe, I need to write more down and read what I've written and check it's right, I need to see my other notebooks. but you've taken them away and shown them to the angel. I need to write some more…' She began to sob.

'You are a brave girl, Belinda. You don't have to look at me, but if you can hear me can you raise your hand to let me know? If we give you some more notebooks will that help? You can come in here where it's quiet and you can write some more, and Nurse Gabrielle will come and see if you're alright. Can you raise your hand if you can hear me saying this?'

Belinda was shaking with sobs, she shielded her face and raised her hand.

'That's good, I'm glad you can hear me, thank you for letting me know. So we can give you more notebooks to write in and biros to write with, and you can have some peace and quiet in here.'

'Will you keep him away from me?' she whispered to Gabrielle, 'Will you stop him from coming in here? Will he leave me in peace?'

'Yes Belinda, we'll make sure no one comes in here. You'll be safe, I'm going to get some notebooks and pens for you. Nurse Gabrielle will stay for a bit longer. I'm glad you could hear me today.' The psychiatrist left the room and Gabrielle sat next to Belinda, resting a hand on her arm.

4 SEPTEMBER

'Say it for me.'

'Belinda, would you like Natasha to visit you?'

'Oh... what, Natasha?'

'You said you stayed with her in her flat in London, you told us about that last week.'

'Oh yes. But... how does she know I'm here? Where am I?'

'This is a hospital remember? You are here to get better after being through a difficult time.'

Belinda stared at Nurse Gabrielle. She laid down her biro and closed the notebook with shaking hands.

'I... a hospital?'

'Yes. You were brought here when you were unwell, and you slept a lot, you were in that room to begin with, do you remember?'

'Yes... that's when you came in and that other one, the bad one.'

'Yes, that's right.'

'And she injected me with something. And she's been doing that every day. She always forces me to lie down, she and that other one are so strong.'

'Yes.'

'So... it's a hospital.'

'Yes.'

'For ...'

'I know what you're going to say Belinda.'

'Do you?' For the first time Belinda smiled. 'You don't use the word mad for people, do you? I realise that now. You say – unwell. I think that's because you're being kind. I was... unwell, wasn't I?'

'Yes.'

'I was mad. I ... am mad.'

'No.'

'Well... okay I can call it that can't I?'

'Yes, you can. If you want to.'

'My mind is my own.'

'Yes. That's good Belinda.'

'And I… I ran away, because …'

'Yes.'

'Say it for me.'

'No… you can say it.'

'But you see, I can't,' she whispered, 'I can't say it. You say it.'

'You don't have to say it Belinda.'

'But I do. I do have to. I have to make it real. I have to make you see it's real. It should never have happened. It was very wrong.'

'Don't upset yourself Belinda.'

'No. I'm… I'm not upset. I'm relieved. I ran away because he…'

'Yes?'

'He abused me. He abused me …' She put her head in her hands and sobbed. 'Say it for me. Say it.'

'Tell me Belinda.'

'Say it for me.'

'Say what Belinda?'

'He…raped me.'

Gabrielle put her hand on Belinda's arm.

'He needs… to be punished. Can you help me? I don't ever have to go back, do I?'

'Of course not. And yes we can help you. And there are other people who can help you. You are a brave girl to say this.'

'I feel… very strange today, my mind feels a bit clearer but I'm so tired. I don't think I need to write any more. I think I've written it all down now.'

'So… do you remember, we were talking about Natasha?'

'Oh yes. Well does she want to come and see me?'

'Yes. And she's got a cousin who'd like to come but only if you say so. Jonathan.'

'Oh.'

'Natasha's got a notebook of yours. One you left in her flat.'

'Oh! Oh yes. I'd forgotten about that. I had to write it all again, but it was better the second time.'

'I'll let them know Belinda. Can Jonathan come too, or should it just be Natasha?'

'Um... I don't know. Just Natasha the first time?'

'Good. Now do you think you might like to try the painting group?'

'Oh ...'

'Just come and see the first time, come and watch. You said you liked drawing didn't you, I expect you're very good. I'll stay with you till tea-time. We've got half an hour.'

5   SEPTEMBER
Writing

... The sixth angel blew his trumpet and the angels who were tied to the river were unbound and came to kill a third of mankind, and there were two million squadrons of cavalry... and the plagues were in the fire and smoke and sulphur, and they had tails like snakes... I can remember it, I did learn it... and there was an eagle in the sky and smoke came out of the abyss and the locusts came to torment men who didn't have the mark of God on their foreheads ... they were not chosen and their names were not written on the scroll in the sky...

Belinda looked up from her writing. She couldn't remember it anymore. She could hear the noise of hell in the room next door, but they let her come in here. She had been good, she had stayed on her bed all night under the duvet with the crying and muttering all around and the rushing footsteps and the banging, and sometimes the laughing and whispering. If she kept very, very still they would forget she was there at all. There had been one time when someone landed on her bed and there were some struggles going on, but she stayed very still, and they went away and then it was morning again. And now the dreams would stop for a while, and she could get something to eat and drink before the others started throwing the food on the floor and dancing.

… They are worshipping devils and demons when they dance because they have read the scroll and what they saw on it made them mad, and so they dance and laugh. Their names are not in the list of the living, their legs are like pillars of fire, and they shout and smoke comes out of their mouths, but the nurses come in and seal up their mouths, they are the bad angels who have been planning what to do with me. If I stay very quiet perhaps they will go away and forget I am here. I don't want to forget, I want to remember but it's so hard to remember, I want to show I have learnt it and learnt it well, I am trying to understand. Perhaps if I eat the scroll it will help me remember but perhaps it will then turn sour in my stomach. But if it was in my stomach…

There were sounds of the door opening and the psychiatrist came in. Belinda covered her eyes with her hand.

'Hello Belinda, how are you getting on? It's alright you don't need to look at me. And I won't look at you. I'll just sit over here where I always sit. I'm glad you're doing some writing.'

'I'm trying to remember. But it's so hard.'

'Do you think you could talk to me a little today? If I sit to the side here like this? I'm not looking at you and you don't need to look at me.'

'Where is Angel Gabrielle?'

'She's busy doing a few things today, but she'll come and see you later.'

'Is she helping the mad people?'

'They're not mad people, just a bit unwell. They're here to get better.'

'I don't believe you. They are mad. They're here to … make plans with the angel and they like dancing to the demons. But you make them sleepy and make them forget things.'

'Now, do you remember a few things from before you

were here? Can you tell me a few things?'

'Well… I've been writing about my life.'

'Yes. You've written a lot.'

'Have you been reading it?' Belinda stood up shakily and stared at him, 'I didn't say you could read it, I haven't checked it yet, I haven't made sure I've got it right!'

'Don't get upset Belinda, no I promise you I haven't read it, I just checked all the notebooks were there and I could see there were a lot of them, so that's why I said you'd written a lot. We're keeping them safe for you.'

She sat down and looked at her writing. 'If I swallow the scroll perhaps I will understand.'

'And what is it you will understand?'

'The prophesies. But they're in different languages, and the angel blew the trumpet and stood over the earth, and those who don't listen will be damned.'

'Can you remember a bit about when you first left home Belinda?'

'Oh… I… I was on the train, and it was getting late, and I didn't know where to go… so …'

'Yes?'

'I… I got off the train and I went into a pub and there was this girl there… she looked strong, and she made the boys go away …'

'And what were the boys doing?'

'They were laughing at me and… so she talked to me a bit and she was kind, but she was worried and looking around and waiting for someone…'

'And what happened then?'

'She… well I went with her, she was searching for someone, then she met some people and … and then she was going home, and she let me go with her. And I stayed there for a few days… she was sniffing something and… and then … she would laugh and joke for a while, it was weird, but then she didn't really want me there, I often couldn't talk to her …'

'And then?'

'Well, I could tell she wanted me to go so I left. I went

and slept in the park, it was scary, but it wasn't cold. And then I got ill.'

'And do you remember her name Belinda?'

'Um… it was, um… Tashie, yes that's it.'

'So, do you think her real name is Natasha? And what does she look like?'

'Well, she's um, she's quite big, with thick hair and a sort of long nose. She often looks sulky …'

'That's very good Belinda, you've remembered a lot. Do you want to go on writing a bit more now?'

'Yes please.'

'Nurse Gabrielle will be in soon.'

6 SEPTEMBER
Like a mad dream

Natasha was silent, she sat watching the game of chess, glancing at her watch and reading an old newspaper she had found under the boxes of board games in the small side room. Jonathan was enjoying the game and made a few jokes and Belinda laughed.

'I've…been so scared,' said Belinda after a while.

'Yes.'

'My father …'

'Yes.'

'He made me… learn a lot of the bible. And answer questions. But the worst thing was …'

'Yes?'

'I don't even know if I dare say it.'

'You don't have to say it.'

'He… it was confusing. Because I began to think it was nonsense and then I thought I would be in trouble for thinking that.'

'What did you think was nonsense?'

'Well, all those things in the book of Revelation.'

'Oh yes, I know what you mean.'

'Oh, so do you know about those things? Like who wrote it and that kind of thing? And what it all means?'

'I don't know what I think. But people have been trying to fathom it out for a long time. For centuries. The church in some countries doesn't accept it into the bible at all. Nobody agrees who wrote it or what it's about, it's like a mad dream someone had, and they wrote it down and claimed it was from God or Jesus.'.

'Oh!' Belinda stood up and stared at him.

'Sorry Belinda, did I scare you. I'm sorry if I said too much.'

'I didn't ...'

'Don't be scared.'

'Is it... is it allowed to say that. Are you allowed?'

'Shall we talk about it another time? It's your move by the way.'

'Oh ...' She sat down again and looked at the chess pieces. 'Oh yes... um... oh, look I can threaten two at a time.'

'So you can! Oh dear, I'm in trouble here.'

'I expect you'll think of something.'

'Haha.'

'Um... I'm sorry I got scared ...,' said Belinda, 'What were you saying. About the book of Revelation?'

'Yes, well if you're sure you want to talk about it. It's completely confusing. I expect most people think it's like a disturbed dream someone had.'

'So why did they put it in the bible? Or why didn't they just say it was just someone's dream? It's a bit like my dreams.'

'I have no idea Belinda, no idea at all. But the bible is only a collection of things people wrote at different times. They were just human beings like you and me, they may have made mistakes or even made things up or got details wrong in the stories. They may have *dreamt* things. We can never be sure of anything really. And there are some books in the Old Testament that some groups of people accept and some don't. There it's your move.'

'Yes. Why did they say it was from God?'

'I don't know.'

'*You* don't know! But I thought you did know, I thought… you're the kind of person who knows these things. It's… there are so many frightening things in it. Horrible things.'

'Yes.'

'So… you don't believe any of it?'

'Well, some of the book of Revelation is poetic and you could see symbolic meanings in it. But only some parts of it. Other parts are… bloodthirsty and, well just weird. They seem to symbolise events that do happen like earthquakes and plagues and things like that.'

'Can you hear that noise?'

'No Belinda, what's that?'

'They're listening from behind the wall. They always do. They want to hear what we're talking about today. And they're making plans.'

'Don't be scared.'

'Nurse Gabrielle will come and get me in a minute. Oh!'

'What is it?'

'Oh… I just… I called her Nurse Gabrielle. I usually think… but you'll think I'm mad.'

'No, of course we won't.'

'I thought she was the Angel Gabriel, and that she was going to tell me something important, and that I would sing a sacred song because I am a young girl.'

'And what do you think now?'

'She's not, is she? An angel. She's just …'

'A nurse?'

'Yes. A kind nurse who's helped me a lot. And … um,'

'There it's your move, I'm not doing very well here am I. My plan is in ruins.'

'Hmm. I don't think you're trying very hard.'

'Ha! Well. I am actually. Out of practice. Pam and Natasha won't play chess with me, so this is a real treat. But …

now I've lost the other knight as well, that's bad news.'

'I'll stop talking so you can concentrate.'

'Right. It would be nice to finish the game wouldn't it, before we have to go. Though I'm afraid I think I've blown my chances now.'

'Yes. Can you come and play again?'

'Of course, if you'd like that. Would you?'

'Oh. Yes please.'

'And we can talk again too can't we, if you can manage that.'

'Yes. Thank you. Look - checkmate.'

'So it is Belinda! Well done. I'm glad you'll be able to manage that again, that's very good to hear.'

7   SEPTEMBER
Martha

Belinda had her back to the door of the Day Room and was seated at a table opposite an old woman who was peering closely at a chessboard and talking to the pieces as she moved them around with shaky hand. Her straggly grey hair fell over her hunched shoulders.

'… The black queen's the Goddess and if I worship her I'll become a witch. But she's not listening to me today. She hasn't got time. She can hear the knights talking about the two thousand million horsemen from heaven coming down to the earth. She doesn't know if this is true or not, it's confusing. President Obama won't let it happen though. He's got his finger on the button. The CIA know about it and they're having a meeting right now. They're blowing their trumpets and need to make a plan to save the world from the atom bombs. But they are going to fall, they are going to fall…Look…' she glanced at Belinda, 'She's moved so she can hear the trumpets better. But the white bishop is praying for her soul. She doesn't want him to, it makes her angry, she doesn't want to know about the bible and the trumpets. She doesn't want to die, she's scared. But she doesn't want to take the pills because they make her brain go grey. The black king's moving towards her again he can never leave her alone, it's a good thing he can only move slowly. She can see him coming so it gives her time to plan and she's going to tell the press, and they always come quickly because they want a story, they don't want to miss anything… He's coming and she can't bear to hear him talk, he says crazy things to her, and she doesn't know if he's just joking or what, or maybe he's even flirting with her which is utterly disgraceful, and the white bishop sometimes listens but he's a bit nervous of the king and so he doesn't say much when he's around. The frightening things is that the black bishop is really an evil spirit in disguise, and he pretends to join in the prayers, but really he's in touch with the black knight, but they're careful and don't let others see. People know they're friends, but it's much more than that, it's shocking really… The white queen is an angel, but she wears ordinary clothes, that way she can do kind things and people will never know …'

Nurse Gabrielle came forward and bent down, 'Hello Belinda, can you drag yourself away from Martha for a few minutes?'

'Oh.' Belinda turned and saw Jonathan. She got up.

'Hello Belinda, I came by myself this time. Is that alright? Natasha isn't feeling too good today. But if you don't want to see me I can go away again.'

Belinda stared at him. 'I… I can't …' she turned away.

'What is it Belinda? Do you remember Jonathan?'

'I… I can't talk to him,' Belinda whispered to Gabrielle, 'You see, I pretended last time, I knew he was… he's the bad angel you see, but I felt safe because Natasha was there, so I pretended I didn't know, but all the time he's making plans with the others.'

'I… I'm Natasha's cousin Belinda, do you remember me?' said Jonathan.

'Yes, I remember now …You were following me, then you caught up with me and sat by the hospital bed in the other hospital, and you were waiting ...'

'I did sit by your bed yes, but I went away when I realised you were scared of me.'

'You went away to start planning with the others.'

'Perhaps another day Jonathan,' said Nurse Gabrielle quietly, 'If Natasha can come with you again? Both of you together?'

'How can I talk to him?' Belinda whispered, 'How can I? He just wants to probe into my mind and find out my sins. You're working out my punishment.'

'You'd better go Jonathan.'

'Angel Gabrielle is protecting me from evil.'

'Belinda, I'm so sorry,' said Jonathan, 'I really am sorry that things are confusing for you and... but I'm glad the Angel Gabrielle is looking after you. Can Natasha come and visit again soon? Would you rather she came by herself?'

'Oh. Yes... yes please.'

Martha was talking continuously '...they're breaking down the castle's defences. They've got new technology, though there have been teething problems. And it's not safe, it's not safe, they can get into the computers and read the secret codes. The white knight is going back to get reinforcements, but he doesn't know that the black knight has another plan ...the bishop is very tired now, he can't go on quoting from the bible for ever when no one understands. People are laughing at him, and it wears him out and makes him angry. It's mainly the young boys who laugh and they take drugs and fly in the sky. Though he knows getting angry is wrong and he must ask God to forgive him. He knows about the black Goddess and he's thinking maybe he could learn something from her, but this thought is very wicked and scary. He's never been wicked before. Is there time, oh it's coming it's coming...!'

'Don't get scared Martha,' said Belinda.

'Who are you? Why are you sitting there listening? Has that man gone now? Leave me in peace, oh leave me in peace.

The bombs are coming soon, there isn't enough time to prepare. The prayers are not enough, they're not enough, they got them off the computer and they're not real prayers.'

'And what is the white king doing?'

'Mmm? Oh no! Don't talk about the white king, don't talk about the White King!' Martha was shocked and cupped her shaky, wrinkled hands over the chess piece, and her voice lowered to a whisper. 'We mustn't. We must be respectful.' She leaned towards Belinda. 'You see you may not realise, you are a very young girl and a lot has been happening in the last few years… but the white king is God but he's lost his power. But we still have to be respectful. We must leave him alone and not move him about. He is always in the same place, and he likes to stay there, and we don't know what he's thinking. They're preparing for the coming of the cavalry, and we won't be able to resist. No plan will be good enough… And the bishops need to tear off their robes, they can't fight like this, and they are confused…'

Belinda felt tired and got up slowly so Martha wouldn't notice. The other end of the day room seemed quiet, some people were talking quietly, some reading, some staring into space or at the TV which showed continuous children's programmes with the sound turned very low. As she went to sit in a chair by the window a young man came through the door. 'Go for it Grandma!' he said, swiping his hand across Martha's chessboard. Some pieces fell on the floor, and she whimpered and struggled to bend over to retrieve them. He walked towards Belinda and stood looking at her for a moment, she was staring out of the window at the sun shining through the golden leaves on the trees.

'Lovely day Belinda, really great isn't it. You going to talk to me today? I'll just sit here shall I. I'm here if you want me.'

'I'll wait,' he said, 'I'll tell you my life story, shall I? Pretty girl like you in a place like this.'

'You don't have to talk to me Belinda. It's ok.'

'You don't have to look at me you know, but if you do I won't break up into little pieces. Haha!'

'Though I was in pieces when I first came in here. All breaking up and with the energy draining away. All those precious little bits of me just going down the plug hole. What a waste eh! Don't you want to know what happened, Belinda? How they stuck me together again? How they did it, huh? The question is…' He learnt towards her and she flinched, 'Will I stay stuck together, huh? Will the glue work and how long for? And if it doesn't, well… what will happen then? Could be messy.'

'Are they trying that glue on you too Belinda? But you probably wouldn't know if they were. It's quite hard to detect. If you're still in pieces well I understand you don't want to talk to me. Fair enough. But we can look at the view together can't we. It's really pretty and the sun's shining. There's a normal world out there somewhere and we're in here, but that's ok.'

'It feels odd doesn't it, hmm… being in pieces. You don't know which bit to answer with, or which bit to think with or which bit to work things out with. But I like sitting here with you Belinda, it's so lovely and sunny. Winter will be here soon won't it. Go for it Grandma!' he called out to Martha who had rearranged the pieces and was talking quietly to herself. 'Do you play chess Belinda? Properly I mean. Maybe we could have a game sometime?'

'Yes,' said Belinda, 'I do play chess. I'd like that.'

8 DECEMBER
Visiting the Manor House

Natasha tied the belt of her dressing gown and smoothed back her thick uncombed hair. It had been a particularly bad night, vivid unpleasant dreams and awful cravings for the cocaine. Then waking to remember their arrival at the Manor House the night before with Belinda, the fragile teenage girl who had then disappeared into the pouring rain and blackness of the village night. It was still very early, the grey light of the winter dawn was creeping through the house and when she opened the door of the large old kitchen she was shocked to see her friend already sitting at the table resting her face in her hands.

'What is it, any news Pam? How long have you been up sitting here! We're all so tired.'

'A while. Jonathan's gone out again, he's frantic. I just woke up and I'm worrying about *him* now.'

Yes,' Natasha pulled up a chair and sat down. 'Awful. Did you get any sleep? What are we going to do? Are you sensing anything? Did Jonathan…'

'I fell asleep when we got back, just dried off and fell into bed. We were soaked weren't we. Where can she be. It's… just so awful.'

'I think you knew something was going to happen, I could tell you weren't happy about this trip.'

'Well, yes I did feel *very* uneasy, but I didn't like to say, she'd be with us all the time, but she did seem kind of settled in Jonathan's house … but he's been getting emails from George which were worrying him.'

'Are you … sensing anything's happened to her?'

'No. Not like that. I mean we could all see she was a bit overwhelmed and withdrawn when we arrived. After dinner we were watching the news about Aleppo while you and George were playing another game with Hugo and making him laugh, and then she left the room … Maybe she decided then and grabbed her coat and crept out when no one was looking.'

'She seemed rational, I thought the medication was ok,

she enjoyed that trip to the National Gallery, well of course there were images that disturbed her, some of the paintings are extraordinary, and then there was that moment when she spotted her father in the crowd by the Tube Station and ran off, I had to chase after her.'

'That must have been absolutely terrifying.'

'Mmm. You know there's something I never told you Pam.'

'What?'

'Well, I went to see him. It was a long way on the train. I found his address in Margate, I looked through her stuff, I know that was sneaky, and I took one of her little paintings to give him, the one she threw away, it was rather striking. It was like a struggle. I told him she was safe with us. I scared him, evil bastard. She said he looked a bit like Hitler, and he did ... I said that the police knew where he lived. All that's unresolved, whether they're going to prosecute and all that ...'

'What! Yes, you can be scary, well done. I didn't know.'

'Of course, I didn't tell *her*, Belinda, she's been frightened he would appear again, all through that time when the hospital were discharging her and her mother came, and we met her and she agreed that we could have Belinda to stay for a while.'

'Yes, but it must have been comforting to think that you and Jonathan wanted to help.'

'Yes, I nagged him in the beginning because he always thought it was hopeless looking for someone in London like that.'

'I'm getting sleepy now Tash. Better make some tea.' Pamela pulled herself up and went over to fill the kettle. Natasha remembered the evening she had first seen the short, thin girl with untidy black hair looking lonely and very nervous indeed in the crowded London pub – it was a horrible evening, her usual dealer had vanished, and she was trying to find several tentative contacts – the girl just kept following her, it was annoying ...

Pam put two mugs on the table and opened cupboard

doors, 'Where is the cereal, they won't mind will they. Got to wake myself up.'

'She was scared all the time when I met her …then I came in one day and she was gone. I read a bit of a notebook she'd written in, must have forgotten, it was behind a cushion, it was like a sort of message, *stop this terrible life, stop taking drugs and dealing drugs, go and find this poor girl who needs help.* But then of course we never found her for months, I left my horrible little London flat and found my way to Jonathan's old family house where he was sorting things out after his mother's death, and he just helped me, and he made me get help, while my Dad was wrecking everything and drinking himself silly and …and for ages he wouldn't leave.'

'Yes, you told me a few things about that' said Pam putting bowls and spoons and boxes of cereal on the table.

'Well of course he was still in shock after the car accident. We both were. Mum and Petra gone in a moment, you can't comprehend it. And the fact that Dad and I weren't in the car. Dad went to pieces, I had to leave home, I couldn't watch, he was letting his business go down, and then he actually sold the house. Our old house. I've never even had a proper conversation with him about that in all this time. For some reason Dad resented Jonathan and was hateful to him. They should've helped each other, both going through a crisis. But Dad despised religion, when he was drunk he would say terrible things, it was deeply unfair. You don't have to have the same beliefs to be civil. Jonathan just tried to keep the peace and would escape into his books when he could.'

Natasha poured milk on the cornflakes. There was so much more she could tell … she had owed months of rent and letters from the landlord were becoming threatening, the waitressing didn't pay anything like enough and the chef had turned nasty, but she got away and they never found her, and Jonathan would give her money, he never asked any questions. 'And then after I found him Jonathan found *you* again, thank goodness he did Pam,' she said.

'Yes. We found each other. Thank goodness. But you must worry about your father.'

'Yes, he's never got in touch over the weeks, I've been ringing a few people and trying to find old friends from near our house, but no one's seen him. I even contacted a bloke who used to work for him, he didn't know anything …'

It was nearly daylight. Pamela got up to refill the kettle and wiped condensation off the window. 'Belinda couldn't have been out all night in this freezing rain, surely! At least the weather's clearing.' She noticed Natasha was struggling, breathing deeply with her fists clenched.

'You know Tash I can't stay here, I wanted to get away the minute I arrived.'

'Really! It's a beautiful old house … But yes, it was supposed to be just the weekend.'

'Yes, I've got things to get back to.'

'Yes.'

'There's something… something not right here Tash, I felt it yesterday. Maybe Belinda did too, but then she was a bit lost wasn't she, when we arrived the boy Hugo kept wanting Jonathan's attention and a lot was being explained by George and Sylvia and then what George said about the Manor House.'

'Oh, yes, you mean, oh my goodness.'

'About giving it to Jonathan,' said Pam.

'Yes. Well, that came out of the blue didn't it!'

'Do you think he…'

'I don't know Pam, don't know what he was thinking.'

The door opened and Anthea came in. She was dressed in smart jeans and a fluffy, pale blue jumper with an orange silk scarf around her neck and her hair piled on her head.

'Good morning. Pam and Natasha isn't it.'

'Hello Anthea.'

'Any news of your poor friend?' She filled a bowl with cornflakes.

'No. Jonathan's gone out again.'

'Mmm.' Anthea sat down and began to eat. 'So what's up with her then?'

'She was in a psychiatric ward and we got to know her, I'm Jonathan's cousin,' said Natasha, 'He lost his wife and …well that was several years ago … We thought Belinda would be okay, she was on this medication.'

'Crikey.'

'Very fragile.'

'Poor kid. Not all of us have the luxury of a psych ward.'

The door opened again and Hugo stood staring in. He had a thick black jumper on top of his striped green and white pyjamas,

'Come on in Hugo,' said Anthea, 'I'll get you some breakfast. This is my brother by the way. Oh sorry, you learnt that yesterday.'

Hugo shuffled to the table and sat down. 'Are you going somewhere Anthea all dressed up? Are George and Sylvia going to live in a little house and leave me here all alone in the Manor House? Why did Belinda go out in the pouring rain and make us all get wet and tired?'

'She's worried about something Hugo, now eat that.'

'I don't like it when we're all wet and tired and cold,' he said mashing his Weetabix and adding sugar and milk, 'I like it when we're all happy and playing my number games and drinking wine and hearing about Sylvia's new baby.'

The door opened and George and Sylvia came in fully dressed.

'You've beaten us to it,' said George sitting down next to Hugo and putting a little notebook carefully on the table, 'I hope we all got a bit of sleep and got warm and dry first.'

'Jonathan's gone out again George,' said Pamela, 'He's so desperate to find her, his car's gone.'

'Yes. Very worrying.'

'Are you two going away?' said Hugo, accepting a plate

of toast Anthea put in front of him. 'Are you and Sylvia going to leave me here?'

'Nothing is decided Hugo.'

'George,' said Pamela, 'I hope you don't mind me asking ...'

'Yes Pam. By the way I'm so glad to meet you at last. Jonathan's mentioned you, and you too Natasha, I gather a lot's been going on in your family. You're very welcome.'

'Thank you. It has yes.'

'George, can I ask you something,' said Pamela, 'I'm not sure Jonathan took you seriously last night when you were talking about the Manor House. I mean we were all talking about people we remembered weren't we, and then I asked him later, but he seemed distracted, and then we were about to discover Belinda had run off, so it was all a bit of a muddle and he rushed around looking in all the rooms, I mean… were you *serious* about giving him the Manor House?'

George pushed his bowl away and rested his elbows on the table. 'I wasn't joking Pam. I've never been more serious in my life.'

Pamela finished her cup of tea and got up and went to help Sylvia by the sink. Then leaving the others sitting at the table she opened the door and went down the corridor. There were footsteps and George caught her up. 'I wonder Pam if I could have a word? Somewhere quiet…'

'Why yes, of course.'

'Let's go in here,' he said opening a door, 'It used to be the Guest Room when it was a hotel, a bit cold today I'm afraid.'

They sat down on elegant easy chairs with a coffee table between them. 'Sorry, I ought to get dressed,' said Pamela, aware of George's clean crisp shirt and smart pullover.

'I won't take a moment Pam,' he said, opening the little notebook and handing it to her, 'I found this in Belinda's room just now. I know it's like prying but we're all so desperately worried and I can see you three have been taking great care of her.'

'Oh… oh dear. Shall I read it out loud?'

'Yes please.'

'It looks like she just started a new notebook, it's the first page. She's put…well, the date, and …*arrived late at this Manor House.*'

'Yes. Keep going.'

'…*The dark angel has brought me here to this enormous old house and it's like a party. Everyone is happy and having fun and playing these crazy number games. Jonathan is always talking to the mad boy. Last week when we were playing chess he moved the White King …*' Pamela looked up, 'that's in capitals… *that proves it and now I know this is where they've been planning to bring me. That man showed us round and I saw where it's going to happen. It's a big bare room with no carpet and a ladder and ropes hanging from the ceiling at the side, and table and chairs, he said it was where they played the game 'Mixed Messages'. He said they were having a break from it. And there was a lock on the door. The rocks are coming out of the sky and people are dying, hundreds of people. God is angry. It's all coming true. I need to escape after dinner, it's dark already. Nurse Gabrielle was the only one who cared but they found out and came to take her away. The last thing she said before I left was …* I'll pause there for a moment George. There's a bit more about what was happening in the psychiatric ward, well *her* interpretation of it… she was there in September.'

'This is appalling stuff isn't it? Does it make any sense to you?'

'Well … we thought she was getting better …'

'You've all done a lot.'

'Yes. She always wrote things down, like diaries about her childhood, it seemed to help …oh but you're busy George.'

'No tell me.'

'There was something about her father, it stuck in my mind it was so horrible - his voice was low and menacing when he was furious when she challenged things he said.'

'Yes, I'm so sorry. Can I leave the diary with you Pam, and you can show Jonathan? Most distressing.'

'Yes of course. He must be exhausted.'

'I'm so terribly sorry that all this has upset her so much. The Games Rooms as we called them were set up for these …well, the entertainment that hotel guests joined in with when they stayed here. They're empty now and we're gradually clearing them.'

'I know a little bit about that,' said Pam, 'Quite a long time ago I actually played a Game, the one where you tell your psychiatrist everything. The *pretend* psychiatrist wearing a mask and sitting at a desk.'

'Oh yes, goodness me, you've been through so much haven't you. Yes, I heard about that, Jonathan was going through a lot too wasn't he. His world was falling apart.' Many things flashed through George's mind, and he wondered momentarily if he had said too much …

'I'd better get dressed,' said Pamela getting up.

'It's hard to explain Pam and we're all very tired right now, but Sylvia and I just want to put this crazy stuff behind us and have a normal life again. And with the baby coming.'

'Yes.'

'We could talk more, but now isn't the time. Thank you for letting me give you the diary.'

'I'll look after it and give it to Jonathan. Though he might have glanced at it yesterday.' They moved to the door and George opened it for her.

9   DECEMBER
Blind

Jonathan sat in his car and stared at the drab landscape. He felt unwashed and weary and chilly in his grey waterproof jacket and scarf, still damp from the night before. It had been dark in the early morning when he had driven slowly round the village and back up the hill to the Manor house and then down the steep winding hill the other side and over the narrow bridge and up towards the flat, soggy, featureless fields. He parked in a rough, awkward layby, what was he doing, surely she couldn't have come this far? There was the gentle hum from the motorway to the east and the sun hung just above the horizon, barely visible through a layer of heavy grey clouds.

Remove two letters from her name and you were left with the word - *blind*. She couldn't see that she was safe with them. They had talked and talked, they did simple DIY jobs in his shabby house, it was like family. Pamela was often out, developing her own activities, she needed to do this, she was a talented medium, he didn't understand it but he respected her and didn't interfere and she always came back, and then they were together. On the day when they first met she said completely unexpected things ... He had been packing up and preparing to move out of the New Vicarage, and he was carrying a large, black bag of rubbish and opened his front door to find a girl slumped against the wall and he dropped the bag and bent to try and revive her.

She opened her eyes. 'Oh, sorry ... I must have...'

'Let me help,' he said, taking her hand.

'Yes ... thank you.' She managed to stand up.

'Please feel you can come in a moment.'

'Yes ... thank you. I feel a bit weak. Sorry.'

He opened the living room door and suggested she sit on the sofa. He brought her a glass of water and went into the kitchen to boil the kettle.

When he came back she had fallen asleep. After a while they had talked. She told him she had come over to the village to try and see Annie, her brother's old landlady, but she was away like she often was. And then there was the moment when Pamela told him her brother Matthew had just been murdered on the common during the night. Utterly shocking and unexpected, her eyes brimming with tears as she sat on his sofa holding the mug of tea. When Jonathan realised who she was he told her he had known her father and brother and was trying to re-unite her family. It was complicated and he spoke slowly and carefully.

And then he had driven her back to her house suggesting she go in and face the emptiness and rest, with a promise to meet her the following day, and later she had told him an extraordinary story about meeting her parents in the house. 'But Pam, your parents are dead,' he said gently. But she had repeated it with something her father said to her, and Jonathan had realised then that she couldn't have known this particular thing because he had left the family when she was a baby and she hadn't seen him for seventeen years and then he had died before she had been able to meet him again. And Jonathan himself hadn't yet told her those details about what he had recently discovered …

His thoughts came back to Belinda. He couldn't forget her frightened eyes and how he often wondered what she was really thinking. And was the fact that *he himself* questioned the origins of the scriptures making her *more* fearful? One book had been lying under others on his desk – *Making Good Sense of the Book of Revelation*. He kept it hidden. When he had read the first page himself nausea overcame him, and he had an odd sense that to go any further might give those weird and frightening images a chance to take hold in his *own* mind. He should throw it away.

It was always fear. Belinda was tortured by it. He remembered some reading he had recently been doing, snatching time with his books and the computer. The authorities feared Jesus. The Roman Emperors feared disorder. And almost everyone in the early centuries seemed to fear heresy, it drove them to hysteria and unbelievable savagery. But he had grown weary of trying to understand those obscure and incomprehensible metaphysical definitions …

As he lingered in the car and watched the gloomy sunrise Jonathan suddenly thought of a strange saying from the little-known Gospel of Phillip which had stuck in his memory. *Jesus took them all by stealth, for he did not appear as he was, but in the manner in which they would be able to see him. He appeared to them all.*

He appeared to the great as great. He appeared to the small as small. He appeared to the angels as an angel, and to men as a man ... It's incredible that people *believe* what they read in the bible, and they don't stop to consider *what* they are reading. They ignore the parts that are unpalatable and nonsensical and contradictory. If I ask them a question and they can't reply they will shake their heads sadly and suggest it is I who is at fault and not them, they tell me to have faith. After all they are the chosen ones. The bishop was like this when I confessed everything. He concentrated on the things I had done and ignored all my doubts, he just couldn't see them, and he lent me books to read as if they could just make everything right again.

Jonathan nearly dozed off but then remembered why he was sitting here in the cold car. He must go back to the village and call on people to see if Belinda had knocked timidly on someone's door in the darkness and the pouring rain. He felt awkward, they would wonder what he was doing back here, but he must, it wasn't important what they thought. He started the engine and drove back and past the Manor House where there were several lights at the windows.

The first person he would call on was his old friend Ruby Seth who lived in a little cottage near the church. He parked and walked across the village green, remembering the last time he had seen her on a hot summer's day when they had sat in her garden and talked.

'Jonathan!'

'Hello Ruby.' She looked just the same, short curly hair, shiny earrings and a pretty colourful dress with a soft woolly brown cardigan thrown over her shoulders. A suitcase stood in the hall. 'How lovely to see you after all this time!'

'Look I'll get straight to the point. I'm sorry to disturb you, the thing is, I'm here in the village visiting friends and one of us has gone missing and I'm looking for her.'

'Oh. Oh dear.'

'A vulnerable sixteen-year old.'

'What do you mean? What's happened?'

'She ran off in the pouring rain last night. It would take rather a lot of explaining. Could I possibly look in your garden near the stream. Just to check?'

'Well of course ...'

'I'll just go down the side of the cottage, I'm a bit muddy. You stay in the warm.'

Ruby was about to speak again but he turned and hurried down the rough path by the low wall that surrounded the cottage. She watched for a moment and then shut the front door.

Jonathan approached the long garden where heavy branches of tall trees bent low over the soaking grass. The stream was deep and fast flowing. He remembered Pam had said something about a deep stream and a narrow bridge, he hoped it didn't mean anything. He stood looking down into the swift, dark water and glanced around, Ruby didn't appear, he would go on to the next house, there was no time to lose.

From her living room window overlooking the green Ruby saw him walk down the road. He was preoccupied. She went back and listened outside the bathroom and could hear soft sounds. 'Are you alright?' she called and there was a faint reply.

She went to sit on the sofa and waited. What an extraordinary thing! She had been about to tell Jonathan about what had just happened, but something stopped her, she remembered the girl had begged her '...*not to tell the police or the ambulance people.*' What on earth had been going on?

Earlier Ruby had gone outside to clear some branches that had fallen during the wet, windy night and she had seen what looked like a body lying on the ground and had rushed over to the mossy bank beside the stream. The girl was soaking wet and cold as ice with straggly black hair stuck to her face, at first Ruby had thought she was dead. Now about half an hour later she relived those strange few minutes...

'No, no ...come back,' she had said, and bent to take hold of the cold wet hand. There was a pulse. 'You'll be alright, come back. Not another death in this place, not another death.' She pulled off her cardigan and covered the still body. 'I'll get something, I'll warm you up.' She rushed to the house, nearly tripping over a broken branch, grabbed a blanket that lay on the sofa and a cushion and ran back. She covered the girl with the blanket and gently lifted her head to put the cushion on the wet ground. She sat down and began to rub the arms and bent to breathe warm air under the blanket. All the time she heard herself muttering, could the girl hear, could it revive her? 'Come back, you're warming up and you will come back.' She breathed more air around the still body and watched the pale face.

And then there was a response.

'That's it,' said Ruby, 'You're wet and cold but we'll get you indoors and warm you up. You're going to be alright.'

The girl stared. She saw a worried woman with curly brown hair bending over her and the sun had come out and sparkled in the drops of water on the low hanging branches. She moved her hand up to her face.

'Oh.'

'You're back. You're back. I'll warm you up and help you.'

'Oh. I ...'

'If you think you can, let's get you up and into the house to dry out and get warm.'

'Oh. I was...I was somewhere else. It was so ...lovely. I was...'

'Don't try and talk. Let me help you up.'

The girl smoothed back the soaking strands of hair and started to move.

'Let me wrap the blanket round, that's right. It'll help you get warm. You're going to be alright.' Ruby took hold of the cushion. 'Hold this, it's dry. Now see if you can move your legs a bit...'

They had gradually got her to stand and then managed

to make their way slowly across the grass. And into the cottage where Ruby kicked off her soaking shoes and sat the girl down on a hardbacked chair and went to run a bath explaining that the bathroom was downstairs. She had helped her into the bathroom and then rushed upstairs to find spare clothes, anything dry, they were about the same height. She came back to find the girl staring at the water.

'I'll be just here,' Ruby said and shut the door. There was no lock on it and the hot water should revive her. As long as she could hear movements through the door, she would wait … She had gone upstairs to get another cardigan and put on some dry socks.

Now she sat and wondered why she hadn't told Jonathan. But he was abrupt, almost rude. She remembered their conversation one hot, sunny day when he had called in, as usual he needed to talk about things on his mind – this time it was about how he used to have an imaginary friend as a child – '…I had mine, I was told He was with me always till the end of time. I was told I could always talk to Him, I was told a lot of things …but recently I read about Him, I went back to the stories people wrote about Him. It was mostly crazy stories written by people who called themselves Matthew, Mark, Luke and John … just stories, nothing you could rely on are they! We will never know. All this made me see a different side to Him and I didn't like it much. Utter unkind words against your brother and you will burn in hell. He was good at describing this to people, …*the blazing furnace, the place of wailing and grinding of teeth.*' Ruby remembered making some remark hoping he would be distracted, but he went on, 'And listen to this Ruby, …*At the end of time …the angels will go forth and will separate the wicked from the good …* ' 'Surely no one believes this sort of thing anymore …' said Ruby, '…*when the Son of Man comes … There will be two men in a field, one will be taken, the other left…* we don't hear much of this in church do we, oh no.' 'Well, I don't ever go near a church unless I have to,' Ruby had replied, 'Except of course I live near one. And very pretty it is too.' 'Do you know Ruby,' he went on, *'He said He had come to set fire to the earth.'*

'Do you miss Him though?' Ruby said, 'If He was your imaginary friend for so long,' 'Oh yes, terribly. All the time. but I look back and realise … I made a terrible mistake. I'm leaving the village, it's all over.' Then they had sat in silence. But then she went on to confess it had been her who had told things to the newspapers. And it was because she had seen him with a girl in his car … And he just smiled at her - 'Yes, that was Pam, she had just lost her brother and I was helping her …' He wasn't interested in *her*, these weird ideas seemed to fill his mind, he came to visit and talk but she was invisible, he was preoccupied with the other woman. It was a knife in her heart.

Ruby heard soft splashing sounds from the bathroom. What should she do? She called again and got a faint response … She sat thinking about the day when reporters had been hanging about outside her cottage. She had phoned one to say she wanted to retell the story of how her tiny niece had drowned, she wanted to silence the cruel, untrue rumours in the village once and for all. It had been Jonathan who had suggested she did this in the beginning, it was one of the strange things he had done … Tears flowed down Ruby's cheeks as she sat remembering.

She had called a reporter, not knowing what would happen, and then there they all were. It had started to drizzle and she suggested they went over to the church to keep dry. 'Where's the vicar then?' shouted one, 'Has he gone to play Games at the Manor House?' There was laughter and everyone followed her across the village green. Standing in the church she had told them the facts about the dreadful day when her niece had drowned in the stream and how it had happened, and she asked them to print the story showing how the terrible accident wasn't her fault … As she came to the end they were getting restless and she led them back through the churchyard to see her garden where it had happened and they started firing questions at her – 'What's up with the vicar?' 'Do you know the vicar well?' 'Is it true the vicar has been conducting seances at the Manor House?' 'Are you and the vicar together?' 'Where has the vicar gone?' 'Do they tie people up at the Manor House and brainwash them?' 'What sort of drugs do they use at the Manor House?' They wouldn't stop shouting but she hurried along, wanting to get this over with, and after taking photos of the stream they were all going off in different directions with some looking uncertainly at the plain modern house behind some trees that was the New Vicarage. 'All I can say is, the vicar has moved out,' she said, and went into her cottage and shut the door. But a young reporter was still hanging about and when she asked him to go he came towards her with a blurred photo of Jonathan. 'There are a lot of rumours going round about the vicar,' he said, 'Is this him? Do you know anything about it and are you prepared to put the record straight about that too?' She hesitated, but he seemed a quiet thoughtful young man. 'I will be especially careful to report anything you say accurately,' he said. And she had let him in.

There were more sounds from the bathroom. Now what was she going to do? She was all packed to go away to the Lakes for her usual winter break. It was a long drive and she needed to leave. Should she tell Jonathan about the girl when he came back to his car? ... *Please don't tell the police and the ambulance people*...

10 DECEMBER
Maxwell and Anthea
After a quick bowl of cereal and cup of tea Anthea left Natasha and Pamela and Hugo in the Manor House kitchen, and climbed the wide, elegant staircase. In her bedroom she pulled on her coat and grabbed her backpack and hurried down the other narrow stairs and out of the side door. No one was about. She ran down the drive not daring to look in the direction of Maxwell's house which could be seen through the cedar trees. He might be waiting and watching from his kitchen window.

She had nearly reached the end of the drive when she heard running footsteps. 'Darling wait. Where are you going? I haven't seen you for days since you left … please come back.'

She started walking down the hill towards the church and the village beyond where the road meandered through scattered houses. Maxwell tried to take her hand, but she snatched it away.

'Darling please. Please. Let me talk to you, let me explain. Let me say sorry. I've missed you dreadfully, I've even missed Hugo.'

'Don't mock Max.'

'I mean it Anthea. Please. Where are you going?'

'I'm leaving. I'm finally going, leaving this dump of a village and this crazy Manor House, and… I'm leaving Hugo.' The wind snatched away her words and she wiped her face. 'I can't do it any more Max, I can't do it. I can't do anything for him anymore, I've been looking after him all my life, all his craziness, I've done grotty jobs, I've cooked his meals. Listened to his ramblings. But now he's got a friend and I've got to grab the moment.'

'Slow down darling, yes of course you must. It's been a nightmare for you, of course it has, you've been wonderful. Please let me talk to you. Slow down, what about me?'

Anthea stopped and looked at him. 'I don't know what to think Max.'

'Look of course you've got to get away from here, of course. Look, you keep walking and head towards the hotel on the main road. But before you get there I'll catch you up with the car and we can go somewhere and talk properly. Will you?'

'Oh … But I need to be careful, some of them might be about looking for a girl who's gone missing, they might see me.'

'I'll wait for you, see you in a few minutes.' Maxwell turned and hurried back towards his house. She watched for a moment and then walked down the hill and past the ancient church and the village green. She saw a car parked – was it Jonathan's? There must be places to hide beside the road…

but then she saw him at someone's front door deep in conversation and hurried past.

'All those things that happened,' said Max, 'A lot of it was the stress. Hugo being around, you know. Of course, I shouldn't say this, and I know I should have behaved better, and he's got nowhere to go and can't look after himself and all that… but this is the real me darling, you do know that don't you?'

They were sitting in his car which was parked in a quiet road in the town. Anthea stared out at the weak sunlight breaking through the rain clouds.

'I'm sorry dear girl. Please. Don't shut me out. Tell me what's been happening.'

'George and Sylvia have been very kind to Hugo. He's kind of settled. They give him regular meals and sometimes play scrabble which he's brilliant at… and sometimes he talks that crazy stuff about the grid in the ground and his secret machine, and they just let him talk, but then suddenly they announce that they're moving out. And Jonathan was giving him some attention while…'

'*Jonathan*! He's back here? What do you mean?'

'Oh, he's come to visit, with three girls, one's a cousin and then Pamela, she's his girlfriend, and…'

'Of course, he and George have been friends a long time.'

'Yes. Well … you see they brought this girl Belinda with them. She was very quiet and fragile looking. George showed everyone round, the Games Rooms are deserted now, and then we played Hugo's crazy number games, well it was quite fun, everyone was pretending they understood the rules, it was like a party, and then we had this lovely dinner and people were remembering people and that was sad, and then George made this announcement, Sylvia's pregnant and they're moving out.'

'Good heavens! He didn't show them our room I hope?'

'No, the door was locked and we just went past. You see when I arrived at their front door they just let me in, they were so kind to me too, they didn't ask questions, they knew I'd been living with you next door. And maybe having me there would make the job with Hugo easier of course.'

'And they may have heard some of the things that've been going on.'

'Yes.' She withdrew her hand from his grasp and pulled her coat more tightly around her.

'Darling please don't shut me out.'

'But then, it was extraordinary. George was saying a few things, how so many crazy people had been in touch trying to get work at the Manor House, magicians and theatre groups and people like that, and how it was all too much to cope with, and then he just said he was going to give it to Jonathan.'

'*Give it to Jonathan.* What, you mean the Manor House!'

'Yes. That's what he said.'

'Good heavens. And what did Jonathan say?'

'Well, I don't think he said much at all. I'm not sure he took it seriously. It was … like a party. I mean it was fun too. And after dinner we played more of Hugo's games, Jonathan was always brilliant with him and kind, and people were pretending things, like at Christmas except our family never did anything normal like that, and then… well suddenly a bit later Jonathan was shouting and terribly agitated, and we all realised something was wrong because he was never normally like that, and he'd discovered that Belinda seemed to have disappeared, he was shouting that he'd searched the whole house, and we all went out into the pouring rain for hours to look for her.'

'You must be worn out after all this. And has she been found?'

'No, he's gone out again, he's in the village. He's frantic.'

'But why did she run off, this Belinda?'

'I don't know, there was a story behind it all. I only heard a few things, and maybe she'd stopped taking her pills or something …'

'Jonathan collecting more waifs and strays as usual. You must be so tired my darling.'

'That's unkind. Yes of course, but you see I had a plan, I had to leave now, *today,* because Jonathan's so good with Hugo and it's probably the only time I could slip away without people noticing, but I feel guilty, and I think I'll always feel guilty and heartbroken…'

'Come here my darling, let me hold you.' He put his arm around her.

'But Max I… after everything.'

'You mean…'

'So much has gone wrong.' Anthea watched a woman walk past the car and listened to the footsteps fading.

'You mean …when we were filming.'

'Yes. All that. Stuff about …you were so angry and jealous, and it wasn't my fault. You made me do it.'

'Yes. But that's all over and done with now. George has closed the hotel for the moment and closed the Guest Rooms and asked me not to use our room for the time being. So …can we put all that behind us? Please?'

'It's hard.'

'Look this is the real me, Anthea. I'm not the shallow person you say I am. I was married to Angela for nearly twenty years before she got ill. But then I was lucky to be able to have private nurses to look after her at home. But then I was seeing someone during this because it was so hard, I needed someone else to help me. I loved her, well I loved *both* of them … but then this odd thing happened. Someone was blackmailing me and I had to end it'

'*Blackmailing* you!'

'Yes, someone who knew I was seeing Phillipa. And of course I shouldn't have been…'

'Who was Phillipa?'

'I met her at the Manor House. Right at the beginning when George and Millicent were having some little dinner parties, they'd just won the lottery.'

'Millicent?'

'George's ex. She left him soon after, they both had so much money, and he met Sylvia, she was an auctioneer, and they've been happy ever since. But the point is, what I'm trying to say is, I did love Phillipa, I do feel deep love whatever you say. But when Angie died Phillipa wouldn't have me back. I tried to talk to her, but I think she was seeing someone else. I regretted things… but then that was when I met you, do you remember?'

'Yes. Of course.'

'I could see straight away that life was dragging you down and you couldn't see a way out. And I wanted you of course. And then I discovered who the blackmailer was. When it all came out.'

'What do you mean?'

'It was Jonathan.'

'*Jonathan*! Oh yes, there was stuff about him in the newspapers wasn't there, I guess a lot of it was exaggerated about his weird ideas, and hard to believe when you knew him.'

'Yes exactly. He took Angie's funeral, he spoke so beautifully. He said all the right things, he gave it dignity and meaning. He's someone special. I couldn't hate him for it. It wasn't a lot of money and it only happened once. I never really spoke to him since the funeral, there were things going on. That was why I was surprised when you mentioned that he's come back here.'

'Well, he was looking after Belinda, she was very withdrawn, she couldn't cope with new people.'

'Perhaps he shouldn't have brought her. Another mistake maybe? You know the blackmail was odd, I mean I was angry at first, I couldn't work out who it was, an email with a funny name, but it did me a lot of good, I paid the money, and then I stopped seeing Phillipa and spent some valuable time with Angie during her last days and got on touch with our kids which took a bit of doing, and they came back, it was good that I did that. So he made me a better person.'

Maxwell was looking out of the window as he spoke and she glanced at him, surprised. The sun went in and the sky darkened. He took her hand and she let it rest and then he reached over and turned her face towards him. 'My darling how I've missed you.'

11 DECEMBER
At the Old Vicarage

Pamela and Natasha had put on their coats and scarves and were wandering around the village. They came to the church and tried the heavy oak door in the porch, finding it unlocked. Rays of sunlight slanted across the chancel through the colourful stained glass of the east window.

'Wow, it looks really beautiful.'

'She might have sheltered here mightn't she. Any signs of mud on the floor?'

They moved up and down studying the old pews and then Pamela sat down for a moment. This was where Jonathan went through so much confusion. She felt it. She imagined him taking the services, it was here he had struggled. Unwanted and startling images would come to his mind, words would choke in his throat. Disturbing quotations from the bible would intrude while others were spoken and read aloud.

'Pam, shall we move on?' Natasha sat down, 'I've looked everywhere. That little room is locked and there's no one here and no signs of anything.'

'Yes, let's go. We could call on Annie, Matt was a lodger in her house for a while, she lives right near here. Maybe Belinda's taking refuge there.'

They made their way through the overgrown churchyard and through a little gate into the wild garden of the Old Vicarage and followed a winding path through the bare trees which opened out to reveal the handsome house beyond. Pamela rang the bell and the door opened.

'Pam! What a lovely surprise!'

'Annie!'

'How lovely to see you.'

'I'm sorry to call so early,' said Pamela, 'This is Jonathan's cousin Natasha. We're staying in the village and we're looking for someone who's gone missing.'

'Well goodness me! Come in out of the cold. Excuse my dressing gown. The heating's working at the moment so make the most of it.'

They followed her to the kitchen and sat at the table while she filled the kettle. 'Well tell me more,' she said, brushing back her thick wavy hair, 'You've caught me on a day off and not up and about early.'

'Annie's a TV presenter,' said Pamela, 'She goes away and does filming for that programme about women in the nineteenth century, you know the one.'

'And then I come back and try to stop this old house from falling down,' said Annie making the tea, 'Nothing much with work till after the New Year now. But Pam it's been ages.'

'Yes. A lot has happened.'

The three of them sat at the table. 'Annie we were wondering if Belinda might have come here last night and asked if she could hide here?'

'Belinda? Oh yes, you said someone had gone missing. Well, no, I don't think so. But there's an old shed in the garden.'

'Can I go and check, would you mind?' said Natasha standing up.

'Of course.'

'You two stay here in the warm.'

'What on earth is going on Pam? You said she was Jonathan's cousin?'

'Well yes. It's a long story, Jonathan and I are together now. After a weird time when I couldn't manage to see him.'

'Oh my goodness... And are you alright?'

'Oh yes. Very alright. Look I know you worried that I was being swept off my feet by an older man and all that stuff...'

'Yes, I was. After everything that was happening.'

'Some of it was, and some of it wasn't...'

They heard the front door close and Natasha came back and sat the table. 'No sign of anything,' she said, 'Thanks for letting me look. I got the old door open but it didn't look like anyone had touched it for a while.'

'And yes, the junk hit you immediately,' said Annie, 'Some of it's mine, and a lot was there when I bought the house.'

'I know Annie quite well,' said Pamela to Natasha, 'Matt came here because something odd happened with our father who he hadn't seen for about seventeen years. Jonathan got to know him a bit, it's too much to tell you now. But she's been so good to us, so kind. He loved living here ... although it was lonely for someone his age. He should have been away at uni.'

'It must bring it all back coming to visit,' said Natasha.

'Yes. And something ... truly terrible happened here. In this house,' said Annie.

Natasha looked from one to the other.

'I try to get over it, you try to erase the images, of course the sadness never goes away, and the complete madness of it.'

'Tash, I expect you're wondering what she means,' said Pamela.

Annie stared at the table. 'I'm sorry Pam, I shouldn't have mentioned it. I'm sorry.'

'Is it okay if I tell Natasha?'

'Yes of course.'

'Well, you see, Annie was seeing this wonderful man, Augustus White, he was a surgeon living nearby. But they hardly ever saw each other, he worked long hours and had a wife and family. They just had this – connection – and then one day he called round ...'

'He never would have done that normally,' said Annie, wiping her nose.

'No – he was worried because … it sounds so awful to say.'

'He'd received a threat, a blackmail threat,' said Annie, 'He was worried this affair, if you could call it that, though it hardly was, was going to be revealed to his family. So he came round to see me, but then …' Annie looked at Pamela.

'Look don't tell me if it's too awful,' said Natasha, 'You don't need to.'

'He was trying to tell me about it,' said Annie, 'It's alright Natasha, it helps me to talk about it. Well, he was just trying to talk to me in the hall, he was really worried and then this bloke Trevor I'd been seeing came down the stairs. He was a cameraman on the show, it was just a stupid, *stupid* fling …'

'Trevor attacked Augustus Tash, he was in a jealous rage and he hit him on the head with the door stop. It was cast iron, very heavy. It killed him. Annie saw it all, and Matthew had come running down the stairs when he heard her shouting.'

'And of course I got rid of it when the police gave it back' said Annie, glancing apprehensively at Natasha, 'The door stop I mean, and Pam came round a few times, and that was a great help. A huge funeral, crowds outside the church, loudspeakers. He had helped so many people. And that was the time that …'

'It's alright, you can say it,' said Pam, 'A few people round here knew about the blackmail, though I don't think the police knew. I mean it was odd and hard to believe. I was seeing Jonathan then and it was one of the things that confused me.'

'I'm so sorry,' said Natasha.

'I sometimes think I'll sell this place,' said Annie, 'All that will never go away. It's a beautiful old house and someone will want it, and all its problems. But this is too much talking, if I get dressed quickly I can come along with you to help with the search.'

'I've got a new lodger now,' said Annie as the three of them walked down the road, 'Very quiet and reliable. But I keep thinking Matthew's going to come down those stairs, I find myself looking for those little post-it notes he used to stick on things saying things like, *Mend me before I fall apart* and *Don't eat me you're on a diet.*'

'It takes a long time,' said Pam. 'And none of it ever makes sense.'

'No. you're right ...'

'Now what does this Belinda look like?'

'Quite small, dark hair on her shoulders. A haunted look, worried. Timid.'

'Well she must be *somewhere.*'

12 DECEMBER
Fun to remember

George settled Sylvia on a sofa in the Guest Room and covered her with a duvet. 'Just have a bit more sleep after that terrible night. Let's hope Jonathan will be back soon. I'll just pop out for a quick walk.' Hands resting on her tummy she dozed off. Would Jonathan accept the Manor House, would he be pleased, would he cope? There would be a lot of packing to do and their little house in town was waiting for them. What would she do with the garden to make it child friendly?

George put on his coat and set off. Perhaps Belinda would turn up and things would calm down? Despite the weekend visitors the Manor House felt strangely empty. Those weeks when people came to play the Games had been extraordinary. To begin with it had worked so well, he and Sylvia had done careful planning and preparation. Everyone was cheerful and normal and accepted the rules and regulations while enjoying the hospitality. There had never been a shortage of bookings... as he walked George remembered a particular conversation that had happened in his small office off the hall. There had been footsteps coming along the corridor, high heels tapping on the floor and someone in flat shoes. It was

Petula who knocked on the door, she had been playing referee in a Game, and behind her stood a striking tall woman in a very tight shiny green dress. Petula said how glad she was to find him and this person said, 'I'm angry! I'm very angry indeed!' Petula said, 'George, I'm afraid Carla is very upset and I thought we would see if… you see the psychiatrist had disappeared when she was about to begin her Game.' He had asked Carla to sit down and said he would try and sort things out. 'No psychiatrist!' Carla was examining her face in a tiny mirror and patting her curly blond wig, 'He just didn't turn up! I've paid all this money to play the Game, all this money and I've been waiting and getting ready and…' She sniffed and put the mirror back in the handbag on her knee.

George remembered he had pretended to talk on his phone and then said that the psychiatrist had been taken ill. 'Well can't you find another psychiatrist? I need one *now*.' He said he was sorry and no one was available and he would arrange a refund and that sort of thing, but Carla was still very worked up. 'How is your weekend going so far,' he said, 'Weekend?... Oh, um… – well this place is stunning of course. It's fantastic. But I needed this talk you see, I really needed it. I don't suppose…' 'What's that?' 'I don't suppose *you* could be my psychiatrist. Right now, I mean? It's nice and quiet in here and… I like you…'

They smiled at each other. 'Carla there is absolutely no way I can play your psychiatrist. For one thing, you already know me, and these Games must be anonymous. 'I don't mind,' she said, 'It could be fun. You see – I've been … I need to talk to someone…' George explained that the Game is formal, and that the psychiatrist wears a mask so you don't know them but Carla was getting impatient, 'Yes I know all that, what the brochure says about - you can tell your psychiatrist anything and everything…' she giggled, 'But – well I really like you. It wouldn't take long. Have you got any spare masks in a cupboard somewhere?' She was looking around. 'It would be quite easy!' she said, 'You get us all here, we pay all this money and then this happens!' George mentioned the refund again and got out a form and started filling it in. Then Carla said, 'How did…how did all this start? It's a fantastic set up. Do tell! You've got time haven't you?' She giggled, 'You lot are making pots of money out of people's misery! Pots and pots. And wasn't there something about winning the lottery in the beginning?' He said that was a while ago. 'So you bought this old Manor House. You and…' They talked a bit more about it and how winning all that money made things go a bit haywire and some of the ideas were a bit outrageous, she was very interested. 'You are so lovely!' she said, and she was looking happier again, 'It's all so lovely. *Tie up your partner and tell them the truth.* Honestly! It's wonderful. Do *really* have people who come and play *that* Game? Honestly! …If you were my partner I wouldn't need to play it. I wouldn't need to tie you up. I would be so happy. Oh, I've just thought of another one for you, you could call it – Terrible and Tantalizing Tales at the LGBT Club'. She was laughing. 'I can tell you're a bit nervous of that one. Hmm! The name just popped into my head. I feel inspired! Thousands would come you know. We'd all come. You'd be millionaires! But perhaps you are already.' 'Well, there must be lots more Games we could think of,' he said, and they agreed that communication was such a big thing. He mentioned a new Game he was working on. 'Mixed messages huh!' she said, 'There are plenty of them knocking around. Are we having mixed messages? I do like you. You're so cuddly! And here's another one,' she had chatted on, 'Hey, my brain's in overdrive! It's so lovely! It's called, Let's Play at Being Grown Up.'

They had a laugh then, talked a bit more and then walked to the Guest Room for a coffee and she agreed to have dinner with him and Sylvia later. George remembered all this as he walked briskly along and was now approaching the houses in the village. Surely Belinda might have taken refuge somewhere? Feeling cold and damp he turned around and started back. Carla ended up saying, 'I'd much rather just dine with you alone. But I see you are determined.' Then she said, 'George you've calmed me down so beautifully, you're marvellous. I don't know how you did it. It was probably better than any psychiatrist.'

It was fun to remember. But then things had changed, it didn't feel the same and Lawrence had wanted to develop his theatre group and be in charge of the entertainment. George walked down the Manor House drive and hurried over to Jonathan who was parking his car under the trees.

'I'm very glad to see you back Jonathan.'

'Yes. Obviously no luck I'm afraid. I've talked to a few people who live in those houses near the stream, they're going to keep their eyes open.'

'Should we alert the police?'

'Well – I suppose we must,' said Jonathan.

'Look I'll do it, you look worn out. You go and have a rest.'

'Here are some details about her,' Jonathan pulled an envelope out of his pocket, 'Belinda Lockwood. Her mother said she could come and stay with us for a few weeks. It's all in there. I'll just go and freshen up.'

George took the forms and picked up the day's newspaper from the floor by the front door and went into his little office. He made the call and then walked along the corridor to the kitchen and was sitting at the table reading an article about Brexit when Hugo appeared looking windswept.

'Hello Hugo.'

'Where's Jonathan? Where's my sister? Why is Maxwell's house all empty?'

'I don't know, maybe he's gone shopping. Maybe Anthea went out with the others to have another search, I expect they'll all be back for lunch soon.' George bent again to his newspaper.

'What's for lunch, I'm hungry. Where's Sylvia?'

'She's having a rest Hugo, we need to be quiet please.'

'It's not fair,' said Hugo, 'Why does everyone keep going out and changing things?'

'Well, if you'd been wandering round the village in the freezing rain you'd need finding and looking after wouldn't you.'

'I wouldn't have gone out in the dark in that weather.'

George put a tin of biscuits in front of Hugo and washed up his mug.

'It's not fair!' Hugo shouted, 'I've got a new number game ready and there's no one here. The girl was stupid to go out like that and make everyone tired. I'm going to my room, I've got things to do.' He went out and banged the door.

Pamela and Natasha came in through the front door and wandered upstairs. Jonathan was in bed, fast asleep. Pamela took off her coat and lay down silently beside him. She would ask him to take her to the nearest train station, perhaps Natasha too. But what was he thinking about what George had said about the Manor House?

He turned over and spread himself out, still asleep. Then suddenly there was a great howling from one of the bedrooms. There were running footsteps and voices, and Jonathan woke up looking startled. 'Oh Pam,' he said, embracing her. 'What is *that*!'

Pamela opened the door and ran down the corridor. Hugo was standing in Anthea's room and tearing the sheets on her bed into shreds with his bare hands. 'My sister's gone!' he sobbed, 'She's left me, she's gone off with *him* and they'll never come back. I'll never see her again.'

Natasha came in and approached the bed. 'Come on Hugo, we'll sort this out.'

He turned and struck her on the face and she fell back. 'Where's Jonathan?' he shouted, 'I want Jonathan.'

'He's been sleeping Hugo,' said Pamela supporting Natasha with tears in her eyes, 'Don't you dare do that again Hugo. Jonathan's completely exhausted and needs a rest. Try and be a bit quieter…'

George came in and stood the other side of the bed. Hugo fell to his knees and started winding a strip of sheet around his neck, 'I'd be better off dead,' he whimpered. George came forward and tried to pull it out of his hands, 'Come on Hugo, we'll talk about this, are you alright Natasha?'

'Sort of.' She felt her face. Hugo resisted George's efforts and buried his face in the torn sheet. 'First our dad,' he sobbed, 'Then our mother, I always knew she'd go. She made herself ill. And now… Anthea's been wanting to go, I always knew…she doesn't want to spend any more Christmases with me…' He went on sobbing and George and the girls looked at each other.

Jonathan came into the room yawning and looked from one to the other.

'He struck me Jonathan,' said Natasha, 'He's gone crazy.'

'Oh Jonathan you should be resting…'

'But what's happened?'

Hugo looked up, wiping his eyes on the sheet. 'Anthea's left me,' he said, 'She's… Maxwell's gone, they've gone.'

Jonathan sat down. 'Sit here Hugo,' he patted the bed. 'Now come on let's talk calmly about this. Unwind that, yes, that's it. Now give it to me for the moment. We don't want you to hurt yourself do we? Maybe they just went for a walk. How long has Anthea been staying here mmm?'

'About… three weeks. She came on a Friday and today is Saturday.'

'And if she's decided to live in Maxwell's house again, well she's nearby isn't she. You could see her every day.'

'No. They haven't just gone for a walk. They've *gone,* his car's gone, I've been over to see. I've still got the key and I went in and had a look.' He started sobbing again.

13 DECEMBER

'Why did you call me back?'

Ruby sat and waited, listening to sounds from the bathroom and looking out through her living room window.

And then the girl appeared. Her wet, black hair was neatly combed on her shoulders, and she was wearing one of Ruby's old jumpers and jeans. She stood looking around. 'Um… thank you for looking after me.'

Ruby jumped up. 'That's good. You warmer now?'

'Yes… I've left my wet clothes in the bathroom, sorry I didn't know…'

'No problem, I'll sort them out. Come and sit down and I'll make you some breakfast.'

The girl sat on the edge of the sofa and watched, 'Cup of tea ok? First I'll get a duvet and you'll get really warm then.' Ruby ran upstairs.

A bit later she came in with a tray and saw the girl had fallen asleep under the duvet. So who was she? Had Jonathan said a name, she couldn't remember. But why was she so terrified of the police and the ambulance people? And why had she run away into the black rainstorm in December, it was lucky she was alive. Jonathan must be told surely. But when Ruby moved silently to the window she saw his car had gone.

Where was he staying, had he said? Not many friends here in this village, maybe at the Manor House? It had all been a bit quiet recently, all those cars that appeared at weekends seemed to have stopped coming.

The girl moved and opened her eyes. 'Oh… sorry.'

'You're worn out. Look here's something and the tea's still hot. Do you want to tell me a bit about yourself?'

'Oh… um. Oh!'

'My name's Ruby and I live alone here. There's no one else to bother us.'

'Oh!... I don't remember! I don't remember my name. It's a blank.'

'Drink your tea and try and eat a bit. You've had a big shock, you were freezing cold for hours.'

'I'm sorry. I don't remember.' The girl stared ahead and drank from the mug and put it on the floor. 'I was somewhere else, I was floating and it was so lovely… I didn't want to come back but then I heard you calling. Why did you call me back, I didn't want to come back…' Her eyes filled with tears.

'I'm very sorry,' said Ruby, 'I'm so sorry things are so confusing. It will probably all come back into your mind quite soon. You were very, very cold and wet for hours.'

'Can I stay here? Please don't tell the police and the ambulance people, please don't.'

'No I won't.'

'Can I hide here?'

'Well… I was just going away on a winter holiday.'

'Oh no! No! I'll be on my own and…' The girl stood up, clutching the duvet and knocking over the mug of tea. 'Please don't leave me.'

'No of course I won't,' said Ruby hastily, 'You could come with me, I'm driving up there in a minute, I must leave soon as it gets dark so early. You could stay in the hotel with me, it's a big room. I'll just get a cloth …'

She came back and started dabbing the wet patch on the carpet.

'But… I haven't any clothes. I…'

'I'll lend you some, and those fit, wear them for now. And we can buy some more and a case or a bag.'

'Are you sure?'

'Yes. Now look, try and eat that and stay warm. I'll go and put some things together and we can go in a few minutes.'

They left soon after and as Ruby started up the car and glanced at her bewildered passenger she saw a police car across the village green coming from the main road and turning up the hill to the Manor House. Had they got out just in time? Had the girl seen it too? She was staring out of the window. Was this whole thing going to collapse into chaos before it started? Ruby drove slowly towards the motorway and after a while tried to talk about ordinary things until the girl dozed off and she could concentrate on the road.

14 DECEMBER
A big decision

Keith knocked loudly on the front door of the Manor House and stood still, listening. They must surely be in? Hopefully he hadn't come all this way for nothing. But then – if things were changing then might be a good thing. He must make his visit look awkward, he must say he couldn't email or phone and that he really needed to make things up with George after storming out like he had.

He tried again and then walked round the house to the side door and the kitchen windows. It was abnormally quiet, where were the guests, were they all playing Games? But then next to the two cars parked under the cedar trees was a police car. What was happening? Had everyone come in taxis? Had there been some rather dreadful event finally after months of threatened chaos and emotional turmoil? Even better, that might give him opportunities to move unobserved around the house.

There must surely be a few hangers on in the Guest Room? He peered through the window and saw a woman lying on the sofa fast asleep and covered with a duvet. Was that *Sylvia?* Was she ill?

'George!'

George was walking towards his car and turned. 'Oh, Keith! How nice to see you, what a surprise.'

'Yes – look I'll say this straight away and then get out of your way if you're busy. I just wanted to apologise. I was out of order that day. I wanted to see you face to face and try and explain – why I behaved so badly. I shouldn't have talked so much about all the things that I can't accept and the medications which worry me so much, it was too much and not the right time. You have a perfect right to run this place how you decide and take a break or stop altogether, it was your decision, yours and Sylvia's of course... you know that time a few months ago when I...'

'Oh...' George had walked across the grass and held out his hand. 'It's lovely to see you, Keith. Hope you're well? Don't worry about all that. You have your strong views, and I would never question those and your experience. We were lucky to have you on the staff. But today I'm afraid you've come at a bad time.'

'Well, I won't stay and get in your way. I'm sorry, is there anything I can do? What's happening, do you have guests this weekend? It all seems very quiet.'

'No, no guests for a while. Still having a break. Look at least come in and have something, lunch perhaps. Sylvia will be getting up soon, she's having a rest after a worrying night when we were looking for someone. The police are here searching the whole place which of course will take some time.'

'Oh... oh dear. It's a bad moment to call.'

'It would take a while to explain so I won't now. I was just off to do a bit of shopping, but it can wait. We all gather in the kitchen at the moment, it's the warmest room in the house.'

'You're very kind,' said Keith as he followed George and they went in through the side door.

Sylvia had got up and was tidying up the kitchen and thinking about lunch for everyone and George was giving her a hand. Hugo sat at the table arranging bits of cardboard and writing down lists of numbers and instructions. She broke off to make some coffee while Keith sat watching Hugo and passing him blank pieces of cardboard while making encouraging remarks. Hugo didn't reply.

Jonathan put his head round the door – 'Ah Keith! How are you?'

'Hello Jonathan. Just popped in to er, I am well thank

you.'

'Look I'm very sorry Sylvia but could I borrow George for a minute? It's rather urgent.'

George put the carrot back on the chopping board and followed Jonathan to the Guest Room and they sat down and looked at each other.

'What's Keith doing here? Just visiting?'

'Poor chap seems very down. Wanted to apologise. A few weeks ago he left after a bit of a row, got a bit carried away with his own worries. He didn't like what I'd decided.'

'Hmm. Awkward. But it was good to have a psychologist around, he was always very, very good with people wasn't he. He helped me several times when people were a bit wound up.

'Yes indeed. What was it you wanted to see me about? The police seem to be doing a very thorough search everywhere.'

'Well obviously we're all preoccupied at the moment. But I wanted to clarify something you said yesterday. About giving me the Manor House.'

'Yes. I did yes.'

'Well … I expect it was some kind of joke, I mean… '

'No Jonathan. Absolutely not. Sylvia and I are in complete agreement. We've had some amazing fun with our guests, but we both want a normal life now, obviously we'll be comfortably off in our little house which incidentally I bought with left over lottery money …'

'But, yes I understand all that, and it's wonderful news about the baby of course, but the fact is the Manor House is *yours*. Surely you could sell it?'

'Yes it's mine to do what I like with. And I'm giving it to you.'

'But supposing I can't accept this – enormous gift?'

'Can't?'

'Or decide I won't? Or mustn't?'

'Well – let's talk about it a bit more. As far as I'm concerned you are an… '

There was a discreet knock on the door and two policemen came in. 'I'm sorry to interrupt. We've completed our search of the house and grounds, so we'll leave you for the time being, we have all the details. Please let us know of any developments. Perhaps she'll turn up after a few hours having stayed with someone.'

'Let's hope so.' George saw them out and watched the police car drive away.

'Jonathan you are a talented individual who has been through a tremendous crisis,' said George sitting down again, 'I doubt that many people would comprehend this, and obviously a lot of journalists have been having a field day and would probably continue if they had the chance.'

'Well, I…'

'Hear me out Jonathan. Please. We may be interrupted at any moment, goodness knows who might turn up next. Dozens of people and organisations keep on emailing. But now I want to do something good with that money. And giving the building to you will give you opportunities that you wouldn't otherwise have. I mean you could start up the hotel again and get the Games going, but somehow I doubt that's what you would do.'

'It seems your mind's made up,' said Jonathan. He was overwhelmed by George's kindness. Yes, it was a tremendous crisis but one that was invisible to most people. The loss of a great love, one that could not be measured or defined, that had no beginning and no end. What was left behind when that was gone? And could there possibly be anything that could compare with it …?

'Yes, my mind is made up,' said George, '*Our* minds are made up.'

The door opened and Pamela appeared. 'Oh sorry.'

'Come in Pam. It's cold in here but we can talk. The kitchen's getting a bit crowded.'

'I'll go and see how Sylvia's getting on,' said George getting up. 'You two take your time.'

'Sylvia says lunch is nearly ready,' said Pamela coming to sit beside Jonathan, 'I just wanted to ask you something. Can you drive me and Natasha to the train station this afternoon? We have to get back and it looks like things are getting complicated here.'

'But Pam can't you stay a bit longer?' He took her hand. 'I've got things to be doing. And ...'

'I've just had a talk with George.'

'Yes.'

'Shall I tell you about it?'

Pamela stared out of the windows.

'What's the matter?'

'You must decide what to do. I won't interfere.'

'It's not interfering. You can help me.'

'I can't.'

'It's a big decision. It's huge.'

'I have to go – after lunch,' she said, and stood up, 'I'll see you there in a minute. Hugo's missing you and telling everyone. And a strange guy has turned up.'

15 DECEMBER
The girl sat silent

The quiet hotel stood beside the lake with a few guests coming and going, Ruby remembered it from December two years before. Old couples and young walkers and solitary individuals who kept themselves to themselves. It was already dark when they arrived and after a light meal in the half empty dining-room they had gone to bed early. Ruby was relieved the girl seemed to drop off and sleep soundly. She had hardly spoken since they left the village.

At breakfast there were more people around, one seemed to be a photographer who had a large plate of bacon and eggs and then went out early and was preoccupied with his equipment and often speaking on his phone. Ruby noticed the girl watching him, he looked like Jonathan she thought. But she felt relieved, it was perfect here, peaceful and homely. She had booked the double room and she persuaded the old couple to let them stay over Christmas. She said that the girl had been ill and needed a bit of peace and quiet and Mrs Fawes had been friendly. 'Yes of course stay over Christmas,' she said, 'There won't be much going on here though. Our children are away this year. Something more exciting to do!'

Now the girl was sitting in the twin-bedded room watching the weak sunshine on the lake and the grey clouds that came and went. 'It's really lovely, it's really so lovely.'

Ruby persuaded her to come out for a walk and lent her a camera. She paused and sat on a seat while the girl wandered along staring at the view and taking photos. The path meandered uphill and through some trees. What was going to happen? Ruby found herself craving for the solitude she was used to, everything had happened so quickly. Why on earth hadn't she told Jonathan about the girl there and then?

Now she regretted talking to that reporter about him. Articles trivialised the stories, he had been confused and lonely and talked to people. Seeing him unexpectedly had awakened all those old feelings and unrealistic expectations ... But now here they were. She remembered the girl opening her eyes and looking around the wet garden ... *I was somewhere else...*

Was it a criminal offence to take a vulnerable person away? And would the girl suddenly remember some traumatic event and get hysterical or worse, and would she accuse Ruby of something, and how could she possibly explain any of it to the kind but vague Mrs Fawes and her invalid husband? When she and the girl were here over Christmas it would feel solitary and sad while everywhere else families got together and had wonderful celebrations. She had already noticed several curious glances from people at breakfast when the girl sat silent and picked at her food and seemed nervous when there was a burst of laughter at another table and loud chatter from the other end of the dining room. There must be a correct way to handle this loss of memory, keeping someone in their familiar environment with people who knew them, waiting for an event or a place to remind them of something …

The girl was near the top of the little hill taking more photos and glancing back to see that Ruby was still there. Perhaps she would suddenly vanish, and it would be as if she had never been there at all and everything would then be as it usually was in this lonely winter retreat.

If she couldn't remember who she was, was she in fact *real?* Did she actually exist now her memory was gone. *I see her* Ruby thought, a pale tortured face, worried eyes. But what am I seeing? Phrases came into her mind from her favourite little book of philosophy about whether a table was a product of one's imagination or a very long dream. Could we be quite sure that everything we saw around us was *real?* Though she knew much of the book by heart it would be a comfort to look at it again and realise that many others had thought about such things, had studied them and puzzled over them for hours and days and weeks and even years … It was all madness, and they had only just got away.

16 DECEMBER
Puzzling

Natasha sat back in the train and watched the dull, wintry countryside flashing past. She was on her way to the seaside to try and find her father. Now that Belinda wasn't around to look after it was difficult and depressing having time to kill sitting alone in Jonathan's deserted house, she needed people, distractions, things happening, anything. She needed to get work and earn money, it was more awkward now Jonathan was away and his plans seemed to be changing. She needed to try and remind herself how she felt when the cocaine wore off, and how all those things had been getting worse …Surely the thought of that was enough to make her want to stop?

Her father would still be grieving, he was an alcoholic, irrational and distant. She was dreading a lonely Christmas but the thought of that was nothing compared to the constant images of a dealer lurking in a dark alley, promising moments she couldn't resist.

Her last conversation with Pam had been puzzling, they had arrived back at Jonathan's house after a complicated and annoying train and bus journey from the Manor House and were sitting in the bare living room waiting for it to warm up.

'I've hardly spoken to Jonathan, but I had to get away.'

'But why Pam? He wanted you to stay, surely you could have …'

'Things to do here. He was – so worried about Belinda and busy trying to sort other things out. What to do with this offer of the Manor House …'

'I'm sorry you feel that way. He looked so sad when he dropped us off. But preoccupied.'

'He said he wants me to move, but I've said I can't.'

'Well yes, it's rather sudden. But why? You two belong together.'

'There's something… I can't really explain it. Best not to try.'

'I'm so sorry. Must be so disturbing for you. But can't you tell *him* about it?'

'No.'

'Is it affecting him?'

'I can't really say. It's complicated. He's strong, he can overcome it, it's going to take time. It's something he has to face, something very difficult and complex. I can't go there to be with him and I can't say anything. I have to do what I have to do.'

'I still can't see why you can't just *be* there with him and support him … through – whatever it is.'

'Yes. I miss him like crazy. Every minute. Of course, I'm used to him being distracted, and burying his head in books for a while but this is a massive weight being put on his shoulders. As soon as George made this offer he started thinking about so many possibilities… he mentioned one or two to me already, they're in his mind.'

'But he loves you Pam, he adores you. I know a lot has

happened in the past …'

'It's not that. Our feelings don't change, he'll come back and see me. But I can't tell him, you see, I can't tell him and I can't watch him go through it either. He has to do it alone.'

'It sounds – just awful. If I didn't know you better Pam I would honestly think you were talking nonsense.'

'But you do know me.'

'Yes. I know that you've told me things – that is before you knew me - you knew my mother and sister had died suddenly and you told me they were okay and wanted me to talk to Dad and stop him blaming himself. I know that happened and I can't explain it. It was something I needed to hear which helped me so much.'

'I'm very glad about that. I'll be alright Tash, don't worry about me.'

Natasha remembered the moment Pam had told her this at a demonstration in the back room of a pub. She didn't usually go to things like that and didn't know what to expect. But it had been extraordinary. Now on the train she replayed all this in her mind, it meant she took things Pam said seriously, however strange they seemed. It also made it look like she would find her father eventually. What was he doing now, was he working again and putting his life back together? He had constantly been drinking in Jonathan's house, that must have used up a lot of money. There must be some left surely after the sale of the house? Where was all the furniture and everything?

The train was slowing down as they approached her station, and she gathered her bits and pieces together and stood up. Now she was here where her family had come so many times in the summer, and there were seagulls crying …a lovely sound that brought back memories. She crossed the platform and made her way along familiar streets.

17 DECEMBER
Quite different plans

Hugo pulled his coat more closely around him and bent again to the ground. He had walked the length of the Manor House and back again, prodding the ground and searching. Perhaps he was in the wrong place? He turned a corner and glanced through the windows of the Guest Room where he could see Jonathan and George sitting in a corner, deep in conversation.

The cold finally got to him, and he went in through the side door and walked down the corridor to the kitchen. With a tin of biscuits beside him he pulled various sheets of paper and cardboard out of a cupboard and spread them on the table and was absorbed for a while doing various calculations.

'Yes George. I understand all that, absolutely. But perhaps you could let me live here and run some projects while it was still *yours*. That would be a good solution wouldn't it? It would leave things open for the future. You feel you want to get away *now* but who knows what might happen later on?'

'I'm sorry but my mind is made up Jonathan. I want you to feel free to decide everything. I expect you've got some ideas lined up.'

'Well yes, things are occurring to me.'

'Well *we* certainly had some ideas. Sylvia started it really, she thought of having guests and then inventing some entertainment. But it took off amazingly and it was such fun, she came into my life like a ray of sunshine, she helped me furnish the place with wonderful furniture from the auction house, she was quite happy to give all that up and come here, and then of course Max was always in the background helping with business things, he was brilliant, he was glad the Manor House was being lived in again after lying sad and empty for a while.'

'And you ended up employing a lot of people. What's happened to all of them?'

'I'll need to let them know,' said George, 'It's over. They're all on paid leave at the moment. I must get on with that, I've been putting it off. I'll give them all good references. I had to be sure of course. I presume you wouldn't consider starting it all up again?'

'Well, my thoughts are of quite different plans really. Leasing out space to organisations who need it, helping groups, that sort of thing. And Hugo ... well I think he has potential. I've always thought that from the first time I met him when he lived in the family house in North Road. The way he plays with numbers is astonishing. No one has ever encouraged him to do anything. And there must be others like him who've probably been equally neglected or misunderstood.'

'Mmm. I wonder if I could show you a few things on the computer, then I can give you various passwords and all that.'

'Of course. While we're not being interrupted.'

George arranged his laptop on a nearby table. 'By the way I had a little chat with Keith yesterday and he left. He seemed awfully sad about something, but I didn't have time. And there's Lawrence of course, he never stops emailing. Always full of amazing ideas for his acting group. I wish he could find his place somewhere and get known properly ...'

'Yes, quite. I avoided him when I could.'

'Oh, here's an email from Maxwell,' said George. Jonathan drew up a chair.

Dear George and Jonathan. I'm writing this to both of you because I gather you are visiting Jonathan. I will phone to remind you to read it if I don't get a reply after a week or two. I have spoken with Anthea and I don't know what's happening at the Manor House.

I need to ask for your help, I need to explain a few things and apologise as well.

Jonathan. Anthea tells me you were visiting and there seemed to be a possibility that you might take things over at the Manor House. I heard that you were searching for a missing girl, I'm sorry about the worry and hope that is resolved.

I'm afraid I have to tell you that Anthea has left Hugo for good. I expect you guessed this and no doubt he will have worked it out and get hysterical. I can't excuse her leaving but I do understand, it's been a tremendous burden to her for many years and she needs a break. We'll spend Christmas with friends in France and then have a bit of a holiday, I will probably be selling my house. I will ask the agents not to display a For Sale sign. I am supporting her and looking after her. It's very painful and she feels terrible but on the other hand she looked after him for years working in low paid jobs.

I'm writing also about the valuable photographic equipment in our room. Obviously we won't be carrying on with the project in there and the room could be put to good use.

I would be very grateful if you could sell it for me. I'll give you details in a minute. I'll give information about the stuff and places where you can sell it online, people are always looking for bargains.

I'm sorry this is all rather startling news for you both and I leave you with the delicate task of telling Hugo. It's never going to be easy is it?

Best regards

Max

Please see below the details about websites and professionals who are always looking for good photographic equipment.

'Well, well,' said George, 'The end of a chapter isn't it. Shall I look after all that?'

'No, I can do it,' said Jonathan. 'You start handing things over and concentrate on packing and getting in touch with people.'

'I'll write down some passwords and that kind of thing. And all the household stuff is in various paper files in the downstairs office. And yes there's a lot I'll deal with of course, people to contact. You might need a housekeeper, there's no one at the moment. The gardener is good, you'll want to hang on to him, does a great job and can turn his hand to all kind of tasks in the house if you ask him. And the caterers are excellent, I've got their contact details, they'll be glad to come back if you've got people here. And then there's the business of transferring the house to you. That will probably take a considerable time to achieve, months I expect. There'll probably be all kinds of checks and things, making sure I'm in my right mind and all that. I believe there's a new solicitor in town, he looks alright. So in the meantime you can live here rent free and start planning.'

'And I'll do the job of clearing Maxwell's room,' said Jonathan.

'Do you know what they were doing in there?'

'I had my suspicions George …'

'They were making porn movies.'

'Yes … Well it's a good thing he's moving on isn't it, goodness me! That could still have been going on now! The room will be useful. The main thing is how we handle Hugo isn't it.'

'Well, that's what you're particularly good at Jonathan.'

'George, I wonder…'

'What?' George was looking at the computer screen.

'I hope Anthea will be okay.'

'What do you mean?'

'Well, it's just something she once told me. It was a bit vague and I think she got cold feet and rushed off …'

'Mmm. It's good Max is looking after her now.'

'Mmm. I wonder about that too.'

'By the way, I'm sorry Pam felt she had to go so soon. She seemed – a bit down? Have you discussed all this with her?'

'She didn't really want to say much. All a bit of a shock I expect, rather a lot to take in.'

'I think you should go and see her, make sure she's alright.'

'Oh yes. I'm planning to drive up very soon.'

'And Belinda?'

'We'll have to keep looking and asking people. Of course.'

'It must be so dreadful not knowing. Has she got family?'

'Well best she never sees her father I again. He should be prosecuted, I'm not sure what happens next. Her mother readily agreed she could come and stay with us for a while, I think she was relieved.'

'Do you know the full story of what was going on?'

'No, I haven't asked Belinda much, but I fear the worst happened.'

'Mmm.'

'I thought we were like her new family. That's what we tried to be.'

'Dear me.'

'Natasha was working part time in London – and she latched on to Natasha, well Natasha felt terrible later because she wasn't friendly, and then Belinda vanished, and Natasha glanced at a notebook she'd been writing in and realised how serious it was ...'

'So what happened to Belinda?'

'Well, Natasha learnt later, it's a long story, she was picked up by some young criminals and lived in a house with them, there was something about a robbery that didn't happen, and they just vanished one day, and she was alone and survived somehow, but then one day she went out and when she came back someone had changed the locks on the doors, so she rushed off ... then I just happened to see a little newspaper headline about a girl who had been found and I followed it up and found her in hospital.'

'Goodness me! Quite a story Jonathan.'

'Yes, it was incredible, I knew it must be her because when I arrived she was asleep, the ward was busy and the staff were trying to cope, and I sat beside her bed and had little look in a rucksack in her locker which had some notebooks in it, but when she woke up she was terrified of me and the staff told me to go. But then somehow we managed to trace her to the psychiatric hospital and Natasha managed to win her confidence.'

'And there's this notebook. I'm so sorry.'

'Yes, she was always trying to make sense of things ...'

'I'm so sorry. And you've worked so hard.'

'Yes.'

'There's an awful lot to do here. There are problems with the building, it's all in a file. It must be hard for you to concentrate on other things. I'll put together all the information for you. And goodness me it'll soon be Christmas.'

18 DECEMBER
'It isn't nothing.'

'What is it, Pam?'

'Nothing Jonathan.'

'It isn't nothing.'

'It's hard to say. On the phone.'

'But you must. Talk to me. Please.'

'Oh Jonathan I miss you so much. Will you be back for Christmas?'

'We'll work something out.'

'Everything feels – strange here. Your house misses you. Tash has gone away for a few days.'

'Look I'll pop back and see you very soon.'

'I've got a lot to do – you know. The training. It's very absorbing. We're both doing what we have to do, that's what we say don't we. We have to do it.'

'I've been talking to George, he won't budge, he insists on giving it to me.'

'Won't that be complicated?'

'Oh yes, it'll take months. Meanwhile I can start some projects here while he moves out. I'll look after it for him …'

'So …what about your house?'

'Well that too of course. Be simpler to sell it wouldn't it. If any bills arrive let me know.'

You still there Pam?'

'Yes I'm here.'

'No news of Belinda of course, I would have said.'

'Awful.'

'I go out and wander around. Try to think of somewhere new where she might be. Hopeless.'

'I don't think she's …'

'No, I know you'd say.'

'Pam.'

'Yes.'

'I need you here with me. Please. Please think about it. How it could be done. Did you get my text yesterday? It was supposed to be a joke.'

'No, don't think so. It's a bit remote where you are.'

'Home is where *we* are, remember we said.'

'I remember. Of course.'

'This huge old place. Needs people in it.'

'You have a lot on your mind.'

'What am I thinking now?'

'Don't be flippant Jonathan.'

'Sorry. Look, change of plan, I'm going to get in the car first thing tomorrow before it gets light and come and see you. Is that alright? Will you let me in?'

'Very funny! This is your house.'

'Please let me in and never let me go.'

'I'll never let you go.'

'No Pam …I know.'

'I'll kidnap you and keep you here.'

'Sounds absolutely delightful I can't wait. I know, you can tie me up and tell me the truth.'

'Oh ha ha, very funny, that was one of those Games wasn't it. Oh but what about Hugo?'

'Oh he'll be alright. George and Sylvia are doing lots of packing, it'll take them days. They're leaving the big pieces of course. They can keep an eye on him. He's been disappearing quite a lot recently goodness knows where.'

'Are you sure? He gets upset if he thinks you are abandoning him.'

'No I'll explain that I'm not abandoning him. I'm not abandoning *you* either. Darling I'm coming home.'

'I have to wait till tomorrow.'

'You'll have me tomorrow.'

'Yes.'

'I know it's hard. I want you now, this minute! Text me soon. In five minutes.'

'Till tomorrow then.'

'Text me.'

'I'll text you. And hope it arrives.'

'A few hours and I'll be home.'

'Home is where *we* are.'

'I love you Pam. For always.'

'Till tomorrow then.'

"I'll be up early.'

'Drive safely.'

'Of course.'

'Sleep well.'

'You too.'

'Better go to bed soon.'

'Text me. Precious little messages keeping me alive till I see you again.'

'Yes.'

'Now go.'

'No you go first.'

'Ha ha! Love you Pam.'

'It's not long till tomorrow.'

'Send me lots of kisses. Real ones tomorrow.'

'Yes.

'Till tomorrow.'

19 DECEMBER
Happiness

Jonathan lay in bed watching Pamela and waited for her to turn the final pages. How was such happiness possible?

'Good book?'

'Yes, I'm enjoying it. Though life seems stranger than fiction for us doesn't it?'

'Yes. Can I talk to you?'

'Only two pages to go.'

'Have you worked out who did it?'

'I think so. Well, there are two people it might be…but often it's the one you haven't even thought of, and they turn out bad when they seemed harmless all along.'

'Hmm!'
	'Well?'
	'Ah, so it *was* her…the cleaning lady. She was planning it all along as revenge for her daughter.'
	'Are you pleased?'
	'Huh! It was just a fun read. Helps me unwind.'
	When she put the bookmark in the book he took it out of her hands and laid it on the bedside table. Then he removed her glasses and laid them beside it. 'But Pam you don't seem to need to unwind. Come here.' He wrapped his arms around her.
	'Well – an escape then. You see I can't sense things about people in the book, so it's relaxing compared with real life.'
	'Ah. How interesting! Maybe I should start reading detective novels to unwind. My mother had plenty but I gave most of them away.'
	'Hmm. But surely your mind is on higher things?'
	'Haha! Yes. I'm afraid so.'
	'Afraid?'
	'It's started racing again Pam. You know, since Belinda ran off there's this awful anxiety all the time and guilt of course, but then at the same time my mind keeps on going over and over things, I can't control it.'
	'I know.'
	'Do you know what I worry about?'
	'What's that?'
	'Well … of course I keep trying to remember things she and I talked about and wondering if I said the wrong thing, I was always trying to persuade her that something dreadful wasn't about to happen, and there so many odd and symbolic things that could be explained in so many different ways …'

'Is it like all these crazy ideas will overwhelm both of you?'

'That just about sums it up, yes. But I try to hang on to common sense. I need your common sense so much. And your love.'

'You've got my love. Always.'

'Yes.'

'But surely you have to do what you have to do. Go on studying it and trying to find answers. You can't leave it in the middle.'

'Middle?'

'Well, isn't that where you are?'

'I thought I was at the end.'

'But you're not.'

'No - it's like…you know Alice in Wonderland, or was it the other one, you know running faster and faster and finding actually you have hardly moved, in fact you are further back than when you started.'

'Yes. Frustrating.'

'Drives me mad.'

'Well. I'm sane, so that's one of us.'

'And I need you for that.'

'Yes.'

'You know sometimes…'

'Yes?'

'Sometimes it's like…over two billion people are being conned right now.'

'That's quite a lot of people.'

'That's an approximate number of the Christians currently living in the world. I think.'

'But … does it matter Jonathan? There are different religions and …'

'Well, *I don't know*! I don't know if it matters or not. People say it makes them happier. But then there are all the conflicts and confusions…And look at terrorism. In the early days this new – well shall we say cult, it was mostly spread by word of mouth and little groups of people started forming, and it looks like other people found them rather strange, but of course that's all tied with the Roman gods and all that...'

'Yes. Are there a lot of books already written about this kind of thing?'

'Oh yes, dozens! There's a lot to get through. There is masses and masses of stuff and you can quickly get tied up in intellectual knots. And you need to distinguish between authoritative commentaries, wild speculation and pure brainwashing! There's plenty of *that* I can tell you!'

'You're a fast reader.'

'Haha. There are just layers and layers of it, going back, these crazy heresies started, and all the unbelievable stuff with the Emperor Constantine.'

'Yes. You know sometimes I feel like there are three people in this bed.'

'Haha!'

'And he's not a nice person to be in bed with.'

'Haha!'

'I'd much rather be alone with you.'

'Oh! Sorry! There, he's gone. We are alone.'

'I'm amazed that someone like you would want to talk to someone like me ...about this kind of thing.'

'But Pam ... you help me.'

'Yes, we help each other. But I'm just little Ms Average, though when you explain some of it I can understand a bit more.'

'Hardly little Ms Average!'

'Well thank you kind sir.'

'You ... connect with something else. Something ... unfathomable.'

'Yes.'

'I'm sorry you're living in a shabby, half-furnished house.'

'It doesn't matter. It feels like home to me. I can handle you being away, but ...'

'I know. You don't really understand about the Manor House.'

'Well I do *understand* … it's a chance to help people, of course.'

'There's a but coming.'

Pamela was silent. He kissed her. 'No buts. Find a way to stop me talking.'

20 DECEMBER
Pretending

'Well, what do you think?'

'Very good, you've done well,' said Ruby. She and the girl were in the hotel bedroom looking at some photos on Ruby's laptop, 'You could pick the best ones and delete the rest. We must go out again when the weather clears.'

'Will it stop raining soon do you think?'

'Never know round here.'

'Shall I put the telly on?'

'Why not? I'll boil the kettle.'

'Who do you think that man is?'

'Which man?'

'The man with the stuff.'

'Oh, I think he's a photographer, is that who you mean?'

'Tall and thin.'

'Why do you think he's come here?'

'Well, *I* don't know. Maybe a bit of a holiday like us. Maybe some atmospheric photos, perhaps he's working.'

'Or maybe just pretending.'

'What do you mean?'

'Oh no, please!'

'What's the matter?'

'Please. That scares me. Stones falling out of the sky.'

'It's Syria.'

'Oh please, it scares me, please!'

'I'll turn it off,' said Ruby, reaching for the remote. 'It's the news about this terrible war in Syria. It's thousands of miles away, nothing for you to get worried about. We don't have to watch it, perhaps it's jogging your memory about something? It's Syria being bombed in the war.'

'Oh no, not you too.'

'What?'

'Pretending.'

'What do you mean?' Ruby remembered the odd remark about the photographer. 'If it's reminding you of something well no one knows we're here, you're safe with me you know.'

'But he's here.'

'Who?'

'The tall man. Watching me.'

'The photographer?'

'He's come here to keep an eye on me. Make sure I don't get away.'

'Would it help,' Ruby began, 'To talk to him a bit? You and me together? We could just say hello and isn't the rain awful and things people say to each other on holiday in the middle of winter. And we could ask him about his cameras and things couldn't we, they look interesting. And expensive. He's no one I know.'

'He'd only go on pretending.'

Ruby was silent. What should she say next? Should they leave and go somewhere else? But where? The girl seemed to be thinking, then they both jumped when there was a quiet knock on their door, and Ruby went to open it.

'Hello, I hope you don't mind me calling on you. What a dreadful day isn't it. I saw you both at breakfast.'

'Hello. Yes, isn't it. But the weather changes quickly round here doesn't it.'

'Yes. My name is Tim Aylesford and I'm on a working holiday. Someone has let me down and I was wondering – if I could ask a very big favour indeed?' He handed Ruby a business card.

'Do come in a minute,' said Ruby moving a chair near the others, 'I'm Ruby and this is… a daughter of a friend. She's been ill and we're taking things slowly.'

'Well thank you. Very kind. Well, I'll come straight to the point. You see someone has let me down, she was going to be a model in some photos, and I caught sight of you…' he glanced at the girl '… and I wondered if you would consider posing for me outside, and I would pay you of course, and your friend could be there all the time. You see you've got exactly the right looks for it, pure coincidence. What do you think?'

The girl stared. She looked as though she was trying to work something out.

'I'm sorry,' said Ruby, 'She's recently had a bit of a shock and, well she gets a bit confused.'

'Oh, I'm sorry. I didn't realise. Am I making things worse?'

Ruby was watching the girl closely. 'Well, what do you think? It's a lovely idea, about the photos…'

'No it isn't,' said the girl, 'It's …I don't remember my name or anything at all.'

'Oh. I see.'

'I don't remember anything, it's gone blank.'

'That must be – very difficult.'

'We're hoping…'

'It's not true. I don't know this woman. She's being kind to me and lending me clothes and stuff, and she let me use her camera. But …'

Tim glanced at Ruby. 'I'm being honest when I say you've got the right looks for these photos I need to take,' he said, 'I think whatever you've been through, whatever it is, well it shows on your face. And that's the look I'm after. Do you, um – remember anything at all?'

'The stones are coming out of the sky and God is angry. There's nowhere for me to hide. Nowhere is safe. You want the photos to show to the police and ambulance people. You could have just taken some without me noticing but you come in here and pretend with her which makes it worse. You could have done it when I wasn't looking, I felt safe before.'

'I really don't know what to say,' he said, 'I'm really very sorry.'

'Please don't go,' said Ruby, 'I … well, it's difficult. I've been hoping things would start coming back into her mind.'

'So … you haven't – known her long?'

'Stop it!' The girl jumped out of her chair, 'Stop torturing me! Stop pretending you didn't know each other, you planned all this, and then you waited for a wet day and then he was going to come in and then there is this *story,* and then he'd send the photos off, stop it! Leave me alone!' She rushed to the door and tore it open and vanished down the hotel stairs.

'I must go after her,' said Ruby, grabbing her coat, 'I'm really very sorry. The situation is …complicated. I can't let her disappear. I brought her up here from the village, she was confused and …she'd met someone I know and well, I don't know what's been going on exactly. She's totally vulnerable.'

'Let me help,' he said, following her and they hurried down the narrow stairs and out into the pouring rain.

21 DECEMBER
A clear, mild, moonlit night

The bitter wind had dropped, and it was a clear, mild, moonlit night. Keith walked through the village from the hotel where he was now staying and climbed the hill to the Manor House. He crossed through the cedar trees to the grounds at the side near the kitchen, there were no curtains at the windows and the light was on as usual. Treading silently on the long grass he came nearer, now he could see Jonathan sitting at the table talking on the phone. It was too risky to try the side door, though perhaps he could try it in daylight when Jonathan's car was gone. The boy would be about, and he could feed him more nonsense which hopefully would then be passed on to Jonathan mixed up with Hugo's own extraordinary stories and ideas. It must be difficult living with Hugo, perhaps he could offer to help in some way? Where had he come from, and what future plans were there about that?

George was definitely moving out, there had been large vans unloading in South Street in town where a long row of Edwardian terraced houses stretched from the railway station to the old Victorian park. He had heard George saying - 'I'll stay here Sylvia till it's done, you go and do a bit of shopping, but don't be on your feet too long.' They hugged and she walked down the road towards the shops. It might have been an ideal moment to talk more with George on his own, but too risky and he was busy with the furniture. It was so good just to see him and hear his voice.

As he stood there outside the kitchen he wished he could hear Jonathan's conversation. It might be the girlfriend who seemed to have left in a hurry. Hopefully Jonathan would soon drive over to see her, he had done this before and had been away for over twenty-four hours. He must be patient. On the day he had called and stayed for lunch he had felt uneasy near the girlfriend, he had heard her talking to Jonathan about going back to his house, and everything was a bit chaotic, people were upset and worried and having intense conversations. But this girl - Pamela - had given him a strange look almost as if she was reading his mind. Would she mention whatever it was to Jonathan? With any luck she might be away most of the time.

He walked back towards the drive as there was nothing more he could do tonight.

22 DECEMBER
Dark and empty and cold

'There Hugo, I've got the book on the screen, come and have a look.' Jonathan sat back and drank his tea.

Hugo peered at the book information on Jonathan's laptop. 'What is it?'

'It's a book about learning how to programme computers, for beginners. Maybe you and I could start having a look at it together …'

'Sounds hard."

'Well, if you take it step by step it breaks it down and you might find you can manage it.'

'But why do you want me to do this?'

'Maybe you could learn it and then create something with a story. You know you like inventing things. It's like learning a new language, you just learn a bit at a time.'

'I've never learnt a language.'

'Ah but you have – what are you doing right now?'

'Talking to you.'

'Exactly. Using the English language. You learnt that so you could learn other things.'

'But that's easy.'

'You can make up stories can't you? Well a computer game is another way of telling a story. Inventing people. And pictures. And making things happen.'

'But I've never done that.'

'If I said write a story in English you could do that. Without thinking too hard.'

'Well, I've never been good at writing. But I could tell it to you.'

'There you are you see! Now I'm a beginner too. We need a book that explains it clearly.'

'I've never played a video game.'

'Well Hugo neither have I. We could learn that together. Let's go and buy some today.'

'Today!'

'I've got to go shopping anyway and it's Christmas soon. Look I'll give you that and you can buy me one, and I'll buy you one and we can bring them home and learn what to do.'

'So it could be a Christmas present?' said Hugo peering at the bundle of twenty pound notes.

'Yes. Go and get your coat on. We'll go to MacDonalds on the way.'

'Is Anthea coming back? Can I buy one for her as well?'

'Oh yes of course you must be missing Anthea,' said Jonathan hastily, 'She'll probably be back soon. But we'll be busy with this when we come back.'

'So do you know which games we're going to buy?'

'Not yet. We'll go and have a look shall we? I need your help. Then we can set it all up in the computer room.'

Later they returned with two video games. Hugo helped Jonathan carry the bits and pieces up the staircase and they switched on the light in the old Games Room and moved a table next to the one where a computer was already fixed up.

'It's nice and warm in here Jonathan.'

'Yes, I put the heating on earlier.'

'How do you know what to do with all that?'

'I asked the man in the shop and wrote some of it down. Now where did I put that list?' Jonathan found the piece of paper in his pocket and put it on a table. Hugo sat down and watched.

'Now, that's that, and let's see, that fits with that, oh yes …'

'It's hard Jonathan.'

'One step at a time Hugo. Now let's see, this is the HDMI cable … that goes in there …'

Hugo watched. 'Why don't you look at the video games Hugo, decided which one you want to start with hmm?'

Soon it was all connected and Hugo handed him *The Soldiers of Zema*. 'This one's mine and the other one's yours, remember?'

'Right. That goes *there*, and ah yes …'

'You hold this Hugo and learn how to use it.'

'Do you know how to use it?'

'No, just try it, experiment. That's it. It takes practice.'

Jonathan was relieved to have got this far. He felt weary and sat down to watch. Hugo took a while to get the idea and then became absorbed.

'Hugo I've got some things to do, shall I leave you for

a few minutes to carry on? I'll bring up a snack for you.' Jonathan moved swiftly to the door hoping Hugo could cope with being in the big bare room on his own.

Soon he came back with a tray and Hugo put the controller down and started eating some crisps out of a bag. 'Is Belinda coming back?'

'We don't know Hugo, we haven't worked out where she's gone yet. But yes I hope so.'

'I miss Sylvia will she be back?'

'She'll pop back a lot yes, she's not far away. And they're coming here for Christmas, I told you yesterday.'

'I miss her cooking.'

'Well maybe you and I could make a Christmas cake, we could learn together and give Sylvia a surprise couldn't we!'

'And is Pamela coming back?'

'Well yes – but she's quite busy at the moment.'

'Why can't she be busy here? Why does everyone go away. You're not going away are you Jonathan?'

'Well, if I do I'll always come back Hugo. Like I did yesterday, I went to see Pam and then I came back. She's living in … another house.'

As Jonathan ate a sandwich he glanced at a notebook he kept handy and where he jotted down ideas as they came to him. There were several things he needed to look up when he had time.

Hugo finally agreed to go to bed. It was odd being in this huge, old house with no one except this strange boy for company, George and Sylvia were now sleeping in their new house and coming back most days. There were so many echoes from the past few months but now it was overwhelmingly dark and empty and cold. He got up and tidied the kitchen and drank a glass of wine. As he walked up the great staircase his footsteps were the only sound.

Large old hunting scenes and landscapes hung where in another time old family portraits might have looked down, waiting for another heir to join them, and keeping an eye on the continuity of life within these walls. What had happened to the Green family? He vaguely remembered some stories in the newspaper… something about two brothers and a sister and a family feud and a father with army background where there had been some dispute.

He wandered towards the eerily quiet corridor where the Games Rooms were. They were gradually being dismantled. He remembered a saying which would often haunt him –*If anyone comes to me and does not hate his father and mother, wife and children, brothers and sisters, even his own life, he cannot be a disciple of mine.* Why did He say this, and there was always the question – *Did He really say it at all?* And if He didn't then why did people put in the record many years later that He did? Was there something wrong with the translation of the word hate? Perhaps in the beginning there had been another meaning. Hardly surprising when there were hundreds perhaps thousands of old manuscripts written in so many languages, … Greek, Aramaic, Hebrew, Latin, Syriac.

Jonathan unlocked the first Games Room and went in and switched on the light. A colourful paper lamp still hung low from the ceiling. In the middle of the large bare space the fluffy sofa and an old armchair and the worn carpet were still there, together with comforting homely objects, a coffee table, some magazines, a vase of plastic flowers. This was where the Game - *Go Back and Tell Mummy* had been played. With more furniture it would be suitable for the Women's Refuge to use.

The next room was now the computer room, slightly larger with bare floorboards and a some hardbacked chairs and tables. Hugo had already spread some bits and pieces around and the ladder and ropes had been removed by the helpful gardener. Jonathan remembered the lighting and acting effects that Lawrence had created that went with the new Game – *Unmix the Messages – a Fun Game for Couples.* And in here before that there had been the Game – *Tie Up Your Partner and Tell Them the Truth.* He had made a joke with Pam about that. Surely they told each other the truth? But was she telling him the truth now?

What on earth had Belinda thought that day when George had been showing them round? Jonathan remembered his little book *Games People Play* which lay on the kitchen table. It looked fascinating but there was never time to give it his serious attention.

Finally he came to the mock psychiatrist's consulting room. The couch was still there, and he sat down and stretched out his legs. Old books had been taken out of the glass fronted bookshelves and were piled up on the desk waiting to be sorted out. George must have been in here. He noticed one by Carl Jung, what a lot of attention had been giving to creating this room, it was incredible. *Tell Your Psychiatrist Everything.* Everything? How could anyone ever do that, there was always more and more buried beneath.

Another biblical quotation passed through his mind – *So I say to you, use your worldly wealth to win friends for yourselves, so that when money is a thing of the past you may be received into an eternal home.* What on earth did *that* mean? Was it now acceptable to have wealth? What did having friends have to do with being received into an eternal home? What was he going to do with all this new wealth, the Manor House itself? He wasn't trying to win friends, he was simply trying to help people.

He hadn't had time to absorb the enormity of what he was being given. It was crazy! It was intoxicating, it was … a huge responsibility. And what on earth was he doing accepting such a thing, how was he qualified to know what to do with it? He had made so many mistakes… Pamela probably thought that. Was that what was bothering her? When she had been leaving she had given him that thoughtful look which told him there were things going on in her mind that he couldn't reach. He was fascinated by her, utterly bewitched, he wanted her here by his side and in his bed …It felt all wrong without her.

A bizarre thought crossed his mind. What would he tell a psychiatrist now if one was sitting there at the desk. Would it be a real one or just someone pretending, and did that matter? He could tell him *anything.* But he wouldn't know where to begin, there was just too much. And there wouldn't be any answers, there *were* no answers …

The couch was comfortable and despite the cold in the room Jonathan closed his eyes and fell into a deep and restful sleep.

23 DECEMBER
Brisk, clean air

Natasha wandered along the seafront and leant on the railings and watched the waves swirling over dark clumps of seaweed and uneven pebbles. Further along the sandy beach spread out, she tasted the salt on her lips and breathed in the brisk clean air. It was so refreshing. Could it blow all the bad stuff away? These distractions were not enough. She walked on, searching for a café she remembered from childhood, perhaps she could escape from the cold wind for a few minutes.

'Oh, are you open? Thank you, just a cup of tea please and one of those buns.' She moved over to the bay window and sat watching the sea.

The woman brought a tray. 'Thank you. I was lucky to find you open today.'

'Well, we don't do much this time of year. Mostly refurbishing the place at the moment. Excuse everything lying about.'

'It's lovely here. I remember it.'

'If you could pay now, I'll be at the back doing things.'

Natasha thought about how her father had raged at Jonathan. Why was this? And Belinda, where *was* she, perhaps she had been found by now? Then voices could be heard from beyond the open door behind the counter.

'In a minute Sal. Hold your horses.'
'But where did you put it?'
'It's in that drawer, but I haven't …'
'I'm going to have a look at …'

Was this her father! Natasha sat very still.

'You don't need to.'

'We talked about this yesterday. I want to read it and …'

'I'll do the cooking, that's agreed. That's why we're doing all this. Apart from the place needing it of course.'

'No, you agreed Jeremy, that's easily done. Agreeing with yourself.'

'What's that supposed to mean?'

'I'm not having it. I need to be involved and we need to discuss the detail. Stop being so bloody awkward and put that away till later!'

'I'll have a fucking drink if I want to. Who do you think you are?'

There were sounds of things being moved about and some banging. 'Give that back!'

'Can't you see Jeremy. The whole project is under threat if you carry on like this. The other day we nearly … well perhaps we were right.'

'Now look what you've done. Careful!'

'You make me desperate.'

'*You* feel desperate! Well look at you before I arrived.'

'Before you arrived things were straightforward. I was fine. Life doesn't have to be madly exciting all the time. I didn't have to worry that someone was preying on me.'

'How DARE YOU. I'm trying to help and build something. How dare you.'

'I'm sorry. But it's sometimes so confusing and when you …'

'Stop this. Let's just get on. I'm the one with skills and ideas.'

'Yes but, well before it was seasonal and then I find other things to do in the winter, like my crafts. People just pop in when they're having a day out, they just want simple things, they don't …'

'We've talked about this. You've agreed, you were happy with the idea. You were grateful. What's happened to that?'

'It when I see you drinking I start to …'

'It's just one drink! Don't make a drama out of it.'

'Do you love me Jeremy.'

'Why don't you answer. Jeremy, please.'

Natasha stood up and moved silently towards the door, waiting for the voices to start again before opening it.

'Why don't you answer Jeremy? I'm sorry I asked that.'

'Give me some space Sal, give me some space. I've got things on my mind. I need to get out and breathe some sea air.'

Natasha went out and left the door open. She ran up the side of the building where there was a small car park and hid behind a car at the far end. She saw her father come out, slammed the door and walked briskly towards the beach pulling up his collar and shrugging his shoulders against the wind. He soon disappeared round the corner.

What should she do? The woman must know she might have heard the conversation. Or perhaps she would assume she had already left? Could she possibly – go back inside and talk to her? She walked back and caught sight of her father, now a distant figure on the large expanse of sand. He bent to pick something up and hurled it into the waves.

'Um – excuse me, I don't know what to say.'

'What's that?' The woman was tidying the table and looked up. 'Did you forget something? I'm just popping out to the shops.'

'No … er … Could I possibly walk along with you on your way? I'll be heading back to the train station.'

'If you like. I'll just get my things and lock the front door and we can go out at the back and leave that open in case he hasn't got his key.' She gave Natasha a puzzled look. 'That's someone who lives here I mean, he's just gone out.'

Natasha broke the silence as they walked down an alley

between houses that led away from the seafront.

'I wonder if you'd mind me telling you something?'

'What do you mean?'

'Well, I have something to tell you.'

'I'm off that way,' she said, 'And the train station's that way.'

'Yes, thank you. You see, what I'm trying to say is … I'm … Jeremy's daughter.'

'What?' She stood and stared. 'But you don't look …'

'Is there any chance we could find a café or something. I know it's awkward and you probably think I was listening just now …'

'Oh. That. Well goodness me. His *daughter*. But he's never said. He's never really told me anything much.'

'I'm here looking for him because, well he left our cousin's house after a row, and I've been worried.'

'It's freezing here. Let's go in there and have a coffee.'

They didn't speak again till they were sitting down with their coffees on the table. 'That's better,' she said, 'If I'm going to have some shocks I might as well be warm and comfortable.'

'I'm sorry if it's a shock,' said Natasha, 'If you'd like me to go I will. I just wanted to make sure he was safe and well. We aren't … close, he's never really liked me.'

'No of course you mustn't go. It's just that, well, surprising though it may sound I hardly know anything about him.'

'Well he has a passion for cooking and I assumed you're going to run a restaurant together when it's all done.'

'Oh yes, that seems to be the idea, and one of the few things that doesn't change from day to day.' She sat back and lit a cigarette.

'I'm Natasha. I'm sorry, I couldn't help hearing a bit of your conversation just now, I recognised his voice and heard you call him Jeremy, and I went out and he left, and I thought …'

'I see. He didn't see you then?'

'No, I hid in the car park.'

'Well that a relief.'

'I've been looking for him since he left – a family thing. And I thought I'd come here since we had family holidays here.'

'I see.' She sat back and stared at Natasha. Slim and pale and tired with thin shoulder-length hair that needed attention.

'I'll just go shall I. I just wanted to know he was safe.'

'No. Don't go. I don't know what to say. It's embarrassing.'

'Please don't be. I know what he's like.'

'Mmm. Well, of course you do, yes. A bad moment. We have lots of good ones too. He's unpredictable. The walk on the beach will perk him up, he'll be fine when he walks back in.'

'Yes.'

'Did you hear … everything?'

'Well, I recognised his voice, and you called him Jeremy. And I didn't want him to know I was there, so I had to think quickly where to hide, and he went out.'

'It's a good thing you did. It was just an argument, it'll blow over. But I'm sure you understand that, you know him.'

'Yes.'

'Of course we know his drinking is a worry. But if I knew more about what's been happening that would help.'

'Something terrible happened – a few months ago. My mother and sister were killed in a car accident. He and I weren't there. He blamed himself. It's so painful to talk about. Mum was tired but he told her to drive … but it was the lorry driver's fault, there were several reliable witnesses. Turned out he was on drugs, he wasn't badly injured.'

'How … absolutely awful. It's good I know, but I won't tell him I know. No wonder it preys on his mind. But what are you doing now?'

'I'm living in my cousin's house, well it's Dad's cousin,

their mothers were twin sisters. I'm between jobs.'

'Well. This is what I think we should do. You go back today to wherever it is, and then turn up another day and we can take it from there. I'll pretend you and I never met, and he'll never know anything about today. If he did I don't know quite how we could handle that.'

'Yes ... okay.'

'I'd love to talk some more but I ought to do that shopping, you know, with Christmas soon, and get back. He'll probably be a changed man for a while after the walk on the beach.'

'Yes. That's good. Okay I won't say when then.'

'What do I call you?'

'Natasha. But don't tell me your name, at least, you may have, but I'll forget it for now.'

'Good luck then ... it was good to meet you.'

'Yes ... you too.'

24 DECEMBER
A rash promise

'My name is Belinda. I ...remember now, my name is Belinda.' She was standing in the pouring rain outside the front of the hotel by the little low wall on the terrace. Occasional cars went past on the quiet road. Ruby and the photographer were approaching, and he held a large umbrella and tried to shelter the three of them.

'Belinda. I'm very glad you've remembered your name.'

'Yes ...it was raining, and very dark. I was in the village and I didn't know where to go. But I knew I had to escape.'

'What were you escaping from Belinda, can you remember anything else?'

'I can't remember, please don't keep asking, I can't remember!'

'Sorry I shouldn't have asked,' said Ruby, 'Shall we go back indoors? It won't do us any good getting soaked.' The three of them made their way slowly towards the front door and into the hall. Tim paused and shook the umbrella and followed them in.

'Thank you very much,' said Ruby. 'That really helped.' They watched as Belinda combed through her wet hair with her fingers and went to stand by a warm radiator with her back to them.

'Shall I leave you now?' he said in a low voice, 'You've probably got things to talk about.'

'Well yes. Thanks again.'

'Will you be going back to the village? Which village did you say it was?'

'South Witters. I don't know, I don't really know what to do.'

'Quite. Well I'll keep out of your way. I'm sorry if something I said made things worse. I won't mention the photos, she seems to think I'm somebody else, if you need me it's Room Five.'

'Yes. There are all kinds of things going on in her mind. And yes, actually you do look a little bit like …'

'Like who?'

'Someone we know. That might be confusing her.'

'Very difficult for you.'

He gave her a reassuring pat on the shoulder and went up the stairs. Ruby and Belinda wandered into the old-fashioned hotel lounge where watercolour paintings of lakes hung on the walls. 'They're rather lovely aren't they Belinda? That one is … Derwent Water. Like the colours in your photos today.'

'Paintings … pillars, a wide staircase. Weird paintings, frightening. Not nice ones like this …'

'I was wondering,' said Ruby, hoping this was another sign she was remembering things, 'It's such a horrible day. Shall we go Christmas shopping?'

'I haven't any money.'

'Oh, well I can give you some money, if you'll let me. We could get you another bag, a pretty one and a warm coat.'

'But you've given me so much already.'

'That's ok. I'm glad to. Would be nice to go some bright cheerful shops wouldn't it.'

'Okay. Will *he* be coming?'

'No of course not. I hardly know him, never met him before.'

'He's like the dark angel. For a minute I thought it *was* him. Why does he pretend? I suppose now he'll take the photos when I'm not looking.'

'Does the dark angel have a name?'

'His name is Jonathan. Yes I was running away. From the dark angel and the room with the ladders and ropes. It was too dangerous to stay. And stones were falling from the sky and... I had to get away. I just wanted it to end, I wanted to die but you wouldn't let me.'

An hour later they were in the big, crowded shopping centre and after a while found a cafeteria. Ruby told Belinda to grab the one free table and look after their bags while she got them a tray of fish and chips and cups of tea. As she stood in the queue next to crying toddlers and moody teenagers she saw Belinda take things slowly from one handbag and put them into the other one.

Then Belinda turned around as if to check on her and Ruby looked away hastily. What was going to happen now? She seemed to remember bits and pieces but then the weird logic came into that too, and one couldn't argue with that. What could she say? How can you contradict someone who appears to be in a separate world with its own craziness? If Jonathan had tried and had failed well, he was much better at that kind of thing than she was. Would Belinda end up imagining *she* was evil and threatening?

A bit later Ruby stood up, 'I'll just pop to the Ladies, why don't you look all this then you can go, I won't be a moment.' She pulled on her wet coat and made her way to a passage behind the café. Now out of sight she walked along it and found it led to the back of the building, there were what looked like storerooms and then round a corner was a Fire Exit door. She struck the metal bar and it opened.

Without looking back, she found herself on an enclosed roof above a small car park. The rain had eased off and as she came round she saw the way to the crowded shopping street where they had been earlier. She made her way carefully down some metal steps which were wet and slippery. She hurried through the crowds to the multi storey car park and ran up the gloomy concrete stairs to the third floor and found the car, unlocked the door, climbed in, put on her seat belt and started up the engine.

She knew her way out of the city and turned and headed north. Her mind was in a whirl. There was nothing of value in the hotel, she could buy more things later. She would send Mrs Fawes a cheque and a letter with some story about Belinda needing urgent treatment. She would say she would be back to collect their things later on. Perhaps she *might* even go back later on, who knows?

She would go and get lost somewhere, have her hair cut very short, wear more makeup, buy lots of new clothes and some glasses. Pay for everything with cash, invent a new name and sell her cottage, get rid of all that clutter. She would leave her job and her horrible life and do something simple where she didn't have to think about the horrors of the world. It would be risky going back to the village, Jonathan might call again, could she look him in the eye and not tell the whole truth? And there had been that police car ...

Ruby didn't dare imagine the next few minutes in the crowded cafeteria, people would just want to get home with their shopping, no one would care. But eventually *someone* would have to take care of Belinda, *someone* would have to help her, the authorities would intervene. And surely no one would have seen them driving away from the village? There was the photographer, but ... it was all a long way away, and he was busy.

It was too difficult to do it anymore, a rash promise, a foolish impulse, it was better this way, Belinda needed proper help from people who knew what they were doing. The short afternoon was already darkening, car headlights flashed past and Ruby concentrated on reading the road signs which were almost obscured by the driving rain.

25 DECEMBER

A murder

'Don't cry my darling, please, please don't cry. Take a deep breath and tell me the whole thing slowly. I love you.'

'I'm sorry ... I will Jonathan, give me a minute. I wish you were here. I wish I could hold you...'

'I'll come soon, very soon. Is Tash there with you?'

'No, she's been out a lot.'

'Now, just slow down and tell me.'

'Where had I got to? Oh yes ...'

'These two men came up to you after the demonstration.'

'Oh yes ...'

'By the way, are you sure you're alright? Physically I mean.'

'Yes. Well ... I'd been aware that they were feeling hostile I could tell, but nothing had happened with them during the evening up to then, and then people were leaving, and some stopped for little chats and often thanked me, and that was lovely, and then there they were, they were tall and looked like brothers.'

'Yes.'

'They said something like, people like me are preying on people and taking their money for a load of crap, excuse my language, and so I did what I do sometimes, I offered them a refund, and well they were a bit confused by that, then they said it wouldn't do any good and the harm was done.'

'Well, what did *that* mean? Did your friend, um, Wendy I think it is, did she come and help?'

'No, she was talking to someone. I asked them if they would like a private reading and whether there was something in particular that had prompted them to come that night. At first they seemed surprised that I was calm and then they launched into this angry stuff, Oh you'd love to hear all about us wouldn't you, we tell you about us and then you tell us about us and we think you must be some sort of psychic and isn't it wonderful!'

'I'm so sorry. Did they go away then?'

'Well no, and it was then I saw something. It was the older one of the two, I know this is hard to believe Jonathan, but I knew then that he was going to commit a terrible crime that night and … it was a powerful feeling, though I didn't see anything specific.'

'Oh dear.'

'They left then, just turned and walked out without another word. And then I did something I've never done before. Everyone had gone and we were just finishing tidying the hall, and I took my phone out of my bag and dialled 999 and talked to the police. I tried to get someone to listen to me so I could describe them and where we were and all that, and what I believed was going to happen.'

'That was good. Brave.'

'But you see … it's no good.'

'*What Pam?*'

'She told me to stop wasting her time and ended the call.'

'Oh Pam, I'm so sorry.'

'There's more Jonathan. There was a fight outside that rough pub, you know, *The Old Goat by the River*, it's quite near the hall where we were. A man was found strangled in the pub garden the next morning. They haven't caught anyone.'

'Oh Pam, how dreadful. I'm so sorry. You must make sure you're safe in all this. I wish I was there.'

'I was so frustrated. Wendy was kind, she's always so kind. She'd given me a lift home and stayed for a chat. Though that was before the murder of course.'

'I'm so sorry. Has it helped to talk about it?'

'Sort of. Thank you. How are you?'

'Maybe you could go to the police station yourself and ask to see a detective. Tell them what you've told me. They might listen and who knows … they might get you to help them. It does happen.'

'Yes. Maybe. Thanks for the suggestion. How are you?'

'Well apart from worried about *you* I'm ok. Getting on with a few things, making enquiries, dealing with some of the emails George was talking about, checking some household things, seeing Hugo between all this and worrying where he's disappeared to and trying to make sense of odd things he tells me, sometimes he seems to imagine people are around and he's had conversations with them, you know the kind of thing. A psychologist who used to work here had turned up and talked to George who was of course very busy, and then Hugo seems to have had a chat outside and said he was telling Keith about something, one of his mad stories, I don't know what he was doing here if it was him, and George and Sylvia are nearly all packed now, they've already moved to their little house, but that's more than enough for now. The point is, I will have to come up and see you again very soon. Very soon. We've got to work out what to do at Christmas. Are you a bit better? You didn't feel that *you yourself* were in danger did you?'

'No Jonathan. I didn't.'

'I have to go but I'll ring again this evening.'

'Promise?'

'Of course. If you're not there I'll text.'

'Signal's a bit funny.'

'Talk later.'

'Yes.'

'I can't come back for Christmas Pam, I'm so sorry. But surely you can come to the Manor House? And Tash too? How is she getting on?'

'Jonathan I'm sorry, I'm going to Scotland, remember those cousins? They've invited me, they rang this afternoon and I thought it would be a good break since you're so busy.'

'Oh Pam. But I want you here. Please!'

'It's only for a few days. They were so kind to me when my mother died do you remember? And I haven't seen them since I lost Matthew. It'll help to see them.'
'Yes. Of course. It is a good idea. But how will I cope?'
'Well …'
'When are you going?'
'Tomorrow.'
'Can you go the next day? There'll still be trains won't there? Please. I could drive over tomorrow. I need you'
'But I … trains get crowded and …'
'I'll be there early. I'll leave very early. I must see you. Specially now.'
'Well …'
'Say yes Pam.
'Okay. Of course I want to see you,'
'What's happening with Natasha?'
'Well she's found her father, but she hasn't spoken with him yet.'
'What! That's good news. Where?'
'In a café by the sea. It's quite a story I'll tell you tomorrow.'
'There won't be much time for talking.'
'Hmm!'
'I must go now and sleep early. Tomorrow George will be here for Hugo.'
'Goodnight Jonathan.'
'Goodnight my darling girl. Till tomorrow.'
'Drive carefully. Weather's bad.'
'Give my love to my house till I get there.'
'Yes. It's missing you. It's lonely without you,'
'Now go to bed.'
'But you're not there.'
'You make me cry you make me laugh.'
'You're a bit mad you know.'
'Feed little kisses into your phone and send them.'

26 DECEMBER
A peculiar story

Natasha stood at the door to the café. Her father was painting a far wall and looked up as she came in.

'Dad! It's you! That's amazing.'

'Well well. It's Natasha.'

'I've been wondering where you could be and I thought of this place where we used to come, I'm so glad to see you!'

'Well well.' He went on painting the wall as she approached through the empty tables and chairs and sat down to watch.

'So ... how are you Dad? Are you working here now?'

'I'm soldiering on. Yes I live here now and we're doing the place up. There's a lot to be done and we have deadlines.'

'You don't seem surprised that I've found you. It's really incredibly lucky isn't it! You could have been anywhere.'

'Yes, it's terrific. And this will be when it's finished. Structurally sound.' Jeremy bent down and moved the roller up and down in the paint tray and then straightened up and continued applying the pale yellow paint to the wall with long smooth strokes.

'Don't you want to know how everyone is. Jonathan and ...'

He glanced at her, 'I don't need to know anything thank you Natasha. I'm busy and settled here now, I wasn't welcome in his house anyway.'

'Well Jonathan is fine and busy and he's got Pam now and she's lovely and we're living in his house and it's like home and ...'

'I'm very pleased for you.'

'Dad please. Talk to me. Don't be like this.'

'Very delighted Natasha. So glad Jonathan has a settled home and everything is going so well for him. I don't need to worry about him anymore then.'

'Don't be sarcastic! Well actually, he's not really alright

at all, he's living in a strange house and Pam is all by herself, and all kinds of weird things have been happening.'

'Oh indeed. Taking care of more of the homeless and helpless is he?'

'What's the matter with you! He's ... the kindest man I know.'

'I think this paint will *just* last, now must finish this corner then I'm done. If you want a cup of tea or something Natasha just ring that little bell on the counter and Sally will come. She's not far away.'

'Sally? Who is Sally?' Natasha got up and went over to the counter and after a moment Sally appeared.

'Hello. I wondered if I could have a cup of tea and a bun if you're open.'

'Certainly, I'll get it. Please excuse the mess, we're decorating.'

Natasha hesitated and then sat down again. 'Who is Sally Dad? Aren't you going to tell her who I am?'

Jeremy glanced at her and went on painting the wall. Sally came back with a tray.

'Sally this is my daughter Natasha,' he said, 'She's just popped in for a visit. Natasha this is Sally whose café it is.'

'Oh, how nice. I didn't know you had a daughter.'

Jeremy bent down to the paint tray and behind his back the women smiled at each other.

'Have you come far Natasha?'

'Just a short train ride. It's so lucky I found Dad.'

'Have you been looking then?'

'Well yes, it's complicated. He hadn't left a forwarding address.'

'Well, you're welcome. Have the tea on me.'

'Thank you. I love the new colours.'

'I'm planning some curtains and other bits and pieces. I love colours and your father adores cooking.'

'I know. Is that what he's going to be doing?'

'That's the plan. What are you doing at the moment. I

mean, do you have a job Natasha?'

'Well, a bit of temporary work. Just sorting out a few things.'

'Yes, you said about your poor mother and sister.'

Jeremy put the roller back on the tray and straightened up, turning to watch them and wiping his hands on his shirt. 'But just a minute Sally, how on earth did you know about them?'

'Oh. Um …'

'*I* never told you about them. How do you know? Did you read some newspaper when it happened? Oh … I see.'

'What do you mean?

'You two must have met before.'

'No, I ...'

'Don't pretend Sally. I never told you about Pauline and Petra. You and Natasha must have met before. What's going on?'

'Nothing's going on! I'll make you some tea, that wall looks finished now, well done.'

'Just a minute!' He walked over and took hold of Sally's arm, 'How do you know about Pauline and Petra?'

'Dad, calm down! Yes alright, I'll tell you, we have met before. I called in the other day and we got talking. And we thought …'

'When? Where was I? Which day was this. What did you think hmm?'

'We thought that I should call another day. When Sally had got used to the idea, and that's why I'm here now.'

'Why?'

'Well, it was a lot for Sally to take in, I mean I didn't say a lot, she suggested I came back another day, you must have been out somewhere.'

'Which day was this?'

'Oh … I think it was Thursday. I caught Sally just going out to do some shopping. You weren't here. Well actually I saw someone walking on the beach a long way off and I wondered if it was you, but I couldn't really tell, I hoped it was of course.

So I had a cup of tea and mentioned it to Sally, about seeing you and did she know you.'

'So you meet a complete stranger and start telling her all about your family, is that it?'

'No, it wasn't like that at all. Stop being like this Dad.'

'This is a very peculiar story,' said Jeremy, '...very peculiar.'

'I'll tell you what's peculiar,' said Sally, 'It's why you're so suspicious about everything. Natasha's really relieved to have found you, isn't that the important thing?'

'Yes, I am very relieved. And it's been lovely to meet Sally.'

'Now I'm going to make some more tea Jeremy,' said Sally, 'Why don't you sit down and have a rest, that wall looks lovely.' She disappeared through the door behind the counter.

Jeremy stood quite still. 'Why did you say...'

'What Dad?'

'You said to begin with, you'd called in, and then there was this *story* about seeing me on the beach.'

'It's not a story Dad, I saw someone on the beach, and I thought it might be you.'

'There's something you're not telling me Natasha and I don't like it.'

'Well there's nothing I can do about that!'

'Here you are Jeremy,' said Sally carrying a tray with cake and cups of tea, 'Let's all sit down and have a rest, shall we?'

'Thank you. Sally, that looks lovely. Did you bake it yourself?'

'Well, I must tell the truth. No. But I do bake sometimes. But not to Jeremy's level of course.'

'Hmm.'

'I've had an idea, Natasha. Can I ask you something?'

'Of course.'

'If you're not too committed where you are, why don't you come and stay here for a while? The flat above the café is very big, several empty rooms. My boys have gone now, though they'll be back at Christmas. We could have a party!'

'Are you sure?'

'And … well you could help with setting this place up. If you were willing to and we'd get it done all the quicker.'

'Not a good idea Sal. Natasha prefers towns with night life and plenty of low life.'

Natasha looked at Sally. Did he know about the cocaine? Had he guessed? Had he told Sally? But surely not, he had no experience of that kind of thing, and Jonathan wouldn't have said anything. Her father was just being rude as usual.

'Well, if you're sure.' said Natasha. Perhaps she could help for a while and then get a job.

'Yes. Please think about it.'

'Well thank you, I will.'

27 DECEMBER
Christmas shopping with Ruby

The cafeteria was emptying. Belinda had finished transferring things to her new handbag. Comb, make up, a purse with some money Ruby had given her, a new diary for 2017, two biros, some tissues. Other bits and pieces. She wrote her name in the diary. *Belinda.* Belinda what? What else could she write? *Christmas shopping with Ruby.* Didn't she used to write a lot of things? Some notebooks somewhere … lying on the ground. With other bits and pieces … But they were all there, she had counted them and put them back … in a rucksack. And where was that? And where had she been living? How did she end up in Ruby's garden? There was something about struggling through the pouring rain along dark roads and down hills. Why was she there, there had been people around she didn't know, a strange boy talking to Jonathan …

Did Ruby know Jonathan? Maybe she would tell him about her. She hadn't thought that before. Now Ruby had gone to the Ladies she could escape. Now. Before Ruby came back.

She could leave the big bags of shopping. Just take her new handbag, the lovely one with the silver chain strap. No one would know and she could get lost in the crowd. She got up and pulled on the lovely, warm coat Ruby had bought. She found her way through the crowded tables and out through the department store and down the escalators to the crowded street.

It was easy. No one would see her, they were busy, carrying shopping bags, soothing toddlers, wrapping their arms around each other, pushing people in wheelchairs. Cars swished past sending sprays of water across the pavement, colours from the lights and Christmas decorations were reflected in the puddles and wet pavements. Dazzling. She kept turning into different streets and they were getting quieter. She walked past houses and saw beautiful Christmas trees in people's windows. A car drew up and a family spilled out, laughing and joking and carrying packages, they crowded through the front door which slammed behind them. The light went on in the living room and someone drew the curtains. A happy family. A normal family. What had happened to her mother? *What made her think that now?* Yes ... her mother. She remembered how she had been standing at the end of a narrow corridor, while ...*Oh why remember that moment, she wanted to forget it for ever.* Her father moving away from her across the bed and doing up his trousers as he walked towards the door. 'Dress yourself,' he said and went out. After she had struggled to move she had gone to the door which was ajar and there was her mother, waiting, watching. A shadowy figure with her face hidden. She would never see that face, she would never know what her mother had been thinking at that moment ... did she know what had happened?

Belinda walked on, past the pretty trees in the windows and the house with the normal family. It was a long, winding street with terraced houses. The traffic was getting quieter and it was nearly dark and pouring with rain ...

28 JANUARY
The storeroom

Christmas had come and gone. George and Sylvia had been willing to play number games with Hugo and they got through the day somehow. Later Hugo had been happy to go off to his video games and that gave the three of them a few peaceful minutes when they insisted Sylvia put her feet up while they did the washing up. Jonathan had managed to get Pam on the phone in Scotland, he was relieved that she sounded happy with her family, and Natasha had moved to the flat above the café by the sea, it sounded cheerful and chaotic, something about a family party with Sally's sons. With a jolt Jonathan realised that he hadn't thought about Belinda for a while.

He mustn't keep asking Pam to move, he knew he should be grateful for what they had. He had tried so many times. 'My darling I need you there, please. You could go on with your training there couldn't you? And you could have a room at the Manor House all to yourself for readings or anything you want.' All this competed in his head with ideas and plans and problems to sort out. Some women from the overcrowded Refuge in town were already staying and most of the bedrooms were occupied, the two other big rooms were being organised and he still needed to sell Maxwell's equipment and reply to the email.

It was nearly lunchtime when he climbed the stairs and walked along the corridor where the Games Rooms were. A handwritten sign *Alternative Worlds* was stuck on the middle door. Inside a very large used carpet had been laid on the bare floor and more small tables and chairs had been spread around the room. Hugo's two tables were cluttered with his boxes full of bits of cardboard. Jonathan wandered about, perhaps he should leave the beginners book on coding lying about up here and Hugo might read it himself? Had he already been up here today? Jonathan imagined the room filled with individuals at computers being encouraged to develop story ideas – but already he realised there would be a mountain of paperwork to do and enquiries to check everything, who could supervise, who would be empathetic, firm and kind, who would be approved by the authorities. But then, of course! He remembered a few days ago Hugo had been telling him a rather confused story about seeing Keith in the grounds, he had only been half listening … Why had Keith come back at all, something about apologising to George, what was going on there? He must find out Keith's contact details, they must be in a file somewhere …

Screaming could suddenly be heard from the room next door – Jonathan rushed into the corridor. The sign sellotaped the door said *Mothers and Children Welcome*. He went in and was met with the sight of three-year-old Divit lying on a rug and resisting his mother's attempts to calm him down '… No Mummy, no, no!' He wriggled and shouted and struck his mother who looked up. 'Oh Jonathan, I'm so sorry about this.'

'No Mummy, let me go, let me go!'

'It's not your fault Alisha, shall I? Look, take a little break,' said Jonathan. She stood up and backed away while the other mothers hovered. Three women were standing together, Jonathan noticed they were ignoring this and deep in conversation. He sat down on the floor and starting fiddling with some plastic tubes, fitting them together. Divit was whimpering but then sat up and started to watch.

Jonathan didn't speak but carried on fitting the tubes together and Divit handed him one, and they worked together in silence. Jonathan showed him how to do it. When a tiny girl approached Divit turned and began to strike her and Jonathan restrained him firmly and the boy struggled and began to cry quietly while he was rocked to and fro. As Jonathan began to sing quietly other mothers joined in and one bent down and took the girl's hand. 'Shall we let Divit have a nice long hug?' she said, 'You can have one another time.'

Alisha was now sitting in a shabby armchair with her face buried in a tissue. 'It's when someone is kind,' she whispered, 'You can keep going until someone is kind.'

Jonathan held Divit for a few minutes, then his phone

beeped. 'You're alright now aren't you,' he said letting the boy go and standing up. 'I'll see you later, Ladies,' he said, 'And you'll be pleased to know another caterer is coming today. I hope you've got everything you need up here.' As he spoke one of the three women turned and spoke to another. Why did they make him feel uneasy?

'That's excellent news.' He was speaking into his phone as he hurried down the stairs, 'I'm so delighted you feel you want to come and meet him. He really has an extraordinary ability with numbers, and I'm not particularly able to assess it. There are some other individuals I'm in touch with who I hope to have here to encourage and possibly study as well but that's still being arranged at the moment …By the way I was wondering …'

'Yes?'

'Well, if I could introduce you as *Mr* Ennistone? Or perhaps …'

'Yes of course. Or he can call me Peter.'

Jonathan had reached the kitchen and sat down at the table. 'Thank you. You see I don't think he knows what a professor is, and his mind can sometimes shoot off somewhere when confronted with something new or unfamiliar. And that might …'

'Of course Jonathan. That's sensible. Whatever you think puts the lad at ease. It sounds like you've won his confidence.'

'Well, yes I think so. Most of the time. But at the moment he's very dependent on me and of course that's worrying but I want to give him support, it's difficult at the moment as his sister's gone away. Broken home and all that, you know. He can be quite calm but then he can be thrown very quickly, sometimes by something quite small.'

'Yes I'm used to this. My first priority will be to get to know him a bit and that'll probably take time. It's good of you to offer me the accommodation. I understand the Manor House used to be a hotel?'

'Yes. Plenty of space here. I'm starting up various projects, an overspill from a Women's Refuge is here already. Coming back to Hugo, he just seems to want to play these video games all day at the moment, we bought some recently, he's never really had much fun in his life but I suppose I do worry a bit that ...'

'Addictive? Haha yes, my sons play them. Don't worry too much.'

'I try to encourage him, but then he can suddenly get secretive and talk about odd things in his mind, but I mustn't take up too much of your time.'

Yes. These things can be a worry.'

'I've got a beginners book on coding but I haven't got him to sit down and look at it with me yet, he has an extraordinary ability with numbers.'

'Yes you said. Very interesting.'

'I can't help thinking something could come out of all this ... but of course you'll be here tomorrow. You've got the map I emailed?'

'Yes, that's fine.'

'I look forward to seeing you then about ten.'

Jonathan ended the call and sensed he had been talking too much. But it was a relief to share some ideas. Ennistone's book *The Isolated Excellence* had good reviews and he had ordered a copy. As he went back upstairs and past the closed door of the women's room all seemed quiet with the sound of chatting and bursts of laughter. At the end of the corridor was a storeroom half full of old furniture and discarded bits and pieces, with a window looking down over the grounds He went in and looked around. He ought to keep this door locked, if toddlers got in they might hurt themselves, he must find the key.

The air was very cold and for a moment everything was overwhelming, there were so many ideas and plans and there was the sadness and worry that never went away. *Was Belinda alive or dead?* Someone would surely be looking after her nearby, perhaps they knew he was searching and thought they could do a better job. How could she ever recover from the traumas in her life? He had heard of electric shock treatments – they sounded scary and old-fashioned. Perhaps Keith would know. Had Hugo *really* seen him the other day? If so what was he doing back here again? Did children like little Divit ever recover from their experiences? How disturbed were the women here and how could they move on and what were those three women up to? And he hardly knew Diana who he had employed to do the House Manager's job, she had already started work downstairs in George's old office, going through bills and paperwork. And why didn't Pam want to come and live here, what *was it*? She could advise him, she could see below the surface of things in a way he couldn't.

He shivered as he stood looking down at the grass and the cedar trees through the window. Then he heard a sound – an odd sound, a scraping, then quiet knocks. There was no one else here, what *was* that? Probably nothing. Why was he lingering here? A deep sadness came over him and he felt nervous … he picked up a small table and went out and slid it against it the closed door.

Down in the hall he saw a neat, printed note enclosed in cellophane and stuck to the door of the office – *House Manager, my name is Mrs Williams, please knock if you have any problems*. He was about to knock himself but then he walked on, he wasn't sure he could cope right now with what might become an intense conversation.

He went into the kitchen and filled the kettle. He recalled the exhausting afternoon the day before when he had been interviewing people for the House Manager's job. For quite some time he had talked to several idealistic individuals who seemed unable to run their own lives efficiently, let alone organise this big house. Then finally Diana Williams followed him into the Guest Room bringing a hint of efficiency and Eau de Cologne.

'Jonathan Wenders? So pleased to meet you.' She shook his hand.

'Wender. Thank you. I'm so sorry to have kept you waiting so long. There have been some rather long discussions.'

'That's quite alright,' she said sitting down and placing her handbag on the floor and patting her thick, wavy, grey hair, 'I've been having one or two rather unexpected conversations myself while I was waiting … It must be a difficult post to fill, rather unusual.'

'Yes … yes you're absolutely right.'

'Well, can I just say … before you go any further. I am in a very fortunate position in life. I am a widow with no money worries and looking for something to do. I'm in excellent health for my age and have bags of energy. Your advert caught my eye immediately.'

'Oh … I'm glad to hear that.'

'Well yes, and I need to find something worthwhile to do with my time. The smallness of the salary is no problem.'

'Yes, it was quite a dilemma deciding how to word the advert actually.'

'Indeed. I can imagine. Well can I say that I think you did it *just right*. I could read between the lines.'

'So what do you think I'm looking for?'

'Well, someone like me, mature and unflappable, and *extremely* efficient!' They exchanged smiles.

'I'm leasing out space to various organisations,' said Jonathan, 'And if things work out there may be several vulnerable and unpredictable individuals here at any one time. There is one here already, Hugo, and actually an academic is coming to talk to him tomorrow. And there are women here from the Refuge in town which is overcrowded, some with babies and young children.'

'This sounds admirable! I do so much admire what you are doing. Using this *wonderful* old house.'

'And there are a number of other projects I'm thinking about.'

'I'm sure I could think of a few things if you ever wanted to discuss it with me.'

'Thank you.'

'Well, you will be wanting to know about me. I have office and book-keeping experience and can create order out of chaos in no time at all.'

'That sounds … very reassuring.'

This had gone on for a while and there had been a pause and Jonathan imagined her putting her feet up on a coffee table and lighting a cigar … she seemed eccentric but straightforward and very kind. He could imagine her organising his scribbled notes and newspaper articles, it would surely be a relief to have someone like her around.

And now she was already in the office and working but he had an uneasy feeling. He made tea and ate some toast and sent Pam a text. He must talk to her tonight. He needed to sell his own house, what money he had was disappearing fast. He stood up and stretched and went into the hall, put on his coat and let himself out of the great front door. There was no news from the police and he often wandered around the village thinking hopelessly about Belinda.

It was a bleak day with a heavy grey sky and the east wind hit him as he walked down the hill. But then as he crossed the village green he stopped, a *For Sale* sign was standing next to the little stone wall that surrounded Ruby's cottage.

29 JANUARY
The hurt and the pain of it

In the café Natasha cleaned the paintbrush in an old yoghurt pot with a little white spirit in the bottom and watched the swirling shapes. She rubbed the brush with an old rag and scraped fragments of dried gloss paint off her hands. She had done a good job and the painting was now all finished, she would leave the masking tape on till it dried. It was satisfying to do this. A job with a beginning, middle and end, and people to have dinner with. *Don't think about it, keep busy. Got no money anyway.* Gathering bits and pieces on a tray she carried them through the door behind the counter to the kitchen and put them in a corner with other brushes and pots of paint.

Her father was cooking at the new stove. 'Dad that smells amazing. I've finished the window frames, I hope you'll be pleased. Done a neat job.'

'Well done Natasha. I'll come and see in a minute.'

'Thank you I'm enjoying it. When will Sally be back?'

'Soon. Gone to look at fabrics. Got good ideas for colours and designs. Could you have a look at sign writers, here use my laptop. Password's curriedeels49.'

'Haha. Sure. Have you seen any yet.'

'Not traditional ones. I want it done properly.'

'Okay.

'Have you decided what you're calling it?'

'The Windy Restaurant by the Sea.'

'Oh, that's lovely.'

'Yes, it was Sally's idea.'

'Dad.'

'Yes Natasha.'

'Can I talk to you about something?'

'Bit busy.'

'While you're cooking.'

She sat at the table and watched her father's back as he stirred the contents of the saucepan, dipping in a spoon and tasting the sauce. These peaceful moments between them were precious and relatively rare.

'You know I mentioned the message. A while ago when Pam was doing a demonstration nearby and I went along before I knew her. And she mentioned Pauline and Petra, I know you didn't want to talk about it, and you think it's ...'

He was silent.

'And they said to stop blaming yourself, and that they really are alright and you must get on with your life and all that.'

Jeremy put the spoon down and turned the gas a little lower. Still with his back to her he opened a packet of rice and filled a kettle with water.

'Say something Dad, please say something.'

He poured the hot water into a saucepan and placed it on the hob, and emptied the rice into it, stirred it with a spoon and turned on the gas. 'There now, that should be all ready for when Sally gets back.'

'Dad please talk to me. It won't hurt to talk.'

He turned the gas down as the water boiled and finally turned to face her and to her surprise there were tears in his eyes. 'Okay Natasha,' he said, coming to sit at the table, 'I understand you want to talk about it. I can't pretend to believe in this spiritualist thing, but if it comforts you then it won't do any harm.'

'Oh.'

'You will have been wondering,' he said, 'Why I seem rather cold towards you? Even now a long time after we lost your mother and sister.'

'Well, I …'

'I haven't been fair to you Natasha. There's something I should have told you a long time ago. Sally has made me realise. She's … good at talking to me, good at sorting me out. She's a tough old bird, at least that's how she described herself. I'm usually a bit more complimentary! She's noticed a lot about you and me and she won't let it go, it made me a bit mad for a while and then I saw …she was right.'

'What do you mean Dad?'

'You see … in fact I'm not your Dad, Natasha you see, I'm not your father.'

'What!'

'Your father was an old friend of Pauline's. They had a bit of a thing before Petra came along. I always knew and I found I hard, but I tried to do the right thing. But seeing you and watching how you looked more and more like him as you grew always reminded me, I could never forget. The hurt and the pain of it. I'm …I have to say I'm sorry Tash, for not being fair to you. This must come as a shock.'

Sally came in through the door from the café carrying several large bags of fabric. There was a silence in the kitchen,

Jeremy was sitting resting his hands on the table and watching Natasha who had turned away and was sobbing bitterly. Then Jeremy leaned towards her and put a tentative hand on her arm. 'I am so sorry,' he said, 'I've been very unkind.'

'Do you want me to go, Dad … oh I suppose I don't call you that anymore.' She fumbled in the pocket of her jeans.

'No Tash, I don't want you to go. Can you think about forgiving me? I know it's a very big thing I'm asking.'

'Can I … still call you Dad then … you're still my Dad. You're all I've got left.'

'I would be honoured,' he said, 'If you would think about staying and calling me that. It's far more than I deserve.'

30 JANUARY
Sarah Stuart

Ruby fluffed up her spiky hair and rearranged the brightly coloured silk scarf around her neck. As she walked down the suburban street with its elegant trees and tall Edwardian houses she went over the details of her new self again. She was Sarah Stuart. Her father was terminally ill nearby – she had studied Google Maps - and she needed to be able to pop in every day. She didn't want to rent a flat, it would be too much of a commitment, she wanted somewhere cheaper and more flexible. She came to number forty-two and approached the front door, the little front garden was overrun with weeds and there were grubby net curtains hanging unevenly in the bay window. A repulsive looking individual opened the door, his shoulder-length grey hair was matted, his long beard untidy. He regarded her with a watchful eye.

'Ah. Good afternoon. You must be Sarah.'

'Good afternoon.'

'I am Samuel Lees.'

'Yes.'

'We spoke on the phone.'

'Yes. You're looking for a lodger.'

'Yes. I am. Come in.'

She followed him into the gloomy, overcrowded living room.

'Can I get you a cup of tea Sarah?' He leaned on his stick and was struggling to clear a space on the sofa.'

'Yes please.'

'Milk or sugar?'

'Just milk please.'

'Make yourself at home.' He lumbered out of the room.

She sat down and looked around. Scruffy books everywhere, old furniture, paintings in dirty broken frames, some standing on the floor propped up against bookcases. A silent grandfather clock. A rather odd, stale smell in the stuffy air and the grimy windows were closed.

He came in with two mugs and handed her one, put one on a little table and sat down heavily in an armchair, resting his stick to the side. 'Now Sarah isn't it. You said about needing a room for a while, and your father is ill nearby, is that right?'

'Yes, that's right.'

'Well it's just me here. And my cat who's nearly as ancient as me. And my very quiet lodger who drives a lorry and sleeps a lot through the day. We need to think of him, are you quiet?'

'Oh yes.'

'It's quite rare these days. Sometimes he and I have a chat, and I don't have a television, I listen to the radio in here. My other lodger moved out, she was a student.'

'Well, I'm still interested please,' said Sarah Stuart.

There was a scratching on the door and a miaow. 'Would you mind letting her in, bit of an effort getting up these days.'

Ruby opened the door and a tabby cat shot in and hid under the sofa.

'Tabitha, your manners please. Well drink your tea and you can go and have a look at the room. I see you like paintings.'

'Oh yes, I was admiring …' She stopped herself. Sarah wasn't that kind of woman, 'I like the one with boats, I like the seaside.' She averted her eyes from the books, Sarah read magazines and posts on Facebook.

'It's a big old house and I like having lodgers. I don't bother them and they don't bother me.'

'Right, I'll pop up shall I?'

'First on the left at the top of the stairs. Cash on the first day of the month. Is it Mrs or Miss?'

'Just call me Sarah.'

'Right you are.' He leant back on the cushions and closed his eyes and the cat jumped up onto his knee.

31 JANUARY
Touring Europe

Dear George and Jonathan

I haven't heard from you so I'll attach my last email to this one. I hope you read it and it will be possible to sort out that equipment. By the way, I was thinking, please give the money to some good cause or other, it will be simpler that way.

Anthea and I are touring Europe at the moment and having a wonderful time. Got the usual photos of her propping up the Leaning Tower of Pisa yesterday.

You have my email address I hope you can find time to reply.

Best regards

Maxwell

32 JANUARY
Hugo and the Professor

Jonathan put his head round the door of the computer room and saw Hugo and the Professor sitting together staring at the screen. Now Diana was around it would probably be easier to start working through the paperwork and regulations required to bring others here.

'I hope you don't mind eating in the kitchen this evening,' he said, 'It's warm and cosy and we're keeping the heating off in other rooms at the moment.'

'That sounds delightful Jonathan, thank you.'

That evening Jonathan laid the table and was having a look at various dishes the caterers had left in the fridge. Diana Williams came in.

'Here's a list Jonathan, I've been putting it together all day and there are a few things I think we should discuss urgently.'

'Oh right. Thank you very much Diana. How about first thing tomorrow morning? This evening I need to look after the Professor who's staying and I'm not sure about …'

'Yes, alright.'

'Please sit down, dinner won't be long. A glass of wine?'

'I never drink.'

'Ah … some orange juice then, will that do?' Jonathan placed the list on the window-sill on a pile of paper while Diana sat at the table and straightened out the knives and forks.

'It's an important day for Hugo,' said Jonathan, arranging dishes on the table, 'A visiting academic is trying to get to know him at the moment and they should be down any minute.'

'Indeed. How interesting,' said Diana politely, 'I've only met him once or twice and he didn't have a lot to say.'

'He'll get used to you,' said Jonathan.

'And where do all the other people eat?'

'The women and kids had some food taken up earlier,

and there's a little impromptu kitchen they can use.'

Jonathan cut a slice of chicken pie and passed it to her, 'Please help yourself to everything, I'll just go and see what's happening.'

In the computer room Peter was typing on his laptop and looked up as Jonathan entered.

'Sorry to disturb you but the meal is ready. Is Hugo with you?'

'Ah yes, how kind, thank you. I think I've got the important things. Oh, Hugo left a little while ago, I thought he was probably with you.'

'Oh. Well, he often wanders off by himself, maybe he needed a bit of time on his own.'

Peter closed the laptop and got up and followed Jonathan down the stairs.

'By the way I've got the new House Manager here for dinner, she's just staying two nights a week.'

'Right.'

Jonathan introduced them and went off to look for Hugo. It was unusual that he was missing at a mealtime. He often tramped about outside, but it was dark and windy. Jonathan called his name a few times then came in and wandered around the house, up and down corridors and up the stairs. All sounded normal in the Women's Room. He turned the handle and went in.

'Jonathan!' Little Divit ran to him and clutched his legs.

'Hello Divit, how's things?'

'Play with me.'

'I'm sorry.' Jonathan gently disentangled himself and turned to the mothers. 'I'm looking for Hugo, has he been in here at all? Big lad, dark wavy hair.'

There was an odd silence and the children quietened down except for Divit who followed Jonathan still calling out.

'Has he … do you know who I mean?'

'You mean the weirdo,' said one of the three women, glancing at her friends, 'He did pop in earlier. Bloody nuisance, we told him where to go.'

'I'm sorry about that ...' There seemed to be two women he hadn't seen before, one was sitting on her own at a little table and reading a newspaper and the other had long dark wavy hair and was pacing up and down rocking a toddler who had fallen asleep on her shoulder. 'I must talk to him. Hello, are you new here?'

The dark girl smiled and nodded and kept walking. 'Nearly off,' she whispered, 'Been very unsettled. Thank you for letting me come here, it's lovely.'

The girl at the table went on reading. He went up to her. 'Hello I'm Jonathan.'

'Yes hello. I'm Francesca Smith.'

'Did you arrive today?'

'Yes.

'Right, I hope it's nice and quiet and people are showing you where things are.'

'Oh yes thank you, I took the bedroom right at the end of the corridor, it was free. Thank you so much.'

'Good. Well, I'll be off for the moment.'

The other Games Rooms were empty. Jonathan called Hugo's name again. He remembered he hadn't yet found a key for the storeroom. As he approached the door Hugo appeared and pushed past him without a word, knocking over the little table. Was he scared? Jonathan followed him down the stairs to the kitchen where he silently helped himself to his dinner appearing not to hear the polite conversation around him.

'Peter has been telling me about his most *interesting* work,' said Diana, 'Extraordinary what the human mind is capable of.'

'Yes, I'm looking forward to hearing more about it,' said Jonathan, 'Also going through the list you've put together. You alright Hugo? That's a nice pie isn't it.'

'Not as nice as Sylvia's.'

They ate in silence and Jonathan poured some wine for the Professor. Hugo sighed and helped himself to potatoes.

'I'm going back upstairs now.'

'Goodnight Hugo,' said Peter, 'Shall I see you tomorrow?'

'Mmm.' Hugo went out and closed the door.

'So … has it been a productive day with Hugo?' said Jonathan, 'More trifle for you?'

'Thank you. Very nice. Well … it's been a completely *unique* day.'

'Yes. I hope …'

'There's no need to worry Jonathan. I do feel I've got somewhere. I have in fact recorded a conversation I had with him this afternoon, he didn't realise I was doing this of course and I hope that you'll agree it was acceptable to do this in the circumstances …for my own research purposes only.'

'I …'

'Excuse me gentlemen,' said Diana finishing her orange juice, 'I think I had better leave you to discuss things. It's been a long day.'

'Yes, thank you so much for your hard work,' said Jonathan, 'I hope your room is comfortable. Shall I come to your office about nine?'

'That would be fine. Goodnight'

'Goodnight.'

'Well, going back to first thing this morning. To begin with naturally he just wanted to play the game and I thought it best if I just sit back for a while and we chatted as he played and I paid him a few compliments.'

'He's been practising using that controller.'

'Yes … well as he was playing he started telling me about the dimensions of the buildings, and distances, you know as the soldiers jump over obstacles and that kind of thing.'

'Oh yes?'

'His mind seemed to be racing. Things like the speed at which he was travelling, then the, er …well to begin with I thought the numbers were just random but then I realised …

well it all seemed to make a lot of sense. Some remarkable calculations. I jotted some down and had a look at them later. Then there was a bit about this character he's created who is a version of himself, and how brave and clever he was and how he could anticipate what was going to happen …again it seemed just good fun but then well he was really involved in this whole thing and it seemed to cheer him up considerably.'

'Yes …I wasn't sure I'd done the right thing, but that's good news.'

'Yes, of course it's tricky. But then something remarkable seemed to happen. By this time I had managed to wander off and turn on the digital voice recorder hidden in my case. Would you like to listen?'

'Oh … um, well if you think …'

Peter lent down and opened his case and got the recorder out and put it on the table. 'I hope most of it is clear, though a few words got muffled once or twice.'

The two men sat listening. They heard Hugo's voice. 'There now, he's going inside.'

'Is he tired Hugo?'

'Tired? Don't be silly, this isn't real.'

'No of course not. Haha.'

'So why did you say that?'

'Just joking.'

'It's not a joke you know. The game I'm going to write isn't a joke. It's really happening, and the Manor House is going to fall down. Jonathan doesn't know yet and he won't believe me.'

'Do you want to tell me a bit more?'

'Why do you want to know?'

'I'm interested. But only if you'd like to tell me.'

'Why did you come here?'

'Well because Jonathan told me you were good at certain things. Like numbers. And maybe thinking of stories. And I've met other people who are good at numbers and I wondered if you were like them.'

'Why?'

'Because it's interesting talking about numbers.'

'I will tell you about it. Though I don't know if I can create a game with it. Jonathan says maybe I can. But you have to learn how to do things first, like coding and people always told me I was no good. They said I was stupid, so I said *they* were even more stupid. And they didn't know what was going on in my mind. It's all about the dark energy. We can't understand it, and we can't stop it. It's come into the house from the grid. It got into the grid because there was a black hole in it which was sucking everything in. Not many people know about this, and I have to keep my eye on it. But I have to be careful not to go too close or I would get sucked in too which is absolutely terrifying. The grid is in the ground around the Manor House. When I first came here I couldn't find it for a while and I was very worried. People don't want to admit the black hole is there because it's so scary, it's one of the scariest things in the universe.'

'Yes indeed, very scary.'

'Everything's getting bigger. But it's happening so slowly that people don't notice, and pretend it isn't happening. Everything's expanding. That's why the grid is collapsing, that's why things can't go on as they are. Now my game will be very important for the world because it's about real things and not pretend. Many buildings are going to collapse. But then I get scared … it's all too frightening to think about.'

There was a silence on the tape, but Peter sat staring at the floor and let it run on.

'Tell me what scares you, Hugo.'

'The dark energy has come inside the house now. And it draws me to itself. Jonathan saw me up there today, he hasn't felt it yet. It likes to hide from people. It's stronger than me and I'm scared. I try to run away and play the game again and keep my mind on that and think about my own game. But then whenever I think about my game the dark energy is just on the edge, just … hovering there and threatening …'

'Can you tell me a bit more Hugo.'

'It's …it's here …right now, it's telling me not to, I can't say, I've got to …'

There were sounds of a chair being knocked over and footsteps. Peter pressed the off button. 'Extraordinary isn't it?'

'I'll make some coffee.' Jonathan got up, remembering how Hugo had appeared from the storeroom and pushed past him without a word.

'Oh yes, thank you. That would be lovely. Strong and black will probably help me clarify my thoughts!'

'Yes … so what happened then, did he …run off?'

'Yes, he stumbled out of the room. He seemed overcome. I didn't know what to do for the best so I thought I should leave it, you said he often wanders off by himself. He had talked to me a lot.'

'Yes. What sort of time was this?'

'Um …late morning. I came down to the kitchen and you'd left those sandwiches on the table with a note.'

'Ah yes. And you didn't think you'd …'

'What find you, I did think about it, but he'd talked a lot and maybe he'd come back in his own time … I realise he's very alone in the world and I greatly respect that you're caring for him and what a tricky task that is, I thought perhaps if we rushed around looking for him it might not help. I mean he knows you're around somewhere in the house doesn't he.'

'Yes, most of the time, or George is here, and Diana of course, though I don't think he's talked to her much. Yes, you did the right thing. He's not told me these kinds of things, well there are hints now and then. He used to invent what he called number games and that's what started me thinking about all this, and I gave him a bit of my time which probably helped him … but there's so much in his mind.'

'Some of his ideas are extraordinary. About the dark energy and the expansion of the universe. I mean where could he have picked this up?'

'Yes, I see what you mean. No idea. Maybe he saw a TV programme and absorbed some ideas he didn't really understand.' Jonathan finished his coffee and got up to clear the table. 'I do find it worrying,' he went on, 'Because recently I tried to help a very disturbed teenager and I seem to have done more harm than good.'

'Oh. Yes, very worrying ... but maybe you didn't.'

'She's run off.'

'I'm sorry to hear that.'

'We've been searching, and the police are supposed to be. But coming back to Hugo, did you speak to him anymore, did he turn up again?'

'Well yes, things got even more strange if that's possible. I've been writing about it ... But it's getting rather late now, shall I see how things go tomorrow? Are you willing for me to carry on?'

'Yes of course. He's always moody and unsociable, nothing new there.'

'Thank you for dinner.'

'I hope your room is comfortable.'

'Yes, thank you, what a fabulous house!'

'We can talk more tomorrow. Goodnight.'

'Goodnight.'

Jonathan pulled on rubber gloves and filled the sink with warm soapy water. *Why had Hugo been in the storeroom?* Had he too heard those strange sounds? What *was* that? He longed to speak to Pam, what would she say about this. She would see *beyond.* Should he ask her to marry him? Then she would come here. *But then what if she said no and insisted on staying in his house?* And there was so much going on. He thought of her family house in the town near this village. He rinsed the dinner plates and put them in the rack. If only all tasks were as simple as this. Then he sat down at the table and dialled her number, but it was the usual message.

'Pam darling, please talk to me. Or are you asleep now. I don't want to disturb you but I so much want to talk. It's nearly a week since I saw you. When can I come over again? That nasty frost has gone, it's a bit easier on the roads. I'm sorry it's late, I was rather involved in talking to someone …goodnight … my darling girl.'

The house was quiet. The women and children must all be in bed. Was there something … something evil …getting at Hugo? This bizarre and unwelcome thought surfaced in his mind. Were demons and evil spirits only to be found in the bible stories, or maybe this was some sort of challenge to *him* to deal with without help from anyone, least of all from the One who he constantly questioned and tried to understand, making a tortuous journey back through the centuries. Who was He anyway, just one of many charismatic Jewish leaders? How was He different from the others? Why didn't He make sure His words and His life were properly recorded at the time? If He could work such miracles surely He could have taken care of this important detail? How was the rest of mankind supposed to manage, what use are these records if they can't be trusted? At a young age He discussed all kinds of profound matters with educated men, but then this confusion was allowed to develop, He must have known that the words He is supposed to have said would be contradictory and misleading …

Jonathan felt weary of it all. I suppose You want me to ask You to help here. *To drive it out in Your name.* Is it damaging Hugo? Could it damage the children? Would I be failing them if I didn't ask for Your help? And so, supposing I did that very thing, supposing I said the magic words and suppose, *just suppose it didn't work.* What then, the demon would win, and the horror would really start. But how *could* it work? Perhaps if I really believed then my faith would make it work. *Your faith has healed you.* Am I afraid? Jonathan realised that he was.

He rinsed the cutlery and laid the knives and forks on a flat tea towel. He wiped the gloves and pulled them off and covered half-empty dishes with clingfilm and found spaces for them in the fridge. Then he sat at the table and took his copy of the New Testament from the pile of books and worked his way through the pages, there was a strange story he remembered reading.

...some strolling Jewish exorcists tried their hand at using the name of the Lord Jesus on those possessed by evil spirits; they would say, "I adjure you by Jesus whom Paul proclaims." ...when the evil spirit answered back and said, "Jesus I acknowledge, and I know about Paul, but who are you?" And the man with the evil spirit flew at them, overpowered them all, and handled them with such violence that they ran out of the house stripped and battered ... and the name of the Lord Jesus gained in honour ...

What did one make of this story? He could read all night, but he must get some sleep. He left the kitchen and climbed the stairs. What had Hugo said? ... something about the dark energy coming inside the house and drawing him to itself. And how he ran away and tried to escape by playing the video game. And it was stronger than him and he was scared ... it was *threatening.*

33 FEBRUARY
On the hotel balcony

The sparkling water of Lake Garda lapped gently against the low wall that ran along the edge of the hotel garden. Anthea and Maxwell were sitting in the shade on their hotel balcony which looked across the lake.

'Max why are you angry? Please ...'

'It's an email – from the agent. Damn damn damn!'

'What? Has something happened?'

Max glanced at her and began to type.

'Please tell me ...' she began again.

'Don't interrupt, let me think! Your damn brother causing all this trouble.'

'What do you mean? You're scaring me, what trouble. Oh, do you mean ...'

Maxwell went on typing. Anthea didn't move. The smooth lawns and pretty flowers were out of focus now, she was back in the Manor House, her brother was pacing the corridors, bursting into the kitchen, storming off into the grounds, demanding food, and were George and Sylvia still there, what was happening, and had they found that poor girl yet, and was George actually going to give the Manor House to Jonathan, and what would happen. Jonathan was kind, he was lovely, but surely even he would find Hugo a handful day after day, she should never have left like that, she should never have abandoned him, she should have found a way to live with it, she had probably made things ten times worse ...

'The buyers have pulled out,' said Maxwell, closing his laptop. And he sat staring ahead.

'I'm sorry. But there'll be others won't there?'

'Word gets around.' He glanced at her, 'It's such a beautiful house, it was where Angie and I lived ... for years. We were happy there before ... now all this nonsense next door. All those so-called weekends going on, and goodness knows what in the grounds, some acting company.'

'But I think that's all stopped now hasn't it?' said Anthea, 'George said he needed a break. And there was something about Jonathan taking over ...'

'That's exactly what I mean,' said Maxwell, 'It seems like there's all kinds of goings on there now.'

'What did the agents say then?'

'Your brother ... he must still have a key. I told them to check, I *told* them. I expect they overlooked it. Hugo's been going in and there are some women there apparently, I mean at the Manor House, Jonathan's up to his usual tricks taking in every Tom, Dick and Harry and giving all kinds of undesirables a home, and there's something about them chasing Hugo and taunting him, yesterday the buyers were viewing again and measuring up for curtains and things, I said they could, and they saw something going on outside, some shouting and laughing ...'

'Women! What women? Jonathan's not like that ...'

'Not like that huh! He's flesh and blood like the rest of us.'

'That's not what I meant. Please don't be angry Max, it's not my fault.'

'Jonathan this and Jonathan that. Why do people think he's so bloody marvellous eh! What the hell does he think he's doing. People spilling over into my garden and wrecking the peace and quiet. George was completely mad to do this ...'

'I think George and Sylvia were ...'

'Don't argue with me! Anyone with half a brain cell could see this was a disaster waiting to happen.'

'Don't be unkind Max, he's my brother, it's not his fault his brain isn't right, it's not his fault. I should never have left him.'

'No.'

'Is that what you think?'

Maxwell watched the pleasure boats full of tourists moving slowly on the sunny water.

'In the beginning ... ' Anthea began, 'You said we'd start a new life and you, well you encouraged me to leave him, you were kind and sympathetic about what it had been like, you knew I did my best.'

'Max please talk to me. You never said ... that I should stay and get on with it, you knew how I felt, you said you couldn't manage without me, you said ...'

'Please be quiet Anthea, let me think.'

'You said nice things about Jonathan, he said nice things at your wife's funeral, and ...'

'Anyone can make speeches Anthea, it's not difficult. People do it all the time, politicians, vicars, everyone. Anyone can put words together and paper over the cracks and disguise the untruths and put off the difficult decisions and pretend everything's alright and ignore the real problems, indeed I've done it myself on many occasions! But the point is, what am I going to do? Is there anything I can say to the buyers to make them change their mind? Or how can I prevent this happening again, word gets around. Maybe I should fly back and try and sort it out.'

Anthea got up and stretched. She bent and kissed Maxwell on the lips and began to undo her bikini top.

34 FEBRUARY
A bit odd

In the estate agents' office Maggie looked the Detective in the eye, 'I don't really know what to think,' she said feeling a little foolish, 'It's just a few things that seem a bit odd. Not a lot of information.'

'Well tell me,' he said, sitting down awkwardly and glancing out of the window. He was young and rather offhand.

'Well, this girl disappeared in South Witters – a few weeks ago now. I think the papers said the police had got involved with the search.'

'Yes. Belinda. We searched for quite a while but no luck so far.'

'I just thought I should let you know something.'

'What's that?'

'Ruby Seth has been in touch and we're trying to get a buyer for her cottage, one of those pretty ones near the church, number Four, The Green.'

'Yes, I know where you mean.'

'Well, you see it feels a bit odd. That's all really. She popped in here just before Christmas, she seemed to be in an awful hurry and looked anxious. And then she's away somewhere, hasn't given an address, just emails and phone calls. She wanted us to go in and measure up and all that while she was away, and we decided on the price then. She was vague why she was selling and of course we don't have to know the reason though it often helps if you can tell the buyers something, some normal reason, nothing sinister or they might start imagining things like Japanese knotweed and stuff, it's a big garden.'

'Right. And has she been back at all?'

'No.'

'Is that all?'

'Yes, well er … Steve, that's the other agent, well … after he took photos and all that he went back to check something, and he said there were several odd things in the cottage. That you might not expect.'

'Such as?'

'Um … some very damp and rather pongy clothes in a washing basket, a blanket with mud stains hanging on a radiator and a very muddy cushion on the floor. I mean people usually clean up and leave places as smart as possible don't they?'

'I see. Well could you show me round and I'll have a look. When are you free?'

Maggie waited by Ruby's front door, enjoying the peaceful scene and the winter sunshine, the village green, the historic church and the sound of occasional birdsong. After a few minutes the Detective came out carrying a blanket and a bag. 'Right, thank you,' he said giving her the key back, 'I'm taking a few things away.'

They walked to their cars parked under the great oak tree. 'Can you keep this to yourself at the moment?' he said, 'Here's my card. If anything else happens or occurs to you can you …'

'Yes.'

'Can you give me Ruby's phone number?'

She pulled a business card out of her bag and wrote it down.

'Can you let us know if you get a buyer?'

'Yes. I don't think it'll be long. It's a great location and not far from the motorway.'

'Thank you.'

He drove away without smiling. She was glad she'd done that, it had been bothering her.

35 FEBRUARY
Lies

Ruby scrubbed the old-fashioned draining board and paused to listen. The old man's radio could just be heard through his living room door and upstairs the other lodger was asleep. She tried to avoid them and cleaned little bits of the dirty kitchen each time she made a quick meal or snack. Now she put the cereal and toast on a tray and carried it up to her bedroom.

It was a pleasant room with basic furniture. She ate her breakfast sitting by the window and looking down at the view at the back of the house where there was a large expanse of overgrown grass with bits of garden statues and old dustbins standing among uneven shrubs and small trees. And the whole garden was dominated by a very large ancient oak tree which reminded her of the one by the village green.

An offer had been made on her cottage and thinking about it now in this bare room in this neglected house with these lonely people she realised what a wrench it would be to see it go. Could she go back after all when things had died down? Would she be safe? What had Jonathan been doing since that day, was he still in the village? Had someone found Belinda and was she being looked after, perhaps she was back in hospital. Had Belinda remembered anything about *her* and told anyone about their trip to the hotel by the lake?

Sadness and guilt and fear. She faced another empty day after being busy getting cash out of the bank and opening new accounts in other places, and making enquiries about selling her car and buying another, but things had been tricky with documents and sometimes people gave her odd looks, and there were awkward moments, and the previous day she had abandoned something she was doing and walked away filled with panic, she had no proof of her new name, it was more complicated that she had realised.

It was all connected with that moment when Jonathan had called and she hadn't told him the truth. And she couldn't shake off the memories of Belinda's haunted look. What had made her abandon her like that? ... it was cruel on top of everything.

She needed to decide about the cottage and phone the agent. Maybe she could pretend to be Sarah and say Ruby was ill ... but that was risky.

There was a gentle tap on her door and she put down the tray and went to open it.

'Hello.' Samuel was leaning on his stick. 'Miss Sarah, can I speak to you for a moment?'

'Yes of course.'

'I wonder if you could come down?'

'Yes of course, is everything alright?'

'I'll just make my way down. You ... follow when you're ready.' He limped away and began the awkward walk down the stairs.

'How are you getting on? How is your father?' He sat holding his stick and his direct gaze was disconcerting.

'He's struggling. It's very heartbreaking, but I'm glad I can see him every day.'

'It must be very hard for you.'

'Yes.' As they talked Ruby reminded herself that Sarah wasn't very bright. 'But I felt so guilty about my mother who died two years ago, I was so busy I didn't see much of her ...'

'Is your room alright?'

'Yes, its fine thank you. It's nice looking over the garden and getting the evening sunshine.'

While he was speaking Ruby noticed an old newspaper lying across the crowded coffee table in front of him and caught sight of part of an article near the bottom of a page – *car accident where a teenage girl was knocked over as she crossed the road* ...

'... is always open if you ever feel like a chat.'

'Yes, thank you.' It couldn't be, it mustn't be ... *in front of an oncoming car and was pronounced dead at the scene. The driver* ...

'I see you like books.'

'Oh – not really, they just reminded me of some I saw in a charity shop...' *and two passengers were taken to hospital with minor injuries. The girl was carrying a brand new dark brown leather handbag with a long, silver chain strap ...*

'Forgive me Sarah, I can't help being a little curious ...' *with a diary in it with the name – Belinda - written in it. Police are appealing for witnesses and anyone who might help identifying ...*

'I was thinking you know that maybe we could have a little talk about this and that.'

She heard herself asking if he'd like a cup of tea and managed to get to the door and open it. *It couldn't be, it mustn't be. But there it was in black and white. That was the bag she had just bought her.*

Keep going Sarah ... She came back with a tray. Samuel was reading the newspaper and that page was now hidden. 'Hmm, Brexit eh,' he said, creating some space on the table. 'Long article here, been keeping this paper. Goes on and on doesn't it. I can see both sides, my heart says leave and my head says remain.'

'I don't really understand it at all,' said Sarah.

'No.'

'What are your plans today, Sarah? But perhaps I shouldn't ask. You will be concentrating on your father in his hour of need.'

'Yes. It's hard to think about normal things.'

He was drinking his tea. 'Did you say you were selling your house? That must be hard for you.'

'Yes ... it's hard.'

'Is there something the matter Sarah?'

'No ...well I'm finding it very hard yes. It's a difficult time with my father, sorry.' She wiped her eyes on her sleeve.

'Have you any other family perhaps?'

'No.'

'And your mother, you said that ...'

'She died. Three years ago.'

'Very sad.'

'I'd better be going in a minute.'

'Well, perhaps you had better, or perhaps not. Or perhaps you could stop telling lies.'

'What?'

'Don't pretend Miss Sarah. You're not very good at it. Oh, I can see you're upset about something that much is obvious. Perhaps it was unkind of me to ask questions.'

'Lies? What do you mean?'

'Yes. And off you'll go in a minute like you do most days, and then you'll come back, and more time will pass. Making your way to the car you pretend you don't have which is parked near Sidney's house, oh yes, he's noticed you coming and going, mentioned it to me the other day when he called in to trim my hair. And then you'll go out again and so it goes on.'

Sarah wouldn't know what to say, she would look blank and just get more upset.

'But what would the philosophers say about all this I wonder, hmm?'

'What?'

'I saw you looking, quite a collection, eh? More than interesting. But you look away then and think I haven't noticed.'

'I'd better go now, I'll take the tray.' Sarah got up and reached for his empty mug and he put out a hand and grasped her arm. 'Tell me the truth Sarah. And what has just upset you so much?'

'I don't know what you mean. Please let go. You've been saying some horrible things to me, of course I'm upset.'

'Something has upset you seriously since you came into this room. It's not me, something else.'

'Of course I'm upset.'

'What has suddenly upset you so much?'

'You said I'm telling lies. I don't have to talk to you. I have to go.'

He let go of her arm and she sank back into the chair and covered her face with her hands. He watched her for a minute.

'There is no father,' he said eventually, 'And I believe you're running away from something. You're a lovely woman trying to hold it all together but it's too much for you. You think I'm a stupid old man who doesn't care what he looks like and sits here day after day with nothing to do. And doesn't notice anything. But you don't know what's here inside ...' he laid his arm across his chest, 'My soul and my heart and my mind. There is so much in here it's bursting and roving around the world like a lost soul with no home, endlessly looking and searching. I feel the mystery, I sense the mysteries – and the endless joy and the wonder and incredible beauty of the world and the pain and the cruelty. You feel all this too Sarah, but you pretend you're a shallow woman with some sort of story, and underneath you think about ... many things. Which of my books are you itching to get your hands on, huh? And you're carrying the pain around with you, and something has just happened, and you are worried and, something has happened in the last few minutes and it's all more than you can bear, and you need to tell me, yes me, Samuel. I am so much more than you think I am, and I can understand, and I can help.'

Ruby looked up startled and their eyes met. 'I am so tired,' she said, 'Yes, you are right. I am so very tired of it all. Yes, I have just lost someone ... but it would be hard to explain it.'

'But you must,' he said, 'And you can. And you will. When you are ready. You can share this terrible thing.'

'But ...' her voice was a whisper, 'I've done something really bad.'

'I won't condemn you, I'm sorry if I said you were a lovely woman, I spoke out of place, I got carried away.'

'It's ...alright.'

'It's true.'

'I'm beginning to see you ... in a different light.'

Yes. You will. I did tidy myself up a bit, but you mean now you're seeing beyond ... that happens when you talk to someone doesn't it, you start to see beyond. The person inside.'

'Yes.'

'Tell me. Tell me everything. When you're ready.'

'Everything?'

'I will understand. Why you've done it. Whatever it is. It might have been me that did it. We can understand each other, Sarah.'

'It's not Sarah … it's… Ruby.'

'What a beautiful name. That suits you so much better.'

'My name is Ruby Seth and I've done something really terrible. And now … it looks like she's dead.' Ruby wept. Then as she began to speak Samuel put his hand underneath some untidy cardboard packaging on the coffee table and silently turned on the cassette tape recorder. The little light glowed.

36 FEBRUARY
Keith hovered in the dark

It was no good. There were too many people coming and going. Keith hovered in the dark near the Manor House with his coat collar turned up and his hands in his pockets. He must be careful going near windows with no curtains. From this distance he could see women moving around in an upstairs room, as he waited another one came to the window and peered out, then turned and spoke to someone. They looked like youngish women and a few days before he had seen several walking up the hill with buggies. They must be a group of mothers, what were they doing here?

He caught sight of Jonathan in the kitchen, he was talking to someone who was sitting at the table. Earlier on Hugo had been tramping about and muttering to himself. There had been no sign of George and Sylvia, had they really gone now? He longed to see George, but it was more important that he get into the house. There was no time to lose, and now there was no alternative, he must call again. There must be something he could offer to do that Jonathan would find it difficult to refuse, he must be busy and under pressure with some new projects.

37 FEBRUARY
God is everywhere

'I really do have to go now,' said David, finishing his pint, 'Natasha, you are unquestionably the darts champion!'

'Yes, haha!' She gave him a quick kiss. 'I'll call round later, Dad's trying out these recipes most nights and it's a free meal worth staying for.'

'Hmm! He's keen. Are you two getting on alright now?'

'Well, he's mostly on his best behaviour with your Mum. She does bring out the best in him.'

'That's really great. I'm pleased for them. Do they know ... we're seeing each other?'

'Well yes, but I made it sound casual, you know, he can be tricky. Though there is one thing ...'

'What's that? I really must be going ...'

'I don't like to ask him for money, and they're not paying me, just letting me stay.'

'And you'd like some?'

'Well, obviously I'll be getting a proper job soon, but I feel I should stay with them till the Grand Opening. Give them my support.'

He felt in his back pocket and handed her a bundle of notes. 'There. Now make sure you turn up later, I'm looking forward to it.'

'Thank you, David.' She slid them into her handbag and pulled on her coat as she watched him leave.

She picked up her phone. 'Pam?'

'Hi Tash. How are you. Haven't spoken for ages.'

'How are you?'

'Busy. Missing Jonathan of course. He comes when he can. Nothing really changes. And you?'

'Pretty good. Seeing one of Sally's sons.'

'That's nice. Café coming on?'

'Yes, it's going to be lovely. It feels strange not seeing

Jonathan and him being so far away doesn't it.'

'Yes. I'm kind of used to it though. Would you think of going down and helping him set things up?'

'No … it's creepy down there, and in the middle of nowhere. Miss him though.'

'Yes. Oh. Look I'm sorry, someone's at the door and I've got a meeting.'

'Talk soon.'

'Nice to hear from you.'

Natasha put her phone back in her bag and left the pub. It was a bleak, grey day and the seagulls were calling. She could walk on the beach, breathe that pure air and wear herself out. Then back to her Dad and Sally. *But it wasn't enough!* She made her way down the street and a tall, gloomy church building stood in front of her, towering above the surrounding terraced houses. Would there be anyone in there? Who might it be? She opened the heavy door.

For a while she sat and listened to the silence. This is what people used to do in the old days. Did they still do that now? She imagined it in countries like France and Spain, but it was sunny and women wearing veils would come in and pray and go into the confessional booth. All part of a normal day. Here it was dark and deserted, she sat thinking of her mother and sister, the usual sadness was becoming less intense as the days went by.

Then she heard quiet footsteps, and someone sat down in a pew nearby. She stole a look and saw a young man in a black cassock. He didn't look at her … but they seemed to be be sharing the space, it was strangely comforting, she was safe for a few minutes.

Was he praying? What was that like? Did it mean he found all the answers to everything, did it mean he was never alone and lost and fearful? How wonderful that would be. To have the strength to pass by a dealer in the street without a second glance and forget the longing or at least perceive it as the dangerous illusion it really was. To have something real and worthwhile to think about and do instead of stumbling from one moment to the next.

'Excuse me,' she said eventually.

'Yes?' A gentle voice, a question without pressure.

'Could I talk to you?'

'Yes, of course.' He moved a little closer leaving a discreet distance between them.

'I don't usually go into churches.'

'No.'

'I … it's peaceful in here. It helps me.'

'We all need help.'

'And … sorry I don't quite …'

'Ask if you would like to,' he said, smiling, 'Or if you prefer, we could just sit.'

'But I guess you're not just sitting.'

He smiled again. 'No.'

'So … are you praying?'

'Yes. I try and pray a lot.'

'Can I pray?'

'Yes. Of course.'

'I think … maybe …'

'Yes?'

'You are praying that I might be able to pray. Because you know that I don't know how to.'

'Yes, I am. And I believe you will be able to. There is something you need help with, and you will get that help.'

'So … is God there then?'

'Yes, God is there. God is here. Everywhere. He wants you to ask for help and He will give it. He wants you to know what to ask for. You can ask Him anything.'

'Anything?'

'Anything at all. Absolutely anything at all. He will give you strength and guidance and protect you from evil.'

Natasha sat very still and wiped away the tears. She wished she could believe it.

Two hours later she emerged from the church and made her way towards the sea front in the semi darkness of early evening. There was help and safety. She could ask and get the strength whenever she needed to. God would always be there. She could keep telling herself this until she believed it, like a magic spell, and it would work. She could *make* it work. She didn't have to tell Jonathan, she wondered what would happen if she did, he would surely be surprised, perhaps shocked, concerned for her as he always was ... an extraordinary thought. But she needn't tell anyone. They would all think she was the same and that was okay. She approached the café and saw the beautiful new curtains were hanging at the windows, the lighting was all fixed up and the sign was in position. *The Windy Restaurant by the Sea.* It all looked so lovely.

38 FEBRUARY
Pouring with rain and very dark
'This is Diana Williams, our new House Manager. She's got a little office in the hall and the door is always open if you have anything at all you want to mention to her. By the way as it's such a lovely sunny morning, can I just say that you are all welcome to go outside, there's a lot of grass for the children to play on. But they must be closely supervised at all times, nothing is fenced off at the moment.'

As Jonathan was speaking some of the women were quietly wandering about, some in dressing gowns carrying half-dressed toddlers, some sitting feeding babies. There was that dark haired woman again sitting on the edge of an armchair. As Diana began to speak Jonathan caught her eye and they smiled.

'Yes, as Jonathan says my door is always open. This is an old house which was converted into a hotel so it should all be very convenient, but please let me know if anything isn't working or something needs attention. You all know you can stay here for a maximum of six weeks, and we hope you'll find it a peaceful and welcoming place to be. Are there any questions?'

Jonathan waited. She reminded him of an old-fashioned headmistress and three women standing together were the troublemakers.

'Well then, we'll leave you to have a pleasant day.' As she and Jonathan turned to go Francesca Smith approached. 'Hello, um …I'm Francesca.'

'Oh yes, we met didn't we. How are you?'

'I'm sort of ok, thanks. But the thing is …well I've got a lot of time on my hands. I don't have kids you see and I was wondering …if you'd like any help with anything. While I'm here.'

'Oh, I see.' Diana looked her up and down. 'Jonathan we need to be more organised about who is in the building at any one time. I'll get that organised straight away.'

'Yes of course, sorry.'

'I've got office experience and if you want any help I'd be very glad,' said Francesca.

'I see. Well … would this be alright with you Jonathan? I could certainly use a bit of help, there's a lot to do.'

'Whatever you think,' said Jonathan politely.

'Jonathan and I have a meeting now,' said Diana, 'But perhaps you'd like to pop down to my office about twelve, and we can discuss it.'

'Thank you.'

Jonathan followed Diana down the stairs and into the little office and closed the door. It was very tidy, and a number of new files were arranged on the shelves. He hadn't slept well, he couldn't get Hugo's haunting words out of his mind. He realised with a nasty jolt that there hadn't been any answering phone call from Pamela that morning, he should have phoned her first thing …

Diana was laying some paperwork on the desk between them. 'This is the urgent pile, things that need your signature immediately, and ah yes, here's a list of the women and children who are here, I'll start a system where people sign in and out. The men are coming to service the boiler today, I'll look after that.'

'Oh yes, thank you, it's good that George updated the whole heating system, one thing we can rely on.'

Diana went on to talk about other things, appliances that needed attention, bills and questions about insurance. Jonathan's mind wandered back to the conversation with Peter.

'And finally Jonathan, what do you want done with these files?' She bent down and picked one up from the pile on the floor. *Tell your Psychiatrist Everything.* 'I presume you have no further use for them?'

'These were the Games the guests used to play,' he said, 'I'd like them safely stored somewhere. There's probably some interesting reading there, I need to get in touch with George who used to run it here.'

'Mmm.' She opened another file and looked at the first page. 'Extraordinary!'

Why did that word keep cropping up at the moment? It was one Peter had used. He and Hugo were probably getting together at this very moment. *Was this a good thing?* There had been so much to talk about last night and they had run out of time. 'Well, it was mainly a way of enabling someone to speak to someone, but in a light-hearted setting,' he said, 'It worked well. You can see all the comments people have written. The Mummies were played by kind older women who were – broad minded. And it was confidential of course.' It was odd trying to explain this to Diana.

She closed the file and put it back with the others. 'Yes, well it's not my place to comment. Shall we get on?'

'Please just store them safely for now.'

'As you wish. There's a spare box here I can put them in.'

'And now, if that's everything, I need to pop up and see how Hugo and Peter are getting on. Things are a bit tricky.'

'Here are your appointments,' she said, handing him a brand new diary, 'I've been through all the emails and arranged interviews with the ones you shortlisted.'

'Ah yes, very helpful. He turned the pages. 'Oh. I see there's one tomorrow!'

'Yes. The new Political Party.'

'Did I really shortlist that one!'

'Yes ... you seemed impressed, look here are the comments you made and all the information they sent with their application. I've checked they're coming.'

'Oh, right ... so I did. Hmm.'

'Yes, and you've got the urgent list with you now haven't you?'

'Absolutely. Thank you so much Diana, you're doing a wonderful job.' As Jonathan left the office and closed the door he saw Peter approaching down the stairs. 'Do you have a minute, Jonathan? I think Hugo may have had enough for the moment.'

'Oh yes.' Jonathan glanced at his watch. 'Coffee in the kitchen?'

'I was going to tell you what happened later, wasn't I,' said Peter settling himself at the table and getting the laptop and digital voice recorder out of his case. Jonathan placed the appointments diary and list on the window-sill next to other papers and measured coffee beans into the machine.

'Well, first I sat looking at the numbers he's come up with and was starting to see that they made sense as far as I could judge, it was quite advanced stuff.'

'Yes.'

'So ... when he came back I was hoping we could talk more about that kind of thing.'

'Yes.'

'So, we chatted a bit and then I asked him if he'd had any more ideas about the story for a video game. Well, all sorts of things started coming out about the relative body weights of the two protagonists, and the speed of their walking and running and the gravitational field of this ...imaginary world beneath the Manor House, and how it changed according to their moods and other extraordinary things ... I say *imaginary world,* though of course it's very real to him ...and there were more formulas to do with time passing and even the relative positions of the planets at any one time, it was well above anything I could just check there and then and I asked him if he minded if I jotted a few things down. Later I put it all together into some sort of coherent form. He was quite happy just talking about this, and even cracked the odd joke about the story line now and then which was surprising, and I was very pleased about that of course. Well after a while I had pages of the stuff, and then I suggested he might do something else while I did some more work by myself, and he seemed quite happy with that. Now I'm coming to the really astonishing thing. I spent several hours typing it into some sort of document and then sent it off to a mathematician friend of mine.'

'Really, how interesting.' Jonathan put two cups of coffee on the table and sat down.

'He emailed several hours later. All the numbers made total sense! This is the extraordinary thing. He was absolutely flabbergasted!'

'Good heavens!'

'Absolutely flabbergasted. I need to take all this information away with me and write it up, will that be alright? And there seem to be several aspects to it ...'

'Well well, I'm very pleased ... that you've got so much out of him so quickly. And that it's of interest. I wasn't able to judge in the same way.'

'Yes, and of course there are still many unknowns, one of the chief ones being about the coding. I don't suppose you've managed to get him to read that book at all. Or perhaps had time to look at it yourself?'

'No, I haven't yet I'm afraid,' said Jonathan, 'I should study it myself, but there are always so many other interesting ones to read! And when you arrived I thought it was best just to see how things went.'

'Yes quite.'

'Well well, it really is ... unbelievable isn't it. And unusual?'

'Aspects of it are *very* unusual. I don't really know what to make of it.'

'And what happens next?'

'I'll talk to my friend again, we were both in a bit of a hurry. And there are one or two other people, and I'll look around and see what I can find.'

'Yes.'

'And ... I think it would be wise if I just ... er leave quietly for the moment. Rather than making a big thing of it which might upset him.'

'Yes. That's a good idea.'

'Perhaps you can ... follow it up and encourage looking at the coding, though it might be difficult to pin him down.'

'Ha! Yes.'

'But you have great empathy, that's so valuable.'

'Thank you.'

Peter glanced at his watch. 'So ... shall I just slip away?'

'I'll come and see you off.'

'No need, you're busy. Can you tell Hugo – I'll call again soon. If he asks that is.'

'Yes of course.'

'You're sure – this is the best thing, to slip away?'

'Yes, I think so.

'It's been extraordinary. Thank you so much.'

'Keep in touch, look forward to seeing you again soon.'

'Yes. I will.' Peter left the room and closed the door, and after a few moments Jonathan heard his car drive away.

He felt little unreal as if he had been in a dream world which would quickly fade. He went out of the side door and walked across the grass at the back, heading for the outbuildings behind two great oak trees, all the doors needed to be securely fastened. Several of the women had taken his advice and a few toddlers were running about.

On his way back he nearly bumped into the girl with the dark wavy hair. 'Oops.'

'Hello Jonathan.'

'Everything alright?

'It's so beautiful here, thank you for having us.'

'Yes. It is. I hope you feel safe, well comparatively safe, and ...'

'Jonathan, can I ask you something? Well, you never actually feel *safe* ...'

'Is your ... child ... okay?'

'Little Andy. Yes, thank you. He's with Pat at the moment, and her friends Marissa and Julie, he loves them, like having new Aunties, they make him laugh. Though they're a bit outrageous at times. And he likes the other kids too. You see I was wondering if ...'

'Yes?'

'Do you do counselling here? Are *you* a counsellor. Because if you are I ...'

'No. Um sorry, what do I call you?'

'Jan.'

'Well Jan, I'm running the place and arranging for the space to be used in various ways, not a counsellor.'

'Well, could I talk to you anyway?'

'Well, it wouldn't be appropriate Jan. There are people who will help you.' He noticed a freckle on her cheek and the way her hair framed her face.

'Oh. Ok.'

'I'm sorry for whatever it is you have been through, and I hope you can get some support.'

'Oh yes, we all support each other. It really helps.'

'Yes. Look it's nice to have spoken to you Jan, but I have a lot to do. Have a good day.'

Jonathan strode off towards the side door of the Manor House. He had the impression several women were within earshot behind a group of trees. He remembered the first time he had seen Jan in the Women's Room and tried to put her out of his mind.

He saw a police car parking under the cedar trees and walked quickly over. Was this news of Belinda? The policeman approached, he was carrying a newspaper and a dark brown leather handbag with a chain strap.

'Jonathan Wender?'

'Yes, that's me.'

'D C Saunders. I met you when we came over after Belinda ran away.'

'Yes, I remember now.' They shook hands.

'Could we go inside Sir?'

Jonathan led the way to the kitchen, apologising that other rooms were cold. He felt sick. There was a silence while he boiled the kettle. 'I am very afraid you don't have good news,' he said as he placed two mugs of tea on the table.

'Yes, I am very sorry. Here is something I'd like you to read and then I need to show you something.' The detective handed Jonathan the newspaper where an article was highlighted with biro, and sipped the tea while Jonathan read it. Then he opened the bag and drew out a diary and opened it. 'This is what she was carrying, and this is what Belinda wrote in this diary. The question is, do you recognise the writing, and do you have anything she wrote we could compare it with?'

Belinda. Christmas shopping with Ruby ... Jonathan struggled to speak. 'Yes, I do recognise it, and yes, I have some notebooks she wrote in, she left her things here when she ran away. I'll go and get them.' He hurried up to his bedroom and found Belinda's rucksack in a wardrobe next to some of his bags. *Dead at the scene ...Shopping with Ruby? ...*

'You can see from any of these – the writing does look the same.'

'Yes. Indeed ... it does. I am very, very sorry. That's the confirmation we need.'

'Was she ... killed there and then, how did it happen?'

'It seems like she walked into the road, the car was very close, it was pouring with rain and nearly dark. We have several witnesses. It wasn't speeding. I'm very sorry.'

'Would she have been …'

'It's likely she was knocked out and didn't know anything.'

'Was she … *with* anyone at the time?'

'We're still looking into that. It looks like she was on her own.'

'Thank you for telling me.'

'Would you like to keep the bag and the diary? We've traced her parents, but we learnt a bit about her family from the hospital.'

'Yes, I will keep them safe.'

'I wonder if … Do you know … anything about how she got so far from here? Someone called Ruby was mentioned.'

'We're looking into it. When we know more we'll let you know … so you can piece it together.'

'Thank you.'

'I am very sorry for your loss.'

'Thank you.'

'Tash?'

'Hi Jonathan, how nice to hear from you.'

'And how are you? Still living by the sea?'

'Oh yes. The café's looking lovely. The Grand Opening is next week.'

'That sounds lovely. Look Tash …'

'Oh Jonathan. Please don't say you've got bad news. I've got an awful feeling.'

'I'm very sorry Tash. I have terrible news.'

'Oh no!'

'She was found after a terrible car accident. She was knocked over and killed on a quiet street in Manchester. In the dark and the pouring rain.'

'Oh no, are they *sure*! But how can they be sure?'

'She was carrying a handbag and she'd written her name in a new diary.'

'But surely …'

'We compared the handwriting. With her notebooks. I'm so sorry to tell you.'

'You still there Tash? I'm so very sorry to tell you this. I'll ring again this evening. You look after yourself.'

39 FEBRUARY
Stuff in the files

It was two o'clock in the morning. Francesca pulled on her dressing gown and opened her bedroom door. Not a sound. Then a baby crying in one of the bedrooms and quiet voices. She crept down the corridor and headed for the staircase. Once in the hall she tried the key Diana had given her to the little office and opened the door.

She switched on the computer, turned out the light and locked the door on the inside. She then looked for a box she had seen Diana tidy away under a bookcase and moved it to where she was sitting. She began to type an email.

Hi Hazel

Well here I am in the office and it's dead quiet. What I'll do is email pics of some of the stuff in the files and the comments with them. This is exactly what you wanted – stuff about the Games people played together with comments people made. Perfect! Perhaps you could write an article a bit like the other one you wrote a few months ago, that was cleverly done, it suggested you had been here (which of course you had) but as a guest (which you pretended to be) and what it was like – the atmosphere – and your experience of playing that Game called Mixed Messages. And I'm sure you remember, there were things 'happening' unexpectedly all over the place and startling the guests, like enactments in the grounds and 'ghosts' in the corridors, I think that was getting a bit over the top. But then I think

'Mixed Messages' was a bit tame compared to the other Games, though I could be wrong there.
Hope things are going well your end. Any more exciting contacts and articles? F

She sent the email and then bent down and took some files out and started reading. After scanning through pages of handwritten comments she put several in a separate pile together with Instructions for the Games and Instructions for the Referees and Permitted Words for some of the actors playing certain parts. She took photos of everything with her phone and sent them to her email and attached the photos to emails to Hazel and then carefully replaced everything in the files which then went back into the box.

These are from the files. There are a lot of comments with the Game – 'Tie Up Your Partner and Tell Them the Truth'. I think you know this involved an actor playing the part of someone's partner, of course it all had to be prepared beforehand using someone with similar build to the actual partner and making them up to look like them, or fairly close.
The instructions: 'Permitted Words for the Partner' are quite interesting to read, all about how to respond to a disturbed person and maybe get them to solve their own problems. And how 'Silence is Golden' and how the referees are trained to intervene if necessary! And making sure there's no contact between the Game Player and the actor afterwards!

I'd better go now Hazel, I'll see if I can find anything else tomorrow night. F

40 FEBRUARY
This was Italy, beautiful but cruel
'Max please!' Maxwell removed Anthea's hand from his arm and strode out of the hotel room, down the stairs and into the lobby. She took the key card and closed the bedroom door and followed him. It would be better outside where other people were about. He was heading for a shady part of the garden near

the lake. It was such a beautiful place, more gorgeous than anywhere she had ever been.

He sat staring over the water and she approached quietly and sat down.

'Please don't go. Please don't leave me in a country where I don't speak the language. I wouldn't know how to get about and how to ask for things.'

'I won't be away long Anthea. Just stay here, everything is paid for, they can always get in touch with me. You can go for boat trips, most people speak English. Have a look at that phrase book I bought the other day.'

'What are you planning to do when you get back?'

'It's difficult to make plans.'

'Might you change your mind and ...'

He turned to look at her and spoke in a low voice. 'So many questions Anthea. Perhaps it's time I asked *you* a few questions.'

'What do you mean.'

'Who were you thinking about? This morning?'

'What? You mean when we ...'

'You know what I mean. *Who was in your mind?*'

'I don't really think while, you know ... '

'I don't believe you.'

'Please, *please.* Don't do this. You've asked me before and I ... I told you, you can't erase everything from your memory, it's all there and sometimes things come to the surface, it doesn't mean ...'

'What! It doesn't mean what!'

'I love *you.* I've told you and told you.'

'And you love him too.'

'Well, I may have said that once, I only said it because you made me angry, and anyway what do we mean by love, and you made me do it and it was the filming wasn't it, it wasn't real.'

'It was real. He's in your mind and that's real.'

'You made it all happen. It's not my fault.'

'How am I supposed to feel when I know you're thinking of him!'

'I'm not. I'm thinking of you, I'm with *you.*'

'It may appear so Anthea.'

'Please don't do this Max, please don't. I've got no one. This place is so fabulous it's like heaven. And I love *you.*'

He turned and looked at her and she felt frightened and helpless. The jealousy seemed to take him over. He had loved his wife – for years. Then he had loved Phillipa. She accepted that, it was how things were. But she wouldn't dare mention this today, it wouldn't help. There was one rule for him and one rule for her. Crying now would only annoy him so she sat quietly and waited. Other people wandered around the garden, enjoying the flowers and the fountains. Perhaps when he'd gone she could try and chat with them, they might be English. This was Italy, beautiful but cruel.

41 FEBRUARY
Something rather scary

Oh Jonathan!

I don't normally write emails. But we often seem to miss each other, and then your phone is engaged, I did send a text but you didn't seem to get it. Something rather scary happened and it would take rather a long time on the phone, and you'd probably be tired out.

Well, I was doing a demonstration and there was a disturbed woman who was worried about her son Daniel. Her Uncle Jack is in spirit and asked me to tell her that she mustn't blame herself for things that happened during her son's childhood. Then he said these things were not the reason why Daniel is where he is now. (This might sound a bit complicated, I don't necessarily think about the messages or even understand them sometimes.) I try and be tactful if I think it's something worrying. The main purpose of the messages is to reassure people.

Anyway, I had no idea what this was going to lead to. The name Daniel was significant, and the woman (who I later found out was called Kathryn

Winter) seemed on edge and didn't say much and didn't thank me for the message.

Later I was clearing up after the evening and I overheard a conversation going on between this Kathryn and someone called Caroline she'd come along with, who I later learnt had a son the same age as Daniel. Basically Kathryn was angry about a few things, she hated this Uncle who was mean to her and didn't leave her any of his money and she was furious that he didn't apologise for the way he'd treated her when he was alive. Well that was understandable.

Kathryn was crying and saying things like – 'This is just the kind of thing he'd do when he was alive. Tell me something which has nothing to do with what I'm really worried about, and he'd laugh and enjoy my misery, and tell me I was just like my mother who he hated. But for God's sake, my son's whole life is in danger right now. Uncle Jack must know what's going on and he doesn't tell me! And you're in the same boat. But it's all crap anyway.'

Well Jonathan this sounded like a serious situation so I stood nearby and pretended to be moving chairs around. She went on talking, 'I mean you've told me a lot Caroline, if it weren't for you I don't know what I'd do. If only Daniel would stay in touch with me like your Tom does. But knowing just a little bit makes it so much worse ...' The other woman said, 'Well we know that Tom and Daniel are together, Tom texted me this morning in fact.' And Kathryn said, 'Well how can they be alright? This – whatever you call it, this cult has got hold of them, they probably make them send these texts after censoring them. I mean we don't even know where they are.' And Caroline said, 'No we don't, I only know that stuff about their Facebook page because you told me, some of the things Tom told me in the texts sounded convincing, and I didn't think it looked like those had been censored, they were about the activities they were involved with.' And Kathryn said, 'The trouble is I can't believe any of it, when I look at the group photo on Facebook I can just make out Daniel in the back row, what are they doing to our son's minds Caroline, what are they doing? And I came here to try and find out, and Uncle Jack must be laughing his head off, God knows how that woman knew about him, and she mentioned Daniel, how did she know his name - that's really spooky, but it doesn't help does it, nothing helps. It's crap isn't it, talking to the spirit world, it's really crap and it's not helping. I wish I'd never come.'

Well Jonathan by this time I had a rough idea of what was going on and I went on moving the chairs and walked back towards Wendy ... I'm sorry, I'm too tired to finish this email, I'll try and tell you the rest tomorrow. I'm back from hospital now, they have been monitoring me but I still feel a bit shaken. That's not the end of the story, I love you, Pam xxx

42 FEBRUARY
Julie

Jonathan was busy after an interview with three idealistic young men which he had enjoyed while knowing it was a waste of time. He printed out Maxwell's email together with the list of the photographic equipment and other things. He hurried upstairs. He would take photos of everything and put it online. But as he walked down the corridor towards the Games Rooms he heard sounds of children screaming and women's raised voices, and broke into a run.

The noise was coming from the storeroom. It was chaos. Two small children were crying, and several women blocked the door.

'... a bruise on his head, look!'

'Marissa you said you were keeping an eye. It was only for a few minutes, I was just ...'

'I was. The weirdo came in earlier and we had a bit of trouble getting him to leave. He trod on some toys and I didn't understand what he was saying ...'

'So you left the door open, and ... don't cry baby, Mummy rub your head.'

'Look he's not badly hurt, stop make such a drama out of it!'

'No, we were lucky, *you* were lucky. Don't you realise this could have been serious!'

Jonathan elbowed his way through people crowded together

by the door and everyone fell silent. Julie was rocking her
toddler to and fro. 'Was there an accident?'

Eventually Julie spoke. 'Probably but nothing very much.
Marissa was watching them and ...'
　　'Yes?'
　　'Well Hugo came into our room as Marissa says, he's
clumsy and we asked him to go and he's so peculiar and we
were trying to talk to him, and the kids must have wandered in
here and there were a few things that fell down and scared
them, but it doesn't look like anything much ...'
　　Jonathan glanced at the crying children and began
tidying up the bits of furniture and piles of magazines and
some boxes. 'And where's Hugo now?'
　　'He ran off.'
　　'He was laughing.'
　　'I expect ...'
　　'Yes Julie?'
　　'Well, you know what kids are like. They like building
things,' she said, looking uncertainly at Marissa. Jonathan
pushed a pile of boxes against the wall. 'I've been meaning to
lock the door. I am so sorry, this is my fault. I'll sort it out
straight away. Is everybody better now?'
　　'Yes, it's calming down now,' said Julie, handing him a
box. 'I'll watch them for signs of concussion, but it wasn't
anything heavy. Luckily.'
　　People were drifting back to the Women's Room. Julie
watched for a moment and lingered. 'Jonathan? ...'
　　'Yes Julie, I am very sorry. I'll pop in later and see how
little ...'
　　'Andy.'
　　'Andy is doing. And the others. Are there two Andy's
then?'
　　'Ha yes. Same age too. I'm a trained nurse so I can keep
an eye on everyone. They just had a fright, that's all.'
　　'I must talk to Hugo.'

'Yes, but don't worry, there's always lots of us watching the kids.'

'Yes.'

'It must be hard work for you Jonathan, sorting all this out.'

'Ah, well. Yes, a lot to think about. My House Manager makes lists of appointments with people I thought I'd already crossed off the list.'

'Oh dear! What happens then?'

'Well, I have to bluff my way through. I don't want to hurt people's feelings. I talk to them for a while and then I have the difficult job of turning them away. And some of them turn out to be extraordinary conversations!'

'Haha!'

Jonathan straightened some tables and Julie came right in and closed the door.

'Hadn't you better get back Julie?'

'I just wondered Jonathan … if I could have a bit of a chat with you.'

'What is it?'

'I think you're great doing all this for people.'

'Well, thank you.'

'I …' she came up close to him. He noticed her curly hair and sparkling earrings, she reminded him of someone … ah it was Ruby. What was happening there? Was it *her* who took Belinda away? Had she actually been there in the cottage with Ruby when he called that day? The police would probably tell him more soon … And why was Ruby selling her cottage? He realised he would miss her in a strange way. Then he suddenly felt an unbearable sadness, it came over him and gripped his throat. It was delayed grief, he told himself, he had been feeling numb since he heard the news. He imagined Belinda walking alone down a dark street in the rain and the car a sudden shadow in the dusk …

Julie stood watching him. 'It's magical here, what you're trying to do … Are you alright Jonathan?'

He took a deep breath and opened the door. 'Please can you go now Julie, for the time being I've been putting this table against the door on the outside, at least that should stop the children …'

'Can I speak to you Jonathan?'

'No, not now Julie, will you go please. I'm sorry I'm rather busy.'

'I think you're … really special. Life is such an effort when we've got to sort things out and move on, it's so tiring.'

'Well, yes it must be, and I wish you well. Now I need to get on with what I was doing.'

'Please Jonathan.' She laid a hand on his arm. He removed it gently. 'We must get on Julie. I must phone a locksmith straight away.'

She shut the door again and studied his face. 'There's something … terribly sad, have you had some bad news?' she said, 'Has something happened?'

Jonathan hesitated. 'Yes … I have actually, but nothing you need worry about. Something dreadful happened to someone I know.'

Julie put her hand on his shoulder and tried to pull him towards her.

43 FEBRUARY
This suffocating room

'But you didn't break the law. Did you?' Samuel watched Ruby who had closed her eyes, resting her head on the back of the scruffy armchair. She had been speaking for some time.

'I don't really know. But it hardly matters now does it.'

'Are you sure this is her?' He indicated the newspaper.

'Yes. The dark brown leather handbag with the silver chain strap, I'd just bought if for her, and a diary, we talked about diaries a bit … and the name. She couldn't remember her surname. It must be her. She must have wandered off, or perhaps she was looking for me which is even worse.'

'But … you did what she asked. You didn't tell anyone,

162

she had reasons for what she asked, you don't know them, but you did your best.'

'I don't think *reason* is the right word. She had *lost* her reason. Isn't that what we used to say?'

'And why, do you think? And you mentioned Jonathan. Who is that?'

'Oh, it's a long story. He called at my cottage looking for her, and I was about to tell him when ... something held me back.'

'Was it what she'd said? And how terrified she seemed, you said.'

What was she doing sitting in this suffocating room with this stranger who was now interrogating her endlessly? Ruby thought back to that day in the shopping centre ... it felt like a long time ago. Would she always feel so guilty, would this stay with her? 'Jonathan was ... used to be the vicar in the village. He was visiting with some people, he was in a hurry, unfriendly. I expect he was looking after her, perhaps after some trauma.'

'You're being very hard on yourself Ruby. You seem very tired. Do you think you could make us some bread and cheese? We've been talking for some time and ...'

'Oh yes, of course.' She got up and took the mugs and went out. She bent down and stroked the cat who purred and rubbed herself against her legs. She put the mugs on the draining board and went quietly up the stairs, avoiding the step that creaked. She grabbed her bag and stuffed it with some clothes and bits and pieces. She had been preparing for this moment and tidying up as she went along. There wasn't much here. She came down the stairs and opened the front door and closed it as quietly as possible. She ran down the street and round the corner and up two more streets and crossed the road. 'Will I be safe from him?' the girl had said. *And will I be safe from Samuel?* She reached her car and threw her bag on the front seat and sat holding the steering wheel.

Where to go, where to run to?

44 FEBRUARY
Praying for her soul

Jonathan was standing in front of the Manor House waiting for the arrival of a photographer who had texted to say he was nearly there. He was thinking about the previous day when Julie had seen his grief, and for a moment he had been tempted to talk about Belinda to someone who might understand. But when she tried to kiss him he quickly realised this mustn't happen and opened the storeroom door again, demanding that she leave – and she had gone, she was too intelligent to linger and try anything else.

He had closed the door then and sat down heavily on a broken chair. *No, no, Belinda couldn't be dead. Such a waste, such pain and confusion. Her eyes were looking at him, worried, puzzled, hesitant, confused.* Such vivid and odd images lingering in her mind, day after day, such disturbing questions, was her name written on the scroll in the sky? If not, what did it mean? Did she have the mark of the beast on her? As he sat there for a very long time with his eyes closed it seemed to him that he was praying for her soul.

Then he had roused himself and remembered he had been on his way to get Maxwell's room cleared. As he walked down the corridor past the Women's Room it was quite strange to think what had been going on in this other room. Good thing no one here knew about that, particularly that group of three women…

Now the car was arriving, and Tim Aylesford got out and extended a hand, 'What an interesting place! I've heard about it somewhere. And a sweet little village.'

'Yes indeed. Do follow me,' said Jonathan slightly shocked, Tim looked so like himself it was almost like meeting a brother. He wondered if he thought the same. 'Can I offer you something, tea perhaps?'

'No, thanks a lot but am in a hurry. Was glad to come

straight down, been in the Lake District working on various projects. Terrible rain up there.'

A large heavy chest had been placed across the top of the stairs with a hardbacked chair wedged in place – 'Sorry about the inconvenience,' said Jonathan lifting the chair so Tim could walk through, and they made their way past the Women's Room where several toddlers were playing in the corridor and on the landing. Jonathan caught Julie's eye as he went past, she gave him a knowing look and turned to one of her friends. 'Jonathan's brought his lookalike friend along,' she whispered, 'Double fun.'

'Bugger, I missed it,' said Marissa, 'Is he as sexy as Jonathan?'

'Could be almost as much fun as Hugo.'

'Where have they gone Julie?'

'Into that big room where the door's always locked.'

'Exciting! What goes on in there?'

'Must be something. Well …'

'Can you hear anything?'

'No, they've closed the door.'

'Must try it later.'

'Keep a watch for when they come out.'

'I've been keeping it all locked away out of sight,' said Jonathan, 'Please have a good look.'

'Ah … right. Oh, splendid, the Blackmagic Ursa, splendid. Let's have a look, a good tripod and um let's see …'

Jonathan waited while Tim examined everything. 'It's all very good,' he said, 'I could take the lot off you if that's alright. Several things I've been looking for and some will come in handy when mine wear out. Let me give you the cash right now, I brought it with me, keeps things simpler.'

'Well thank you very much indeed,' said Jonathan accepting a bulky envelope, 'I'll get someone to help us move it.'

He came back with Francesca and together they carried everything down the stairs and out to the car. Julie looked the other way and kept watch at the top of the stairs and then moved the chest and chair back into position. Outside Tim was about to leave, he paused and looked around again. 'South Witters,' he said, 'Why does that name ring a bell?'

'Well, it was in the news a while ago. Something and nothing really.'

'Oh ... oh yes, are you the um ...'

'I used to be the vicar here.'

'Ah. Yes, it's coming back now. Wasn't there a woman called Ruby something?'

'Well, the papers, you know what they're like. A few years ago her tiny niece drowned in the stream in her garden, terribly tragic.'

'How awful.'

'I'm very glad you're happy with all the stuff,' said Jonathan, 'Thank you for coming all this way to pick it up, it belonged to someone who's gone off somewhere ...'

'Mmm. It was an interesting trip. And some great bargains. Goodbye!'

Jonathan waved and watched him drive away. Something had seemed odd about this conversation.

He went back to Maxwell's room and folded the silken cover on the large double bed and took down the colourful wall hangings. He carried them along to the storeroom and went in and placed the folded fabrics in a drawer. He paused looking out through the window. He couldn't help remembering how Belinda had climbed nervously out of the car the evening they arrived. He should never have brought her here.

None of them had seen her put on her coat and open the front door and walk away from the Manor House in the darkness and the rain, or perhaps she had run ... Perhaps she might have been knocked down by a car right here on that night, the roads were very narrow. But then what on earth had happened after that? It was such a shock to think Ruby must have been involved ...

He wondered what Tim had been thinking. Then he heard the strange sounds again. It wasn't exactly a knocking noise, more like a soft scrape and something like soft footsteps. What *was* it? He mustn't linger here, he must protect the children, and he went out and placed the table in front of the door.

It was late and Diana would have gone home. It would be a relief to sit in the warm kitchen and have a bit of a rest. Hugo appeared and silently shared some leftovers from the fridge and then disappeared without a word and Jonathan didn't have the energy to try and suggest they look at the coding book. He also felt nervous in case Hugo asked about Peter.

He needed to distract himself and glanced at the pile of books on the table, picking up the New Testament which now fell open at a place where he had left off. The story of St Paul's travels was always so interesting and impressive, so much more readable than the tedious letters about sin and divine retribution. Here was a passage about Paul being held prisoner in Caesarea while the Chief Priests and Jewish leaders were plotting to kill him. The Roman Governor Festus was speaking to King Agrippa.

…we have a man … left in custody by Felix; and when I was in Jerusalem the chief priests and elders of the Jews laid an information against him, demanding his condemnation. I answered them, "Is it not Roman practice to hand over any accused man before he is confronted with his accusers and given an opportunity of answering the charge." So when they had come here with me I lost no time; the very next day I took my seat in court and ordered the man to be brought up. But when his accusers rose to speak they brought none of the charges I was expecting; they merely had several point of disagreement with him about their peculiar religion and about someone called Jesus, a dead man whom Paul alleged to be alive …

Jonathan read on, fascinated by the story, there were so many interesting details. But then he paused – was it the *true* story it said it was? He skimmed through the pages …

… Festus shouted at the top of his voice, "Paul, you are raving; too much study is driving you mad." "I am not mad, Your Excellency,' said Paul, 'What I am saying is sober truth. The King is well versed in these matters and to him I can speak freely. I do not believe that he can be unaware of any of these facts. For this has been a no hole-and-corner business. King Agrippa, you believe the prophets? I know you do." Agrippa said to Paul, 'You think it will not take much to win me over and make a Christian of me. "Much or little," said Paul, "I wish to God that not only you but all those also who are listening to me today might become what I am, apart from these chains…"

There had been the account of the time when Paul was in Jerusalem, Jonathan turned the pages -

"… the whole city was in a turmoil, and people came running from all directions. They seized Paul and dragged him out of the Temple; and at once the doors were shut. While they were clamouring for his death a report reached the officer commanding the cohort that all Jerusalem was in an uproar. He immediately took a force of soldiers with their centurions and came down on the rioters at the double. As soon as they saw the commandant and his troops, they stopped beating Paul … Some in the crowd shouted one thing, some another…

Paul was allowed to address the crowds. What a powerful presence he must have been! And a linguist, he spoke to the people in their own language … he gave them a detailed account of his own background and then he made a startling claim, and the crowd went mad. Why is this, Jonathan wondered. Was it because Paul claimed that he had actually *seen* Jesus and heard words spoken by him?

'… up to this point they had given him a hearing; but now they began shouting; 'Down with him! A scoundrel like that is better dead! …'

There wasn't enough time to read it all now, let alone work it out. The story of how a devout and powerful Pharisee had persecuted those loyal to this new religion on a vast scale and then had somehow had a vision and had completely changed. How was one supposed to make sense of that? Paul himself was reputed to have said that the voice of Jesus spoke out of the blinding light – Jonathan turned some pages to find something, yes there it was – *I send you to open their eyes and turn them from darkness to light, from the dominion of Satan to God* ... ' This was the writer's account of *Paul's own words* about what had happened to him which was already a subtly different account from the one in an earlier chapter. So already two versions of the same incredible event, and there were differences. But of course there were, how could it be otherwise? And how could it be that everyone up until that moment had been in the grip of Satan? Whatever *that* meant, it was utterly absurd ...

And there was a lot about prophesies ... Jonathan was getting sleepy and put the bookmark back in its place. As usual the little book *Games People Play* still lay on the table. With a start he looked at his watch, it was late. He had meant to phone Pam, but now she was probably asleep. He must see her soon, it had been too long. He sat for a while drinking a glass of wine ... Too much to think about. Everything was such an effort and a lot of time had been wasted with fruitless interviews. And when was Peter coming back?

45 MARCH
A platform on the cliffs

'Will you come with me today, Natasha?' said Jeremy, 'It's not a long walk, and it's a beautiful view. It would make a change. Sally's nearly finished the curtains and printing out the menus and I'm soon going to be very busy indeed!'

'Why this particular walk Dad?'

'You see ... I want to take you to where I scattered Petra's ashes. I want to share it with you. It was a bleak rainy day, but today is beautiful sunshine. It would mean a lot.'

They set off along the seafront heading for the cliffs at the end and the path that wound its way upwards through twisted, wind-battered trees. As they listened to the gentle unending sounds of the ocean they were both thinking of Petra, in Natasha's mind there was a constant shifting, now she understood why the sister she had adored had always lived within the warm embrace of her father's love, while she herself had felt somehow alienated. Petra's young life had been carefree but as she grew she lacked ambition and drive, while Natasha somehow had needed to strike out and create something different. But now she was caught in a sinister net she could never have imagined. Still her father didn't know, he had no idea. David had been difficult recently, he didn't understand she needed time to herself. She thought he probably suspected something but didn't like to mention it. She liked him, but ... not enough to worry if he got angry and her being unpredictable kept him on his toes. It was a huge relief that she and Jeremy could now just share some peaceful times, she didn't want to spoil it by asking *him* for money. They left the seafront and started the climb.

'This is where I said goodbye' said Jeremy at last as they stood on a platform on the cliffs with strong railings protecting them from a drop to the swirling water and black rocks many feet below. 'It was a grey day with rain in the north wind. I needed that sort of weather, and I needed the wind. I wanted it to blow her to Italy, that magical place that always fascinated her since I read those books when she was little – do you remember them? Eccentric little books, stories with pictures of statues and lakes and odd Italian words thrown in, they were beautiful books.'

'Oh yes, I remember. They were beautiful. Have you still got them?'

'Probably in a box somewhere. I'm afraid a lot of my stuff is in storage. I just bundled it all together when I sold the house. It was a bad time. I neglected everything, it was my fault.'

'Yes.' She had intruded during that bad time when Jeremy was living in Jonathan's house.

'Petra. A beautiful name.'

He turned to her and held out his arm and she moved towards him and stood leaning on the railing and wiping her eyes. And they listened to the wind and watched the fluffy white clouds, letting their eyes rest on the sea and the distant horizon.

46 MARCH
Marissa

Quite early the next morning was grey and overcast and Jonathan was climbing the hill from the church. He had been out for a brisk walk through the village, hoping the sun would break through the clouds. As he walked down the drive to the Manor House he saw Marissa coming towards him. Tall and quite heavy with hair scraped back in a ponytail and a sullen expression.

'Good morning, Marissa. How are you getting on?'

'I need your help Jonathan, I can call you Jonathan can't I?'

'What is it?'

'Could we go somewhere so I can tell you?'

'Well yes if you like. Come to the kitchen, it's warm in there.' She followed him through the side door and down the corridor.

'Come and get warm. Sit yourself down and I'll make you a cup of tea.'

'Oh thank you Jonathan. Two sugars and milk please.'

'Now then, what is it? How are you getting on and how are your friends, Julie and Pat wasn't it?'

'You've got a good memory. They're ok. Though we're all a bit worried.' She drank her tea and stared into space.

'Whatever you've taken refuge from here,' said Jonathan, 'I hope you at least feel safe for a few weeks. Do you feel safe?'

'Sort of. But I need someone strong and manly to look

after me.'

'Well, let's hope you find that person soon. Meanwhile maybe you can make some plans and take a bit of time to think things over.'

'When you're nearby ... I feel safe,' she said, 'I so look forward to you popping in to see us.'

'Well ...'

'I can't think straight Jonathan. It's bad. It was so bad. I need ... someone kind and strong, someone ... like you.'

'I'm just running this place Marissa,' he said, sitting down at the opposite end of the table, 'Think of me like a gardener come bottle washer. That's all.'

'Oh no, it's so much more Jonathan, what you do is so much more than that. You're so manly and strong ...'

'Drink your tea Marissa, and let's leave it there shall we?'

'You don't know how terribly attractive you are.' She was staring intently at him, 'Please let me say. Oh Jonathan, I think I've fallen in love with you.'

'Marissa we need to end this conversation,' he said, 'Just drink up your tea and take my good wishes with you please.' If it wasn't rather tragic to see this awkward, overweight woman sitting in his kitchen talking nonsense it might have been quite amusing, but he had no trouble keeping a straight face. No doubt everything that was said and done would be reported straight back to the gang of three.

'We can all have strong feelings when we've been ... under pressure ... and worried about our children and ...'

'I've just got the one.'

'Our *child* ... and often we don't know where we might be living, and ...'

'Well *some of us* ... might be. *Some of us* might be living in a fucking great Manor House. Only trouble is there aren't enough servants.'

'Melissa we need to end this please, drink up your tea and ...'

She put the mug on the table and got up and came close

to him. He stood up. 'Kiss me,' she said, 'If you don't I'll scream. I'll say you attacked me. And then what will happen huh!'

'Melissa, this is not helping anyone. Please go and we'll say no more about it.'

'Oh, so fucking kind! *So fucking good to everyone aren't you, Jonathan Wender!* But what about all the things the press found out hmm! Not so good then were we. The disgraceful vicar the press absolutely *adore.* And they'd love a bit more, like dogs with their tails wagging waiting for dinner.'

'A lot happened, and a lot was said. Some of it was lies and I expect you know that. Now please just leave.' He walked to the door and opened it and stood with his hand on the handle. 'People come in here all the time, the caterers are due any minute, they do a whole batch of cooking every morning, and George is due for a visit, he still has some packing to do and Hugo often pops in …'

'Well, that would be such fun now wouldn't it! Hugo the weirdo. Might get upset if his darling Jonathan was found with his arms round someone.'

'I'm waiting. If you don't go I will leave and then there will be no point in your being in here.' As he spoke Jonathan remembered there was a pile of paperwork on the window-sill.

She came up to him and removed his hand and shut the door and stood close. They were about the same height and she looked into his eyes. Hers were lined in black and there was the suggestion of a faint body odour – she kissed him on the lips. 'There now. That was lovely wasn't it.'

'Get out of here Marissa, right now.'

'I'll open the door and scream.'

'It won't do you any good. Who will believe you?'

'Oh …plenty of people.'

He moved past her and opened the door again. Then he moved swiftly to the window-sill and gathered up all the bits and pieces. He mustn't lose any of it. He stood looking out of the window. He remembered the day after they had all been searching in the pouring rain in the dark, and he had stood here with Pam and she had been distant, he had thought she was probably tired, she had pulled away when he tried to put his arms around her. What had been happening during those moments, was she *seeing something* and not able to tell him. That could be the only explanation. And things had somehow never been the same after that. He needed her here. *He must speak to her* it had been too long. But during the day she was often out and about and didn't answer her phone ...

Melissa was still standing near the door watching him. He walked past her and hurried down the corridor, not waiting to hear what she did next. He saw Hugo approaching looking muddy and cold and walked past him and knocked on Diana's door and hearing her voice, opened it and went in, closing it quietly.

'Ah Jonathan. I was about to ring you. Your nine-thirty appointment has arrived and is waiting in the Guest Room.'

'Thank you, Diana. Remind me who it is.'

47 MARCH

'What was she up to?'

Several mothers were wandering about outside with their toddlers and the sun had come out. They gathered near one of the cedar trees where a few tiles had been laid in the grass, and several helped the children, balancing and stepping across the gaps and playing counting games. Then one put her hand on the arm of another. 'Did you hear that?'

They paused and listened. To begin with it was just a murmur. Several voices all speaking at once. Coming closer. The mothers held their children's hands and looked at each other. People in rural nineteenth century clothing were slowly approaching. Then suddenly there was a woman's cry, and she broke away from the group and ran across the grass. A chase began with shouting. They scattered and re grouped while she was held in their midst. They formed a circle and there were questions and she answered, crying and shouting together with a young man who also stood in the group.

The mothers and children stood very still. As the actors spoke there were other sounds that distracted the ear, a chanting that went on and on, insistent, incomprehensible, there was no sense in it. Suddenly the circle broke up, some began to fight with their neighbours, some ran to the trees and more figures appeared, and there were more sounds that confused the ear, shouts, screams, and music from a medieval instrument, and the sound of monks singing. The young couple broke free and ran to some thick trees where they embraced passionately, there was talking and shouting and fighting. Then a tall man in the midst raised his stick and instantly everyone fell to the ground and lay motionless. Except one figure who appeared from nowhere and began to read from a scroll. But it was in a strange foreign language and made no sense.

As he spoke the figures on the ground began to make small movements and raised themselves, and one by one they crept away through the cedar trees until he was alone. He finished speaking and stood quite still and suddenly there was an explosion, and a puff of dense smoke enveloped him and the tall man, and when it gradually cleared they had disappeared.

'Don't cry Jen,' said one mother, 'They've gone now. Just some people playing a silly game. The mothers stood nervously, unsure what to do.

'Are they coming back?'

'What was all that about?'

Jonathan appeared from the side door of the Manor House. He had seen what was going on from the kitchen where he was making a cup of tea after interviewing a group in the Guest Lounge. He saw the mothers and looked around, and then a tall man with thin grey hair and strong features appeared and was striding towards him.

'Jonathan! Greetings to you!'

'Lawrence? Good afternoon.'

'I trust George is here?'

'Well … no, he's not actually.'

As they spoke the actors were approaching silently from various directions and came together in a group nearby. One of the toddlers began to cry and her mother bent down and picked her up. The others watched.

'Not here! George not here, but why?'

'Well … didn't you know – things are a bit different now, hasn't he been in touch?'

'No! What are you talking about?' Lawrence strode up and down suspiciously. 'I expect he watched from inside the house, I'm going in.'

'Just a minute,' said Jonathan, 'You can't just …' He moved forward but Lawrence pushed him aside, 'Don't get in my way! Stop this. This was for George to see, are there Guests here? If was for them too. They could have all this every day, and more. Wonderful atmosphere, sinister history, ghosts real and imagined.'

'Lawrence I'd better explain,' said Jonathan, 'But just a minute.' He walked over to the women and started apologising.

'Just a minute, what!' shouted Lawrence, 'Excuse me!'

'I'm very sorry,' said Jonathan in a low voice, 'It's a misunderstanding. He used to work here and he thinks it's still a hotel. He wanted to demonstrate a kind of play that they could put on. I would just go quietly now and take the kids indoors. He'll be gone soon.'

'Excuse me!' shouted Lawrence coming up behind Jonathan, and the mothers started to make their way hurriedly towards the house clutching their children, 'What is going on! Where's George! How dare you walk away.'

'These people are staying here,' said Jonathan calmly, 'I was suggesting they went somewhere safe.'

'Safe! Safe! How dare you. What are you suggesting!'

'They need to feel safe. They wouldn't have understood what that was all about. It would have been scary for the kids, you can see what effect it had.'

'I don't know what you're talking about,' said Lawrence, 'You know perfectly well what this is about. I want George to see what could be done, how this ancient place could be transformed. But I haven't had a word, it's been weeks. So I came here with my group and expected a bit more appreciation.'

'Well George isn't here I'm afraid,' said Jonathan, 'I'm sorry he hasn't been in touch. He said he was going to email and explain.'

'Explain what!'

'Well, I think you'd better ...'

'Explain what!' shouted Lawrence approaching Jonathan and staring at him, 'Well, I'm listening!'

Behind him the actors were murmuring amongst themselves, and several detached themselves from the others and began to walk towards the drive.

'George isn't running the hotel now, he's moved out.'

'What!'

'He's not going to carry on with the Games, and he's letting people know that he can't employ them anymore. He's very grateful for everybody's hard work and ...'

'No need for a speech Jonathan! Spare me. So where can I find him?'

More actors were leaving, only two women remained, watching Lawrence and looking around.

'I'm sorry Lawrence, I can't tell you that. He will be in touch I'm sure. Meanwhile I'll tell him you were here.'

'Not good enough!' He came right up to Jonathan, 'Not good enough.'

Jonathan turned and saw Diana hurrying towards him. 'Are you alright?' she said breathlessly, 'Can I be of assistance?'

'Who is this?'

'Lawrence, this is Diana. She runs the house here.'

'Perhaps *she* can tell me where George is.'

'No ... er Diana, Lawrence used to work for George. I think I should leave it to George to get in touch.'

'Well Lawrence, Jonathan had made things quite clear,'

she said, 'I'm afraid that's all we can do for you. Come Jonathan, let's go inside, I have some paperwork for you to look at.' She took Jonathan's arm and turned him round and they walked to the side door and went inside.

After several hours and a tour of the now empty grounds Jonathan went up to the Women's room and spoke to the ones that were there. He explained and apologized. '… it may seem scary but it was just an outdoor play. I'm so sorry. He shouldn't be back.' People looked doubtful.

It was now the evening. Jonathan had managed to get Hugo to sit down after supper and they had read a few pages of the book – 'Coding for beginners.' Hugo had asked a few questions he couldn't answer but it was good that they had some peaceful time together. He sensed there were many things on Hugo's mind but hoped some calm moments would do him good. Would this ever go anywhere? It was impossible to tell. When was Peter coming back? *Was* he coming back? When Jonathan rang him, George had said he would email Lawrence and was going to pop in the following day, and Hugo was looking forward to it.

'Can I go and see them in their new house?'
'Well, you can ask him tomorrow.'
'When will Sylvia have her baby?'
'I think it's due sometime in April.'
'Will they come back and live here then?'
'You could ask him that too,' said Jonathan wearily.
'I'm going to bed now,' said Hugo getting up.

Jonathan tidied the kitchen and dialled Pam's number. If she didn't answer he really would have to drive up there and soon. It was the usual message. Had something happened to her? As he walked through the hall he noticed a light under the door of the small office. That was strange, it wasn't a night Diana was staying. He knocked and Francesca opened the door.
'Oh hello. You're working late, is everything alright?'

'Oh yes … I'm sorry, I felt restless and thought I might as well finish a few things Diana gave me to do earlier. She let me have a spare key to the office, I hope that's ok.'

'Well yes of course, and you will take great care of that key won't you. There are some unpredictable people staying here.'

'Oh yes of course, yes great care.' He knew she understood what he meant.

'Well, thank you for helping if that's what you want to do. I'm sure you'll remember to lock up later.'

'Yes, I've nearly done for tonight.'

'Well … goodnight then. See you tomorrow.'

'Goodnight Jonathan. Oh … um, there is something.'

'Yes?'

'I was wondering if I could mention something to you Jonathan.'

'Fire away.'

'Could you … come back in for a moment? It's a bit tricky and I don't want anyone to … well you know.'

'If you like.' He came back in and closed the door and sat on a free chair. Francesca was sitting at the desk where there were a number of files and some labels. 'Just getting these done,' she said, 'The paper filing system Diana wants as a backup.'

'Looks great,' he said, 'Now what is it?'

'Well, I've been debating with myself what to do Jonathan, I really have.'

'I'm all ears.'

'You see … I need to warn you. Though I'm sure you can look after yourself.'

'Is this a joke?'

She didn't return his smile. 'I suppose it's a joke to *them*, but it could be …'

'To *who*?'

'Marissa, Pat and Julie. You see, they've got a bet on who can get you into bed the quickest.'

'Ah.'

'You don't seem too surprised!'

'No. The thought had crossed my mind actually. Two of them have already been, er, paving the way.'

'Oh!'

'Don't worry Francesca. It's very kind of you to tell me this ...'

'You can't trust those three. Between you and me I mean. I hope you don't mind me saying this.'

'Well, I think we should be very careful what we say Francesca, but I do know what you mean. But don't worry they won't be getting very far. My heart is already taken.'

'It's not your heart they're after.'

'Haha! No, I'm really quite safe, I can cope. It's kind of you to warn me.'

'You see I heard them talking – they didn't realise I'd heard. They're really quite malicious though Julie's a bit more sensible. I don't think she really agreed to it.'

'Mmm. Well you've all been through some experiences and are here to have a bit of time to reflect and make plans ...'

'It's so lovely here. How did it all start?'

'Well Francesca, it's rather late now and it's a long story. For another day perhaps.'

'Yes. I know it's late. Mmm, sorry. Always a bit of a night owl myself. You know my father's father was a bishop.'

'Oh, really?' Jonathan was startled. Where did this come from? Did she ... know something about him from the past?

'My father, well he was the rebel, he was the second son. So he threw it all in his father's face and caused no end of family dramas.'

'I see.'

'I never really knew my grandfather which is a shame. My father wrote a couple of books, think I've still got them somewhere.'

'And so – how do you fit in, with all these family dramas? Somewhere in the middle?'

'I'm not sure Jonathan, I don't have a fixed place, I read

different stuff and realise my previous ideas were all wrong.'

'Ah, well yes I know what you mean, I do that all the time.'

'Oh yes ...'

'You know something I discovered recently gave me quite a jolt.'

'What was that?'

'Well the *order* of the different books of the New Testament is different from *when* they were written and recorded. Well of course all that is quite difficult to establish. Did you know that? Why didn't we know this before and why does nobody talk about this? I suppose it's the so the so-called story will appear to happen chronologically. But when you look behind it all it's a very different picture. Why does reading the wretched thing require such a supreme effort of detective work?'

'I hadn't really thought ...'

'And so, you see, when St Paul wrote all those ghastly letters there were no written records yet about Jesus's life, well, there may have been some, but they would be scattered here and there, a few people might have seen them, it was all just mainly hearsay and conjecture. For years and years. It's incredible isn't it. Think how a story changes in a few minutes and hours, or a week. So what on earth would they have made of it, the people receiving his letters in far-away places? They still worshipped pagan gods didn't they. And sometimes it seemed that they went on with that ... so what could they have made of the things he wrote, the startling claims? What were they based on? They were inspired, and heartfelt and striking but controversial. It was all mixed up with the Jewish prophesies, and it would be an impossible task to wade through all those and have them fresh in one's mind, and when one starts unravelling the Old Testament there seems to be so much that doesn't correspond with actual history.'

Francesca had abandoned sticking labels on files and was watching Jonathan curiously. 'Really? I don't know much about all that. I suppose I just thought, well that it *was* history.'

'Well quite. And you know, we can never be sure who wrote what. And all these old accounts and letters were copied out by scribes and ... surely this is the most significant thing of all, almost all the thousands of ancient texts have been subjected to both accidental and deliberate alterations.'

'Really?'

'Oh, St Paul was an incredible person, oh yes, and if the accounts of his life are to be believed he survived all kinds of hardships ... '

'Really?'

'And there are so many things, so many muddles! What good does it do anyone having all these muddles, nothing is certain is it. I could be up all night going over it all and I would hardly have started.'

'Yes.'

'Can I tell you something Francesca. It's really been bothering me. Talk about detective work!'

'Well ... of course,' she said politely. What on earth was coming now?

'Well, you'll have heard of the Apostles Creed?'

'Well yes.'

'*And He descended into hell. On the third day He rose again. He ascended into heaven.* People recite this week after week, do they actually think about what they are saying?'

'Well I ... '

'Well look at the account in the story according to St Luke. On the cross Jesus said to one of the other men - *Today you shall be with me in Paradise.* Paradise! Well you'd think whoever wrote this would at least try and get their facts right wouldn't you! Presuming Paradise and Hell are actually two different places.'

Francesca was silent.

'Oh look Francesca, I'm talking far too much, a bad habit of mine. Blame your father for getting me going! I would have liked to have met him.' He stood up and stretched. 'I really must go and you must be tired.'

'Yes it's late.'

'Goodnight and get some sleep yourself.'

'Yes. Goodnight Jonathan.'

He went out and closed the door. He walked away and stood at the bottom of the stairs. What was she up to? He didn't trust her or her father or grandfather one little bit. He tip-toed back towards the office door and listened. But there was nothing to be heard.

Francesca tidied up the files and sat thinking about this conversation. It had all come pouring out, he seemed lonely and somehow ... lost. And terribly kind and not really coping with things. Where did this leave her? Could she perhaps have another talk with him late at night perhaps, and confess everything?

She imagined the conversation. 'Jonathan I'm afraid I have something I must tell you ...I've done something rash and ill advised. I'm not who you think I am you see, I'm not from the Women's Refuge at all ... I work for a magazine and send information to my editor who has already written one article about the Manor House, she came here for a weekend.' But it would be impossible to tell him, she would be too ashamed. She imagined how he would listen, he would be calm and it would be difficult to guess what he was thinking.

She began to feel sleepy and checked her emails There was an unexpectedly long one from Hazel and it interrupted her train of thought. She had better read it straight away.

48 MARCH
'I have to resign.'

Fran

What you're sending is great, thank you. Keep it coming. I never did find out enough when things all got a bit intense a while back, though not for want of trying. I needed something really dramatic or catastrophic to happen which had then been covered up, but I know my imagination is working overtime! If you can keep talking to Jonathan and anyone else and you hear about something please keep digging (carefully of course!) you are perfect for the job, you have an air of being so sensible and normal!

I'm writing now because I've just heard something pretty amazing and I thought I'd put it in an email while it's fresh in my mind then I can refer to it later. I hope you haven't been found out by those ghastly women, I wonder what they'd do to you if they knew, I bet they'd eat you alive, it must be nerve-wracking!

Anyway, this is my story, it happened like this. I've managed to rent a little house right next door to the Women's Refuge in town, what luck! Naturally I have to keep a low profile, I go out with messy hair and no make-up and old clothes. (quite relaxing actually!) Well this morning I was wandering about in the garden and feeling uninspired. I have been following one contact in particular recently but it ended up with a wild goose chase to nowhere and wasted a lot of time and petrol. Well with the sunny weather I hoped someone might come outside next door and have a conversation. Well, they did, and boy what a conversation it was. It will make your hair stand on end.

Two women came out and one was crying. They must have sat down somewhere the other side of the fence. One said something like – 'Now you've got my attention Anthea, if you feel like talking a bit that's ok, but no pressure. No one's here to judge you, you do know that don't you. You're in the right place and you'll make new friends. Take your time and start at the beginning.' Well the name Anthea rang a bell and then I remembered that lovely girl who used to work at the Manor House, she was a cleaner for a while and looked stressed out and miserable. I actually had a few words with her once, I said she didn't have to put up with whatever it was, (hoping she might tell me of course) and she seemed very unsure of herself. Well it's probably the same person, her voice did sound familiar. 'Why Veronica, why?' she started saying, 'I've been with this man, and it's all gone wrong and I've nowhere to go and I left my poor brother who's not very bright and can't look after himself.'

'Well, that's a lot to cope with Anthea. Do you want to say a bit more?' 'Well he chatted me up, he's in his forties, really rich and successful looking, and charming with it of course. To begin with I just thought wow, is this really happening. Of course I was glad of the work in the Manor House where George was such a lovely bloke to work for ...' There was a bit of a pause then and then the other one asked, 'What's his name, this

rich bloke?' 'Maxwell. He actually lived next door, and he was helping George with different things, I think just as a friend really. He always looked immaculate and his clothes were expensive and … ' 'You're doing really well Anthea, just tell me what you want to, no pressure.' 'Well, things got, well… you know, we got involved and well it was a bit overwhelming and like a dream really. But then …I hardly dare tell you really, you'll be shocked.'

'Don't tell me if you don't want to Anthea, you know you can stay here while you think what to do next, we've got a bit more space because some of the women have got some rooms at the Manor House …' 'What you mean in the village!' Anthea interrupted, 'Not the Manor House in the village. You don't want me to go there do you?' 'No, not if you don't want to, don't worry Anthea,' said the other one reassuringly, 'I'm sorry if I worried you. No of course not, you stay here and take some time to sort yourself out.' 'Sorry,' said Anthea, 'I didn't mean to get worked up. You see … I've done something really bad … I left my brother there, he's not normal, he can't look after himself and I've done it for years and Maxwell helped me run away. He's still there I think and he gets terribly upset when people abandon him, and I feel dreadful. I'm the only family he's got left.' 'You've got a lot to deal with Anthea, are you still ok to talk?' 'Yes. If you don't mind. You see Maxwell's charming on the surface but underneath he's … it's hard to explain. You see he recruited me to do something. Well I suppose you could say he groomed me … He … talked me into making some movies.' There was a bit of a silence then. 'I think I know what you're saying Anthea.' 'Yes. And he employed this young actor Phil. You can imagine what he was employed to do. With me. And Maxwell was in charge.' 'You haven't done anything illegal Anthea and you're very brave to tell me, I hope it's helping.' 'Yes it is. Well, to cut a long story short, Maxwell was pleased to start with but then … it's like he became jealous of Phil and started accusing me of thinking about him when we were … you know, and I tried to keep telling him I loved him and not Phil, but something slipped out one day when he was being particularly angry, and ever since he's kind of held it against me, it was all terribly intense, and then we went away together and he was lovely one minute and then raging with jealousy the next and then he left me in Italy on my own, something about the people buying his house getting upset and maybe my brother had something to do with it, and it was scary because I *didn't know the language, but I got back somehow, and I came here because I've nowhere to go, but I'm scared he'll see me, so I cut my hair and coloured it and changed my clothes with some of the money I had left, and here I am and I don't know what to do.' Well Fran there was a longish silence after all this and I expect the other one was just giving her a rest after saying all that. 'Shall we go in for a cup of tea Anthea, you must be worn out.' And they must have got up from where they had been sitting.*

Well it's quite a story, and I don't know what to think, I could try and engineer a meeting with Anthea in town and make it look accidental, sounds like she's in quite a state. But she might remember me though at the moment I don't look like I usually do. I could pretend to be homeless myself, though that might be going a bit far! Tell me what you think. Goodness me, maybe I could even apply to stay at the Women's Refuge myself, but that would definitely be pushing my luck!

I'll end this email and wait to hear from you. Dying for more news! H

Francesca read this through twice and then sat thinking for a while. Then she began to type.

Hi Hazel,
Yes it's quite a story as you say. I never met Anthea but Hugo is a disturbed and lonely lad and some of the women are quite mean to him and tease him cruelly. Jonathan was here tonight in the office (where I was 'working late') and we had quite a long chat.
There aren't many people around I could talk to about the time a few months back, I did see a bloke wandering about in the grounds and thought about approaching him, but it seemed risky.
Now I'm very sorry to tell you Hazel, but something has happened to me. I can't spy on the Jonathan anymore and send you bits of information. I'm very sorry, I have to resign.
He just an incredibly kind man who wants to help people and is still very confused with a lot of things and doesn't seem able to move on after the bad time he went through in the village. When I mentioned my father and grandfather who was a bishop that set him off and there was so much on his mind. And actually a lot of what he said made sense, and I thought maybe I might sit down and do some reading myself sometime. I did warn

Jonathan about some of the women, he seems to laugh it off but also seems a bit overwhelmed with everything.

I'm sorry to let you down and I've actually been doing some mundane but useful work for the new Manager who's quite a character but her heart's in the right place.

I'll get out before anyone notices. Yes, I've been very nervous thinking I would be discovered, so it's lucky I haven't.

All the best Hazel, and just keep my name out of it from now on. Fran

49 MARCH

'…absolutely shocking and utterly unbelievable…'
Jonathan walked towards the storeroom with a box of old toys Pat had handed to him. 'These are a bit scruffy Jonathan, would you mind if we got rid of them?'

'Yes of course,' he said, wondering if this was going to lead to another absurd situation. 'I'll store them for now. Let me know if there's anything else.'

He moved the little table out of the way. Once inside he looked around. It was odd. Small things seemed to be different places, though he couldn't remember exactly. He was looking for an empty space for the box in an old wardrobe when he heard the odd sound again and stopped and listened. It seemed a bit louder but there were long gaps between. But then it came again twice and some banging and what sounded like footsteps. He left quickly.

As he walked through the hall there was a knock on the front door and he opened it to find a middle aged man standing there looking rather cold.

'Good morning.'

'Er… good morning. I wonder?'

'Yes?'

'I apologise for calling out of the blue. This is the Manor House, South Witters isn't it?'

'Yes indeed. As far as I know we're the only one.'

'Well, what a stunning place it is too. Look I am so sorry to intrude. My name is Leslie Smith and I'm looking for my daughter, she sent me a rather odd text message and mentioned this place.'

'I see.'

'Her name is Francesca Smith. I know it's a bit of a long ...'

'Can you describe her to me?'

'Ah, um ... well about five foot six, a little overweight, wears glasses, mousy hair usually scraped back, doesn't bother much with her clothes ...'

'And can you tell me a bit more about ...'

'The circumstances? Yes, well we haven't been in touch for a few months and sadly not this Christmas, things were a bit difficult, so it was a surprise to get this short text and completely out of the blue, so I felt I must follow it up, maybe there was something wrong she wasn't telling me, so I looked on Google Maps and here I am. But I realise ...'

'Do you think she would want to see you?'

'Oh, er ... so she *is* here then, is she?'

'I'm just being cautious,' said Jonathan, 'You see there are number of people staying here for a few weeks for various reasons, it's a safe place for them.'

'I see. Though I don't really know what you mean. I'm her father, Leslie Smith. Look I've got a photo of her here when she was a little girl.' He fumbled in his wallet and handed it to Jonathan. 'Well?'

'Um ...'

'Look I know this is a bit unusual and you don't know me ... she *is* here isn't she!'

'Well ... '

'Obviously she's here. I can tell from the peculiar way you are behaving. I'm her *father* dammit!'

'I'm so sorry if I've offended you,' said Jonathan, 'It isn't intended.'

'So what happens next?'

'Look would you mind waiting a moment? I would ask

you in but as I said things are a bit awkward …' As he spoke Jonathan sensed some of the women were in the hall behind him, there were footsteps and sounds of whispering and giggling.

'It doesn't look as if I have much choice does it! And after coming all this way, the traffic was appalling on the motorway with all those road works.'

'I'll be back in a moment.' Jonathan closed the front door and walked slowly to the office, knocked on the door and went in. Diana was peering at the computer screen and writing in a notebook. 'Good morning Jonathan! Almost like spring today isn't it!'

'Good morning Diana. Is Francesca with you?'

'No, she's not down yet. Mind you she often doesn't appear till a bit later. She's being a great help by the way.'

'It's a bit awkward.' Jonathan closed the door, 'Someone is here to see her, I think I should speak to her before … asking him in that's all. Can't be too careful.'

'Oh.' She glanced at him. 'Oh, wait a moment, what's this?' She took hold of an envelope that lay half hidden by a file on the desk, 'It says to Jonathan and Diana.'

He took it from her and opened the envelope and read the note. 'Well well … she's gone. It just says … she's sorry, she enjoyed working here, and thanks us for the hospitality. No explanation.'

'Well well!'

'A bit sudden isn't it?'

'Yes. Curious Jonathan. Seemed fine yesterday, did a few jobs, generally organising the office really but nothing was too much trouble. Hope the girl's alright. Any idea where she's gone?'

'I'll just check her bedroom,' said Jonathan and ran up the stairs and along the corridor. The key had been left in the one at the end and when he went in he saw the bed had been stripped and the room was empty with the sheets and towels in a neat pile on a table.

'I'm very sorry,' he said to his visitor who was still there outside the front door, 'She seems to have gone overnight.'

'*Gone!*'

'Yes, gone, she left a brief note. Didn't say anything much.'

'This is a blow. And I've come all this way.' Leslie got his phone out of his pocket and looked for the text message. 'A bit vague there too, hmm.'

'Look would you like to come in for a moment,' said Jonathan, 'I'm sorry, come and at least have a cup of tea and warm up.'

'Well, that would be very welcome.'

'I'm sorry about before. But I have to be careful.'

'Well, not sure what you mean, but I understand it was awkward,' said Leslie as he followed Jonathan down the corridor to the kitchen.

The two men sat at the kitchen table. The room was cosy and warm while outside a cold wind blew. Jonathan was distracted. He needed to see Pam this couldn't go on. He needed to get away. What were those women up to, what was that odd sound in the storeroom. But he must be polite and vaguely remembered things Francesca had been saying about her father the night before.

'Your books?' Leslie broke the silence.

'Oh yes. Indeed.'

'May I look?'

'Yes of course.' His visitor picked one up from the pile and looked at it. 'A good selection,' he remarked, 'Do you know something very curious, very curious indeed?'

'What's that?'

'I'm sorry I don't know your name.'

'Jonathan Wender.'

'Ah yes. Well, this is my book, one I wrote myself. Look, Leslie Smith. That's me, a little photo on the inside cover.'

'Really! Oh ...' Jonathan was startled. The book hadn't been there before. But maybe Francesca put it there before she left ...

'I'm very interested to see you're reading it,' said Leslie, 'Very interested indeed. Very *pleased*. Would very much like to know your thoughts on the subject when you've read it of course, if you have time ... shocking isn't it what's been going on for so long, absolutely shocking and utterly unbelievable.'

'Yes, I'll ...'

'So you've been doing some reading on the subject.'

'Yes indeed. Bit of an insomniac.'

'Did you ... know my daughter well?'

'No hardly at all. There are a number of women staying here for a few weeks, they've mostly escaped from ... difficult situations ...I'm setting up a number of projects here.'

'Hmm. Worrying.'

'She didn't tell me anything much – about her personal circumstances.'

'No. I see. But then she sent this text. Odd.'

'Yes.'

'I do understand – that you can't necessarily talk much about .... your plans. I won't ask any more. I'm glad she was in good health, I'll have to be content with that for now won't I?'

'Would you like some toast? You've come a long way.'

'Well, that would be very nice thank you. Please don't go to any trouble. This is a subject of endless fascination isn't it. My father was a bishop you see, had an overdose of it all through my childhood so I wandered off and did all the usual things ... but then I came back to history and theology. There's no getting away from it, it hasn't got me yet but it's only a matter of time.'

Jonathan put the toast in a rack and put it on the table together with butter and a jar of honey. He didn't know what to say. Was this really happening, or was it a twist of a game he was being drawn into? How was he supposed to be able to tell? Was he now supposed to start discussing all manner of things close to his heart with a stranger ...but there was the book in black and white, wasn't this proof that this man was who he said he was? What harm could there be in having some kind of discussion? As usual there were many half-answered questions accumulating in his head. Surely it would be a tremendous relief to discuss all this with someone who had studied it and written about it, wasn't this something he had wished for many times?

'What do you mean a matter of time?'

'Well Jonathan it would be difficult to explain it to someone unless they had experienced it themselves.'

'So why does it draw you back?'

'Hmm, now there's a question, there's *the* question.'

'And do you have any kind of answer?'

'Hmm, I wonder why you ask. So, what else have you got here ...' Leslie looked through the pile of books ... 'hmm yes, that's good and ... no haven't come across that one, and yes this has had *excellent* reviews. I did dip in and found it rather badly organised though, pity. And what's this, *Games People Play* ... mmm.'

Jonathan found it difficult to think clearly, he needed to see Pam, he needed a break from these decisions and interviewing people and trying to work out how things could be organised. He needed to get away from seeing Belinda everywhere he went. And where was Hugo today? As usual he had no idea. Were the women chasing him round the house, teasing him ... when was Peter coming back? How would Hugo react if he mentioned Peter now, and would he tell him some of the ideas he had told Peter?

'Are you feeling alright Jonathan?' said Leslie, finishing the toast and drinking the tea.

'I'm a bit ... sorry you've caught me on a busy day.'

'I'm sorry. Thank you for the hospitality, I wonder if I could use your ...'

'Down the corridor on the right.'

What could he ask Leslie that would prove this wasn't a game but real life? Jonathan's brain seemed to be enveloped in a kind of mist and things seemed to be slipping away. Was this man checking up on him and making sure everything was under control? Was he a reporter looking for a story? He hadn't seemed to want to develop any of the ideas they had been talking about. Jonathan couldn't work it out from the inside, he was in the middle and he couldn't get to the end. If he could get to the end then maybe he could look back and see everything more clearly.

Leslie came back into the kitchen and stood by the table.

'Um, Leslie, do you want to know why your daughter was staying here?' Jonathan was watching him closely, 'Can you guess anything about that?'

'I ... er, well she's a bit of a dark horse you see, doesn't talk to me much. I think she had a job recently, was a bit vague. So, no ... I have no idea what this place is or what projects you might be referring to.'

'No.'

'But she's a strong character always very independent, able to look after herself. My motives in trying to find her are entirely selfish, I didn't expect her to need me, perhaps now she's trying to elude me, maybe she regrets that text message. Or perhaps it was a mistake and she sent it to the wrong person, that can happen can't it?'

'Yes. She seemed like a strong character.'

The door burst open and Diana appeared holding a list. 'Jonathan I'm sorry to butt in but I ...'

'That's alright Diana.'

'I've just been on the phone to the Women's Refuge in town. Veronica West, you know, who runs it, she's just told me something rather strange. She's never heard of Francesca Smith, never heard of her! She was never from there at all! So the question is, who *is she* and what was she doing here!'

'Um ... Diana, this is Francesca's father, Leslie Smith. Leslie this is Diana who runs the house here.' Jonathan sat down, he felt a little dizzy.

'Oh, pleased to meet you, oh ...'

'Diana I haven't told Leslie much about Francesca ...

I didn't think I should.'

'Oh.'

'But now … it looks as though maybe she wasn't running away from something after all.'

'Yes. Oh dear. Jonathan I'm sorry if … '

'That's alright.'

'Are you alright Jonathan?' said Diana.

'I'm feeling a bit light-headed. Probably lack of sleep.'

'I think I'd better go,' said Leslie, 'I don't really know what to think. Thanks again. I'm sorry it's a muddle.'

'I'll show you out,' said Diana, 'Jonathan isn't looking at all well. You just sit there and I'll put the kettle on in a minute.

50 MARCH
Pale brown hair with a receding hairline

Diana came back into the kitchen holding a package and handed it to Jonathan. As he opened it he remembered he had ordered Peter's book. There it was, *The Isolated Excellence* by Peter Ennistone. It had taken a while to arrive. It looked really interesting. He opened it and noticed a small photograph of the author on the dust jacket, then he stared, it was a plump, smiling man with black hair and a thick beard wearing glasses and a straw hat and he had his arm around the shoulders of a boy – it was Hugo.

But it couldn't be, of course not! A boy *that looked very similar to Hugo*. A boy who was smiling. Hugo didn't smile. Even when they were playing his number games.

And the Peter who had been here and talked to Hugo had pale brown hair with a receding hairline and a long thin face.

Diana put a cup of tea in front of him. 'Are you alright Jonathan?'

'Thank you, Diana, that's very welcome.'

She sat down opposite and watched as he drank his tea. 'Is there something the matter? You don't look well at all.'

'The tea is very welcome Diana. Is there a sandwich in the fridge?'

She placed one in front of him and sat down again.

'Diana …I'm very sorry but we need to cancel tomorrow's appointment. I have to go and see my girlfriend for a couple of days – urgently. She's living over a hundred miles away and she's not been answering her phone. And also I'm … a bit tired.'

'I see.'

'I'm very sorry. Can you move the appointment to next week? And apologise for me?'

'I'm sure I can Jonathan. I hope nothing is amiss.'

'I really don't know Diana, I am a little worried I admit, and can you keep an eye on Hugo while I'm away? He knows where the food is and he's in and out. I think he's made friends with one of the caterers.'

'Well, we'll do our best. It'll seem odd without Francesca won't it, she's been such a help. I have tried to talk to Hugo once or twice …'

'Underneath that sulky manner there's a very lonely boy who responds to kindness.'

'Yes, I'll do my best Jonathan.'

''I'll try and say goodbye, but it's often difficult to know where he is and he can get upset when he thinks people are going away.'

'Quite. I'll ring you if there are any problems.'

Jonathan packed a few things but left the book in his bedroom and was soon walking through the hall with his overnight bag. It would be a relief to get away for a day or two. As he drove through the gloomy landscape and travelled nearer to Pam he began to feel better – more calm and hopeful. *What does the brain do when something doesn't make sense?* He had read somewhere that it puts whatever it is aside, it pushes it away, it cannot be processed, it's threatening and disruptive.

Who was the man who said he was Peter Ennistone who had come to the Manor House?

He concentrated on the road. The important thing was now he was going back to his own house, *his home. Home was where she was.* What was the Manor House, what had it become? Was it a safe place? It was supposed to be but ... Would Marissa carry out her threat? He remembered the ugly look she had given him as he walked past the Women's Room that morning and her expression that day when she had suddenly become angry and threatened him. He too had felt very angry.

When he finally arrived it was getting dark and his house was cold and empty. He wandered through the rooms. He realised he hadn't been in touch with Pam or Natasha for some time. Then he remembered Natasha had moved out and was living somewhere else. After a snack he went upstairs and through the open door noticed that her room was empty and she had stripped the bed. He opened the door of the boxroom where Belinda had slept. A few possessions were strewn about and the bed was made. 'Thank you, Jonathan' she had said when he first brought her here from the hospital, 'It's a cosy little room, I like it.' He should sort out her bits and pieces ...

In their room the bed was made and Pam's things on the dressing table were tidy. There were no clues, no detective stories beside the bed. He drew the curtains, pulled back the duvet, sat down and took off his shoes and lay back, staring at the ceiling. It was very cold. She would soon be back and everything would be alright. It was such a relief to have a rest. It was so odd that Leslie Smith had turned up like that. And what had Francesca been doing there? He remembered that Maxwell was selling his house, there had been an email ...he had Anthea with him and they were starting a new life. So it really didn't look as though they were coming back, he had vaguely hoped that they might. He took his phone out of his pocket, should he try and phone Pam now? No, he would wait. He put it on the bedside table and stretched out his hand to find her nightdress under the pillow. It was the pink lacy one, he laid it next to him and closed his eyes. He could just detect her perfume ...

51 MARCH
It's angry

Jonathan's phone beeped. It fell to the floor and a voice could be heard.

'Is that Jonathan?'

'Diana?'

'Jonathan I am sorry to bother you. Something serious is happening and I think you should come back immediately.'

'Serious! What do you mean? But I've only just got back to my house. It's a very dark night and I'm very tired.'

'The police are here.'

'Police!'

'A child has fallen down the hole.'

'A child! Which child. A hole, what are you talking about?'

'Little Divit. He was missing and his mum knocked on my door, she was in a state. There's a big hole someone's dug at the back of the house, you know near the outbuildings, it's really deep and we heard ... oh Jonathan I can hardly tell you.'

'What Diana?'

'A faint screaming. Well Alisha was hysterical and she leant over and we had to restrain her, the police and the fire brigade are here now, they've fenced it all off and they've got ladders and lights.' Jonathan heard raised voices talking the other end.

'Are you there Jonathan, I'm sorry I ...'

'Is Hugo around?'

'Hugo ...?' Shouting drowned Diana's voice, then thumps and sounds that gradually faded.

'Diana! Diana! Are you there ...?'

Jonathan jumped out of bed and spoke to the phone. 'Darling I need to see you so much. I'm here, I drove over this afternoon. Where are you? I need your calm. I need your help.

But something's happening at the Manor House. Something dreadful, some sort of accident. Please, please speak to me, where are you? Why don't you reply?' In the bathroom the shower was on and steaming water was flowing in a circular pattern into an enormous drain. The floor was slippery. There were strange sounds in the house, crying and banging and a voice - 'Your fault Jonathan, your fault.' Downstairs in the living room a phone was beeping, it was under cushion on the sofa, it was Pam's phone but it slipped out of his fingers.

As he drove oncoming cars flashed their lights. His own phone beeped beside him and the car was filling up with black water – '*Save me, please save me!*' he prayed, '*I am sorry for my sins. Protect Belinda's soul. Protect Pam from the criminals who want to know the names of the winning horses … Clear the storeroom before the demon gets the children …*' Around the Manor House there were police cars and fire engines lit by bright searchlights, by the side door was a fat, dark haired man with a thick beard talking to a thin man with a long face and pale brown hair – the Peter Ennistones! *Both of them!* They waved and shouted. Women were screaming and held tightly to their children's hands. Jonathan ran towards the back of the house, but Diana was behind him and he turned - 'You never should have gone, Jonathan, this is your fault, you should have kept an eye on Hugo he's been digging this hole … There's a machine down there and the wires have got tangled up, it's a long job and will take many weeks. Divit is down there, *it* needs a child.' Now Diana was rising in the air and loomed over him blocking out the light and Marissa, Julie and Pat were approaching, they spoke together like the chorus in a Greek tragedy, 'She's in a very fortunate position, she can help needy people and organise the office for you. There must be paper, it's safer, but nothing is *really safe,* no one is safe, it's angry and it won't tolerate being locked up …' They held a paper in front of his face and laughed, 'It's all written down Jonathan, but they got it wrong.' They turned and ran off and Diana floated away, there was a crash and the lights flickered and went out and he stood in the darkness and felt cold water creeping up his legs, he was sinking and sinking …

'Darling Jonathan.'

Jonathan opened his eyes. He sprang out of bed. 'No, no! Let me go down, let me find him, I will pray to Jesus, He will save the child. He will send this … this *thing* away. This … evil spirit. He must send it away, it's the only hope. But then perhaps it won't work …'

Pamela took hold of his hand. 'It's me, Jonathan, it's me. Look at me.'

'Where am I, why am I back here? …I was … what's happening?' He sobbed.

'Sit down, here. Have you been asleep? You're in our bedroom. I just got back, it's me, Pam. Have you been asleep Jonathan, have you been having nightmares?'

'Are you … Pam … when did you …' He stared at her.

'I just got back. Been away a few days. Went to see my friend, do you remember her? I had to get away and have a break from it all. What a lovely surprise to find you here. I'm sorry it's so cold, I turned off the heating.'

He looked around the room and back at Pamela. She watched and waited.

'But … I think I need to phone Diana,' he said, 'Is it really you? Were you kidnapped?'

'Kidnapped! Of course not. Don't be silly. That was just a joke we had wasn't it. Of course it's me, I'm solid see.'

Jesus stood among them. 'Peace be with you!' he said, and then showed them his hands and his side.

'Pam is it really you?'

'Yes, I'm here. Hold me Jonathan. It's me. Was it a bad dream you were having?'

'I need to phone Diana.'

'Who is Diana?'

'She's like a house manager. She runs the office at the

Manor House. Something awful has happened.'
'Here's your phone.'

'Diana?'
'Hello Jonathan. Did you have a good drive?'
'Diana … how are things? Is everything alright?'
'Much as usual Jonathan. Enjoy your break. I'll phone if there are any problems. Oh, you'll be pleased to know I had a chat with Hugo earlier.'
'Right. Are you sure everything is alright? You haven't heard any sounds of …well sounds of trouble?'
'I'll go and wander round if you like but it's rather late. But everything seems quiet Jonathan. Try not to worry. You've been working rather hard haven't you! I promise I will phone if there's anything amiss.'
'Right. Yes, I have … thank you.' He ended the call and looked at Pamela again.
'Hold me,' she said, 'You're home now. Whatever it was it was in your head.'
'Darling girl. Oh … how I've longed for this moment. Nothing is real except this.'
'Tell me about your nightmare.'
'Not now. Don't talk now. Oh thank goodness, thank goodness. Oh my darling … I've needed you so much … oh I'm so tired.'

52 MARCH
'I saw her and thought she was dead'
Ruby was wrapped in her coat and sat and listened to the sound of the stream. She had carried a garden chair across the soaking grass near to where she had found Belinda. Would being here help her to understand? *I saw her and thought she was dead and I though no, no, not another death in this place, she must be saved, I felt her pulse and I tried to warm her up and I talked to her and then … she responded. But she was so terrified of everything that I felt I had to protect her … of course I was wrong, but I didn't know that then.*

It would surely sound ridiculous to talk like this. But she had just done what felt right at the time. It was only later at the hotel that she realised Belinda couldn't really hear her at all – something monstrous and sinister was gripping her mind. Who was *she* to try and discover what or who had done this to her and to try and help drag her back from that black world? It was an impossible task. '… *Will he be coming?' 'No, Belinda … I don't know him at all, today was the first time I've spoken to him … does he remind you of someone?' 'He's like the dark angel. For a minute I thought it was him in disguise. Why does he pretend? I suppose now he'll take the photos when I'm not looking.' 'Does the dark angel have a name?' 'His name is Jonathan. Yes I was running away. From the dark angel and the room with the ladder and the ropes. And the stones were falling from the sky and… I had to get away. I just wanted it to end. I wanted to die but you didn't let me …'*

What would she say to Jonathan now if he came walking down the garden towards her? That journey through the crowds must have been frightening for her, or perhaps it wasn't, perhaps when ideas within your mind were utterly terrifying then your circumstances didn't really matter. There were no answers. But then Ruby heard voices and watched the flowing water as the sounds came closer across the grass. Whoever it was must have found the way along the side of the cottage.

The four of them sat at Ruby's kitchen table drinking tea.

'I have something to tell you Ruby,' said Tim Aylesford, 'I have explained it to these two at the station and in my statement. But I would like to tell you personally.'

Ruby was silent. He seemed … a kind man. Someone who had just been normal and had glimpsed something very odd and strange.

'I followed you, you see, that day when you and the girl went shopping. It was such a terrible day, and the thought of bright cheerful shops was comforting. I couldn't understand what was happening and I felt concerned, but I knew I had to keep my distance. When I parked near you in the multi storey car park and followed you I ended up in the cafeteria and it was quite difficult to keep out of sight, and I knew that if Belinda noticed me well it would just confirm her worst fears. But you may not know what happened next.'

For the first time Ruby looked at him. 'What do you mean?'

'Well, you left her with the shopping bags, I expected you would come back in a moment. But then she got up and just took her handbag and found her way through the tables to the main door and went out and down the escalators and through the shop to the street. I followed her outside for a while, but it was raining hard and getting dark and very crowded. I felt very concerned. But then I lost her, I went up and down and it was no good. She had vanished. In the end I gave up and went back to my car and I saw yours had gone. So it seemed like you had both escaped from each other. There wasn't anything else I could do.'

'So …'

'You see, you escaped but she did as well, she must have been waiting for the chance. She didn't hesitate.'

'Well, thank you for telling me this, um … Tim isn't it.'

The Detective Inspector was staring at the table. 'Ruby I must tell you that we know what happened next. We know all of it.'

'What do you mean?'

'Tim told you this because it might help you to see it differently. But we have information from Samuel Lees. He told us everything. He taped the conversation with you and sent it to us. We were wondering if you'd come back here.'

'Well, I did come back. I wanted to try and make sense of it, and I only did what she asked, she was terrified. But of course it was wrong, all of it. But none of that matters now does it. She's been killed. Maybe she walked out in front of the car, who knows? But what had happened to her mind, this is something dreadful that none of us can ever possibly understand. Something we will never experience.'

There was a silence around the table. She didn't know what would happen and she didn't care. She finished her tea and took the mugs to the sink and rinsed them under the tap. Then she stood looking out of the kitchen window at the stream at the bottom of the garden.

53 MARCH
'What are you seeing, Pam!'
Jonathan and Pamela had fallen into a deep sleep together. Now it was daylight, and he watched her face on the pillow. It was always like this when he came here now, it felt temporary and there were so many unresolved things surrounding him which gave him no peace. She woke and moved towards him, stretching out her arms.

Later Jonathan sat up, pulling on his clothes. 'I wonder if you know what I'm going to say Pam.'
'Yes. I didn't want to ask last night. Some news of Belinda?'
'She was killed by a car. They think she walked into the road it was pouring with rain and nearly dark.'
'Oh no! I'm so sorry. Oh, poor Belinda.' Pamela lay quite still, staring at the ceiling.
'I see her everywhere. I try to keep busy. I hope she is at peace,' he said sitting down on the bed and taking Pam's hand.
'I am so sorry.'
'I have a newspaper article I can show you, it's in my bag.'
'Yes. But are they sure, how can they be?'
'We compared the writing in her diary, she wrote her name. She was carrying a handbag and a diary. Belinda still only remembered a few things … The police are still investigating it.'
'Oh Jonathan it's truly terrible.'

'Yes.'

'Oh. It's awful. Have you told Tash?'

'Yes, I rang her. You seen much of her lately?'

'No, she's quite involved with this new restaurant. They've had a big opening day and now they're booked up.'

'Well, that sounds very good.'

Pamela wondered if Jonathan ever thought about Natasha's drug habit. There had been some talk about support groups near his house when she'd been living here ... now she had a cold, sad feeling which was separate from the horror about Belinda ...

'I'll need to get back very soon. I told Diana it would only be a couple of days.'

'Yes, I understand.'

'Come with me Pam, please. You must. I can't bear it any more without you. I simply can't bear it, it hurts too much. I need your help.'

She sat up and he leaned over and took hold of her arm and covered it with kisses. After a moment she withdrew it gently and pulled on her dressing gown. 'I'll just ... let's have something to eat. We could sit outside, it's quite a nice day.'

Jonathan took a snack and mug of tea outside and sat down beside the old table in his mother's garden. The sun shone through the bare branches of the bedraggled apple tree. In front of him were the uneven expanses of bare soil where a few small weeds were growing and there were large piles of dead plants and rotting fruit on patches of straggly grass.

He remembered the summer's day when he had made the garden like this. He had destroyed his mother's garden. It was a crazy memory. He had hated Jeremy being there in the house, it had made him feel the sad loneliness of his childhood all over again ... Pam appeared carrying a tray and he realised he had completely forgotten about Belinda and the Manor House for a few minutes.

'I haven't told you Pam, but it's been feeling like really

crazy things have been happening, not that dream I was having. Real things, I'm serious.'

'Yes.'

'You think I'm imagining it.'

'No, of course not.'

'I know that look.'

Pam was eating some toast and looked startled. 'What look!'

'Stop this!'

'What. Jonathan what do you mean?'

'Stop this.' He leapt up, slamming down his mug of tea. 'I need you to stop this, it's not fair. Not you too. I don't know from one minute to the next what those women are up to ... and Hugo's in and out of the place and as mad as a hatter.'

'Calm down Jonathan, I ... don't know what to say.'

'No! I'm *not* calm, how can I be calm? How can you do this to me!'

'But I'm not doing anything. I tried to say ... weeks ago, well actually I decided I wouldn't say anything.'

'Say what?'

'Well ... when George said about giving you the Manor House, well you knew I was unhappy, but I kept quiet. I knew I had to keep quiet. But you never asked, you never noticed really. It wasn't for me to say.'

'Unhappy! But why? What a fantastic opportunity. And it was something I had to do, remember we always said that, we have to do what we have to do.'

'Sit down Jonathan, calm down. All the neighbours will hear you and I'm not dressed yet.'

'Something's got to change Pam, it's not right. It's not fair, I need your help, now, today, tomorrow. Please. I need you to accept that ...'

'Accept what? I understand you have to do it.'

'No, *you don't understand anything!*'

'Sit down Jonathan, stop shouting at me! That's awful, it's an awful thing to say.'

'I have to shout at you. I can't get through to you. You give me that look as if to say …' He gripped the side of the table. Pamela got up and picked up her plate and mug and went back into the kitchen, he followed her and watched while she stood at the sink.

'I need you there. Pam. Please.'

'And I'm sorry Jonathan, I can't come, I'm in the middle of something. And *I needed you.*'

'Well, you could have come …'

'Remember Christmas mmm! Actually I had a lovely time with my cousins in Scotland. Thank goodness they were there. It was snowy and magical. Cousins are good, they're family. They lost my mother and Matthew too, they miss them too. And then I wrote you that email the other day, you didn't even …'

'What email? When? Why write an email?'

She turned and faced him. 'About … two weeks ago. And then I texted you to say. I was too tired to finish the story, but you never even phoned, you never …'

'I never saw any email! What text? I never knew. Of course I've been phoning you, it's often your voicemail, I've been trying to talk to you, I've left lots of messages …'

'Something horrible happened, I felt … out of my depth, it was really frightening, I described some of it in the email and then I was tired.' While she was speaking he picked up his phone and was going through his messages.

'I couldn't take it anymore, so I went to see my friend for a few days.'

'No Pam, there's no text here. I would have read it if I'd known. But I've been snowed under with emails, people wanting this and that, magicians, actors, organisations, groups, even politicians, the list is endless. Difficult decisions.'

'Yes.'

'Well, I'm so sorry Pam. But what's this all about? You must tell me.'

'I could find the email,' she said, sitting down at the table and opening her laptop, 'It would be easier to read it and then try and remember the rest ...'

'By the way, did you take your phone with you ... when you went to see your friend?'

'Yes of course.'

'You didn't leave it on the sofa in the living room?'

'Why would I do that?'

'Mmm. Never mind. Let me read it.' He drew up a chair.

'Here it is,' she said, and they sat reading the screen.

'Hospital! How long were you there. You mean something happened that you didn't put in the email? Are you alright now? What else happened!'

'Yes. I'm sort of alright. Well, what happened was this. I went back to the main door and stood there, I was hoping these two women, Kathryn and Caroline would leave then, Kathryn was angry about this message from her Uncle Jack and worried sick about her son Daniel who she thought was involved in some sort of cult with this fake Facebook profile ...'

'Yes.'

'Well, they came up to me, luckily they hadn't noticed that I'd overheard them talking ...'

'Yes.'

'I just wanted to say goodbye, I was hoping they'd leave. But then I ...'

'What Pam?'

'I saw. Something about this Daniel. He was in trouble. He was being drugged and ... sort of brainwashed ... or what's the word – radicalised. I can't think what else to call it.'

'How frightening.'

'He was in a room with some men ... and there were books on the table.'

'Go on Pam.' He took her hand. 'You poor love.'

'He was being trained ... to kill.'

'What!'

'It's difficult to describe. And it doesn't seem credible.'

'You must tell me, you must.'

'They were training them ... to kill Moslems.'

Jonathan pulled her close. 'You poor love,' he said, 'What a terrible thing to see. And then what happened? Did all this come to you in a flash while the women were still there?'

'Yes, yes ... I became aware of it very quickly and I had to decide what to tell them.'

'So ... what happened?'

'Well, they were standing watching me. They were hostile. I think they sensed something was up. I ... knew I had to tell them.'

'And so ...'

'I said ...' Pamela blew her nose, 'I said I'm very sorry that you had such a short message from your Uncle Jack, and then Kathryn said something like, her son was in trouble and this was all crap and she wished she'd never come.'

'Was her friend still there, um Caroline I think you said.'

'Yes, she was there, she was worried, I don't think she knew what to say.'

'Well, Pam keep going, tell it all to me, you must.' He wiped her tears with a tissue and smoothed her hair.

'Yes, I said ... I'm very sorry, I have something to tell you.'

'Yes.'

'Kathryn was still hostile. I'm very sorry I said, but I believe your son and his friend are with some evil people who are ... but as I said it she came towards me, she was about to strike me, but Wendy came forward and grabbed her and said something like – 'No you can't do this, you must stay calm please,' and Caroline helped as well, so they were both restraining Kathryn, so I said that she was right to be worried because these evil people were drugging young men and persuading them to kill Moslems, and they're being kept in a house ... and she started shouting something like, 'What do you know about my son, I never mentioned anything about him, what house, where, what evil people, you bitch, how dare you make up such evil lies, what right do you have, my son would never listen to such things, it's you who should be locked up …'

'Oh dear. My poor love.'

'I said, well it was sort of ok to speak again because they were restraining her, I said I'm very sorry to tell you this, and the message from your Uncle will make more sense now because he knew I was going to tell you this later, and he knew the thing he told you would help you not to blame yourself for things you taught Daniel from the bible as a child. Well she stared at me then and looked like she was trying to work something out, and there was a pause, and Wendy and Caroline must have let go, and then she went mad, 'Jack's a bastard!' she shouted, 'he'll be enjoying this, he was always scornful when I tried to teach Daniel things and he said it was dangerous crap you shouldn't inflict on a child and I said I was trying to bring him up right and I had no support from anyone, but you can't possibly know this, it's too horrible, what is it these evil people are supposed to be telling them hmm! You tell me that you little Miss Knowall.' Well this is the worst part Jonathan, I didn't want to say any more but I couldn't leave it there could I!'

'Were you absolutely sure … about what you'd seen I mean. Absolutely sure …'

'Not you too!' Pamela stood up and slammed down the lid of the laptop, 'Not you too! Doubting me. *How can you!*'

'Pam I don't doubt you but …'

'I told her that I was sorry, but her boy is being held against his will in a house and she needs to contact the police, and Tom is there as well, and yes, their texts are being censored. And that was when she came at me, she was completely out of control, she must have knocked me out.'

'Oh Pam … I'm so sorry. Sit down again, you poor thing.'

'Wendy was kind, she came to see me, she told me that

the police had taken them away, and I did speak to the police a bit later … and since then I've been helping them, they're listening to me now. It's like you suggested a while ago do you remember? That's what I'm in the middle of.'

Pam sat down and rested her head in her hands. Jonathan got up and filled the kettle. 'We need to be together,' he said, 'This sounds … dangerous. You could have been badly hurt. Please say you'll come with me now.'

'You're not listening to me.'

'Surely you can do this … by phone. Surely. You say you love me. It doesn't make sense that you won't come.'

'I can't explain anymore.'

'Pam. You're strong. And you're … '

'But you doubted me.'

'No, I …'

'I do understand. We're not always logical are we.'

'We need each other … don't we?'

'Why don't you answer Pam? Mmm? I try to understand. But maybe you're still angry… about other things. Maybe you still think it's my fault Matthew was killed.'

'Let go of my arm Jonathan. Calm down. That wasn't your fault. Don't be ridiculous. We don't need to go over all that again.'

'I could see what hell that man was going through, the doctors just prescribe these pills and don't care, and I just wanted to help, *what a fool* …'

'You're not a fool, of course not.'

'I'm … sorry. That what I feel I have to do is … difficult. Not straightforward. That I can't just put things aside that most people dismiss in an instant or never even consider in the first place. Who knows, or perhaps *you* know, perhaps I might be about to discover something. … and then you give me that look, like you're seeing something and not telling me. It's killing me. Pam I'm … there's too much to struggle with, too much to try and understand.'

'Jonathan you're very tired. You're grieving. Belinda's

dead. Being here reminds you, seeing her little room. You need a rest. You need to escape from this house.'

'*What are you seeing Pam!* I need to know. Please!'

'Jonathan stop shouting.' She turned away.

'So … I'm right. There is something you're not telling me. Why, why! It's me, talk to *me*. *Please talk to me* … Am I mad? To try and help people. To accept a huge gift from a friend? To see potential in someone who's never been given a chance? There's so much fucking misery in the world, is it mad to question all these ghastly religions that distort how people think and cloud their judgement and make them hate, and …well it goes on for thousands of years and most people swallow this nonsense. Where's the love hmm! All you need is love …'

'Stop shouting at me Jonathan please. How can I possibly answer any of your questions. Hmm? Remember I don't understand anything do I!'

'But you *do* Pam, you do.'

'No. You're right, I don't understand … and I *never will.*'

'Come with me. Today. Now.'

'No! I can't.'

'Stop crying. We belong together. I love you I love you.' He pulled her to him and embraced her roughly.

'No Jonathan, not like this. Let me go.'

He gripped her arms and his body shook with painful sobbing. His phone beeped. He let it go on for some time until it stopped. After a few minutes he let her go and pressed Diana's number.

'Ah Jonathan.'

'I'm sorry I missed your call, Diana. Is everything alright?'

'Jonathan I'm very sorry to disturb you but I had to ring. I'm afraid … the police are here.'

'Why? What's happened?'

'I'm afraid they're searching for Hugo.'

'Why? What's happening Diana? Is anyone hurt?'

'Yes, I'm afraid so Jonathan. I'm very sorry to tell you. Hugo has attacked Marissa. She was found in one of the outbuildings. The truth is ... I'm very sorry to tell you ... he's ... raped her. I'm so very sorry to be the bearer of this terrible news.'

54 MARCH
Very worrying indeed

'Something dreadful has happened, and I have to go back,' said Jonathan. Distraught he rushed upstairs and threw his things into his bag and drove away without a word. Pamela watched his car disappear. Was he in a fit state to drive? How would he cope?

Would they ever see each other again?

She climbed the stairs slowly and got dressed, splashing cold water on her face and trying to take in what had happened. Then the front doorbell rang.

It was a shock to see a man so like Jonathan standing there. She quickly realised it was Jeremy, she had met him when he had been in Jonathan's house during those rather strange weeks ...

'Ah, Pamela isn't it?'

'Jeremy!'

'I'm very sorry to arrive suddenly like this. You see I've just driven over, we're very busy with the restaurant which is wonderful, but Natasha's disappeared and we're worried. I just wanted to check that she's here.'

'No, I'm very sorry ... I've not seen her, haven't been in touch for a while ...'

'That is a blow. That is really disappointing. I wonder

if I could come in for a moment? Is Jonathan here?'

'Yes of course, sorry.' She closed the front door. 'I'll put the kettle on. No … Jonathan just left. I'm sorry the house is a bit of a mess, some decorating half done.'

'Thank you,' he said following her into the living room.

'Just sit down and I'll make some tea,' she said.

'Thank you, Pamela,' he said, taking the mug off the tray. 'Are you … alright? Looking a bit washed out.'

'Oh, well, a bit tired, thank you. But tell me what's been happening.'

'I expect you know already.'

She had a shock but then realised he was deadly serious and polite. He seemed … very different. Sober and sensible.

'Well, I'm not sure what you mean,' she began, 'You tell me.' Perhaps he didn't know about the cocaine?

'I expect you've known for a while,' he said, 'About the drugs. I didn't know you see, not until yesterday, Natasha and I have been getting on better, well you see I told her something about her childhood, it's a bit involved, and after that we were like – quite good friends, but then odd things started happening …'

'Was it about money?'

'Ah … well yes, you've guessed, it started going missing, first from my wallet, then a bit from Sally's bag, and Natasha was often not around when she said she was going to do things, and then she was out a lot, and then David came round, he's one of Sally's sons, Sally is the one whose café it is …'

'Yes, Natasha told me about Sally,'

'Ah yes … well, David was pretty upset too and he's a level-headed sort of man, very successful and sensible, and this had all been going on for a while, but he had no idea…'

'I'm very sorry to hear this,' said Pam, 'But sadly not surprised. I'm so sorry I haven't been in touch with her for a few weeks …'

'Well David had finally realised, it took him a while, he

got it out of her eventually and he was furious, and apparently she just left his place, and he thought she'd come back to us which she hadn't ...'

'No. I'm so sorry. I haven't spoken to her a lot lately, I should have.'

'Are you alright Pam, excuse me asking. You're looking ... a bit shaken up.'

'Yes. I am. A bit shaky. But you've got other things on your mind. The point is, she hasn't been here, and she hasn't been in touch. She must have ... contacts, you know, dealers and people she might be spending time with, could be anywhere, but more likely near you. Or maybe near here.'

'Yes ... I was desperately hoping she'd be here. This is very worrying indeed.'

'She may turn up.'

'Are you ...'

'Well, I live here. Sort of. At the moment.' Pamela turned away and took some deep breaths.

'And you said Jonathan's just left? Natasha said he's back in the village at the Manor House helping people?'

'Yes. Well ... a lot's been happening ... and you've got enough to worry about.'

'What do you mean?'

There was a silence and Jeremy watched her as she blew her nose and drank her tea. 'I'll just take these,' she said getting up. He stood up and went over to her. 'Look Pam, I hardly know you, but I can see ...'

'I'll be alright,' she said not looking at him. He took the tray out of her hands, 'No, you're not,' he said, 'Sit down and have a rest for a minute.'

She sat down and buried her face in her hands. He sat beside her and waited and then put his arm around her and she sobbed on his shoulder.

'I'm so sorry Jeremy,' she said awkwardly, 'This is so ridiculous.

You're worried about Natasha and I should be helping.'
'Yes, in a minute.'

'We've … Jonathan and I have broken up … the Manor House thing has all gone wrong, Jonathan just got some bad news and he left, he didn't explain but I know it was bad … it's all a big shock, we didn't … well it wasn't a row exactly, it was like … I haven't really worked it out and I don't know where I should be living, and he needs to sell this house.'

'I'm very sorry to hear all that. But maybe it'll blow over? Have you got anywhere to go?'

'Well yes, my old family house is near the Manor House – there are tenants there. At least that brings in a bit of money. But I don't want to go back there, and getting them out and selling would all take time and … I'm alone you see, my family are all dead.'

'I'm very sorry. It's obviously shaken you up. I always had the impression that … that you and Jonathan were very close.'

'We were.'

'I'm sorry, I don't mean to pry. Look can I impose on you a bit more and ask if you could take me round this town to places that …'

'Oh yes.' She sniffed and blew her nose, 'Yes, I could try. Though I'm not, I'm very sorry Jeremy, I'm not optimistic.'

'Do you … well I've heard that you see things … can you …'

'I don't see anything about Natasha,' she said, 'At this moment I just feel, well very sad, pessimistic, hopeless. She tried to give it up, Jonathan and I encouraged her, she did go to some meetings. I got the impression that … but it's a dreadful thing to fight and people hide what's happening, they need it so desperately, this has been going on a while and we were all busy and didn't realise. I feel terrible, she was my friend. I'm so sorry I didn't help more.'

'I'm sure you both tried,' he said, 'I had no idea. All these months. I should have realised too. I need to phone Sally and cancel tonight's bookings. I was thinking I'd be able to get back, but I need to search now, it's urgent.'

'Yes of course.'

She got up and took the mugs back to the kitchen while he picked up his phone.

55 MARCH
His heart felt like stone

The familiar roads back to the Manor House were a blur of greys and browns and greens and yellows. Jonathan sobbed aloud and then pulled himself together as he drove. More and more impossible questions. Was this Marissa's doing, did it really happen, would he be allowed to try and help Hugo, will there be anything to salvage. *What would happen with Pam, what could happen? Would they ever see each other again?* It truly felt as if the ground had opened up and it was him who had been cast down into the deep pit with a band of ice around his throat making it difficult to breathe. But better it was him than little Divit. Who had dug this hole and what was its purpose?

By the time he got back events had moved on, the police spoke to him briefly and confirmed the facts. He heard Hugo howling in Maxwell's garden when they found him and took him away. Jonathan wasn't allowed to speak to him. Should he tell the police about recent events? It felt a bit like the time before the drug addict Frank Williams murdered Pam's brother, he had wondered then if he should have spoken to the police during the previous weeks.

Ruby had come back, and the police picked her up at her cottage. Jonathan learnt a few things later and there was something in the papers. Did he understand why she had deceived him that day? She was muddling along trying to help someone without really understanding it, she just tried to be kind. But nothing she could do ever changed anything, Belinda could play a good game of chess while all the time the weird and frightening images were paralyzing her mind.

The women were already beginning to leave and most of them looked the other way when they saw him. But Jan paused in the corridor with her little boy. Jonathan said he was sorry no one would be staying and asked what she would do. Well, she didn't really know, reluctantly she said goodbye and turned away and the little lad waved and smiled.

One evening he was finally alone, everyone had gone. Diana had been kind, unexpectedly kind. 'I find it hard to express how I feel,' she said putting down her worn, old suitcase and shaking his hand. 'It's been … a pleasure to know you Jonathan, all this was something quite unusual. What will you do now?' He told her he didn't know and thanked her for her fantastic work. 'It could have been … quite different.' She lingered and glanced around the panelled hall. 'You imagined it quite differently didn't you?'

What he had imagined was now virtually invisible. One day in the future he might be able to have a long and interesting conversation with her. And one day perhaps he might get in touch with Francesa's father and who knows, they might talk for many hours. During the long days after everyone had left the huge rooms and corridors were silent while outside spring flowers nodded in the cold wind. Did George know what had happened, surely he must have heard? Jonathan found it impossible to pick up the phone and waited to hear from him, taking time to think and doing practical tasks. He cancelled the caterers.

He stood in his bedroom and wondered what to do with Belinda's little rucksack, still stored carefully with his bags. Would she have minded if he read her notebooks now? Would she know? What would they tell him? He sat on the bed and laid them out and then put them away.

For a while his comfort was his books and the computer screen. Now he had all the time in the world and would sit in the small office off the hall where he could still remember the common-sense kindness of Diana and Francesca, there had been normal moments when practical tasks were being done. He needed those walls close around him while outside the great Manor House waited. What was to be done with it?

There were many things to read, too many. There was The Essene Gospel of Peace. He no longer had the energy to wonder whether it was true or not, but it was beautiful. Had the church been deceiving people for hundreds and hundreds of years? Surely no one will ever know. The virgin birth of Jesus had long been puzzled over and defended by the authorities. It was at the heart of the whole thing. Had these old manuscripts and scrolls that told different stories always been hidden away? Or perhaps just not yet found. And now would they be ignored for ever? Probably.

What else was hidden under lock and key in the vast Vatican archives? Here was a different image of Jesus who lived with his fiancé who died ... He spoke with God and learned about the birds and beasts and the healing powers of herbs and flowers and the hidden qualities of precious stones and Astronomy and Mathematics ...

Jonathan rushed from one website to another. Since the discovery in 1946 of the Dead Sea Scrolls many questions had been raised. People were stunned to learn that during the first century there was a community which for hundreds of years had studied many old religions and had many ancient manuscripts. The Essenes lives simply, they shunned publicity and shared everything they had and served one another. They wore white robes and were known as prophets. In Jerusalem there is a door that bears their name. People respected their honesty and pacifism, their goodness and discretion, their talent as healers and devotion to the poor.

The exquisite poetic language soothed his thoughts, some of it was the same as the New Testament, but most of it was utterly different, it was like everything that had been left out before, it was like coming home and hearing what he always knew. It made him feel he had been right to keep asking so many questions.

It spoke about the all-powerful protective Mother, her angels and her laws and her great love, it was very comforting. It told him not to seek for laws in the scriptures but that he would find them in the grass and the trees and the rivers and the mountains, and in himself. It told him scripture is without life. When he saw this it was like someone was shaking him by the hand and confirming what he had been doing all these months, endlessly struggling with the meanings of words.

He became aware of the angel of the air and the angel of water, and his confusion was being gently washed away. The angel of sunlight would embrace him. It told him there was no true brotherhood by blood. He thought of the pain Jeremy had inflicted, – his cousin, the nearest thing to a brother. The walls of that small office protected him as him he raced through the text. There was so much of it and it was all so much kinder …

It talked about the sun being like a flame of the candle beside the full light and truth of the Heavenly Father and this reminded him of a dream Pam had told him about, she had written it down for him because it was so strange … he opened the door and ran up the stairs and searched in one of his bags … As he stood in the cold bedroom and looked at her neat handwriting on those sheets of paper, the pain of losing her hit him again and his heart felt like stone.

I am tied to a chair. Jonathan is standing a few feet away, the other side of the line. I only have a few words I can say, they are written in shaky writing on a piece of paper I am holding. 'Untie her!' he is shouting, but some people in the corner are reading something and take no notice. One of them holds a paper up in the air and then begins to tear it into tiny pieces.

'You need to untie her now!' He calls again, then turns to me. 'Pamela I cannot cross the line,' he says, 'I am so sorry, I cannot come closer. I cannot break the rules of the Game.'

I look at the words on my piece of paper but there's nothing there that makes any sense. I want to speak but no words come out.

'They will come,' he says, 'They have the authority to decide. We have to

wait until they are ready. They know what they are doing.'
The man in the corner of the room is still tearing the paper into tiny pieces
which fall to the floor around him and are lifted by the breeze.
I try again to read the words on my piece of paper but the writing is a series
of wobbly lines which start to move over the paper. Then the line of the
writing turns into a thread which starts to stretch over my arms and dig
into the flesh like wire. I shout then, I don't know what and I am being
pinned more closely to the chair. It's hard to breathe.
'You don't need to know any rules!' I suddenly shout, 'There are no rules.
You can go where you want. They aren't watching us anymore, they're
busy.'
Jonathan sits down on the floor and takes off his shoes. 'Help me! 'I shout
again, 'Please Jonathan help me. What are you doing?' The wire tightens.
Now there are other men with him, all sitting on the floor barefoot and
they stare at the flame of a candle standing on the floor in the middle of
the circle. They begin to chant old medieval music.
A man approaches and unties me and I stand up. 'You can go,' he says,
'There will be more Games tomorrow. You need to sort things out and
throw things away. You need to work things out.'
'I need Jonathan,' I say but the man has moved away and isn't listening.
'What do I need to sort out?' Jonathan is still sitting in the circle singing
the old music with the others. He seems far away now and I don't feel I
can interrupt. I stand and feel helpless.
'You need to play again tomorrow,' the man says, turning back to me and
then he points to the corner of the room. Three men are holding papers and
they wave them at me, 'These are the new Games for tomorrow,' they call
out, 'You can come back. You need to decide if you want to come back.'
'How do I decide? How do I know if I should play the Games? Which
Games should I play? And where will I go now until tomorrow?'
'Do what you have to do,' they say, 'Keep the rules. Sort everything out.
It's up to you, you're in charge.'
I walk over to the corner and I want to challenge them, they make me
angry. They need to explain it to me, but they are talking to each other
and looking at papers 'Tell me!' I say, 'Tell me which Games to play and
where I should go!' But they don't take any notice.
I try to grab a paper but they turn and make jeering sounds and their faces
become weird and frightening and they laugh in my face. Behind me the

chanting is getting louder and I turn and see the candle growing taller and the light from the flame expands and gets brighter and brighter until everything in the room is flooded with it.
I can't see anyone anymore. Jonathan has disappeared. I search for him but the light hurts my eyes and makes them water. The tears flow down to the floor and hiss as they hit the floorboards, the water boils and the steam rises and floats in the light. It is very beautiful and very frightening.
There are all the colours of the rainbow and more colours I have never seen before. I have never seen anything more beautiful. The pain goes away from my arms and eyes and all I can see is this light and the rainbows dancing and floating. They move towards me and circle around me. They lift me from the floor and I am weightless. Time has stood still.

Jonathan sat on the bed. Was this all he had left of her now? The meaning of the dream struck him afresh, all mixed up with echoes of the Games at the Manor House and decisions and helplessness and reaching out to him and sensing something was pulling him away from her. Was it always pulling him away, had they finally been forced to acknowledge they could not be together? Was there any hope this might change? He folded the paper and put it back in the envelope and carefully placed it in the bag so he would always know where it was.

So much he thought he had forgotten. But now again he was craving for the comforting walls of the little office, and he walked slowly down the wide staircase. The words were still there on the computer screen. They would always be there as if waiting to be found. There was so much to read. *Here was the gentler prophet he had been seeking and behind the gentleness was the greatest strength of all.*

He opened the office door and went to the kitchen to make a cup of tea. On the way back a little letter lay on the mat by the front door. It was Pamela's writing and he tore it open.

Dear Jonathan, Belinda has spoken to me. She was calm. She wants you to know that you can read her diaries. Read the one that has five blank pages at the end. She wants you to know she is alright. Pam

What! He was running out of tears and looked for the kisses that weren't there. They weren't there. Slowly he grasped the meaning of the words. Again he climbed the stairs. There was her little rucksack and yes there was the notebook with the five blank pages at the end. He looked through it until a particular sentence caught his attention ...

... I was locked out of the house.

I rushed back along the pathway that ran along behind the houses, I didn't look back. He would have nearly caught up now, following and watching and laughing. I saw another path going through between some high fences, there were tall mature trees in the gardens with heavy branches overhanging the path.

I wanted to climb the tree and hide in the branches. There I would not be burnt with the flames, under here it was shady and cool. The path started to go up and came out into a bank of grass and more trees. Great and marvellous are thy deeds, Lord God, Sovereign over all; just and true are Thy ways, thou King of the ages. Who shall not revere thee, Lord, and do homage to Thy name? For Thou alone art holy. The path led back into more houses and out into another street. I began to run. My rucksack was heavy, full of the notebooks, some clothes, and the money, the honest money and the guilty money. I tripped and fell, struggled up and ran and ran. All nations shall come and worship in Thy presence, for Thy just dealings stand revealed. Do not pour Your wrath on me, do not pour Your plagues on me. I do not have the mark of the beast on me, I do not. I came to another road and went down it. At the end of the road there was busy traffic. The Thames will not turn to blood. I am sorry, I am sorry for my sins. Do not pour the flames on me.

I will not sleep, I will stay awake and be ready. I am not strong enough for the battle, spare me. I mingled with the crowds, I bought a bottle of water from a little shop. That man is really an angel coming to find me and pour the wrath out of the bowl onto me. But I will find somewhere to hide where the hail cannot strike me. I am not a whore, he made me, he forced me, I couldn't resist, I was too small and weak. But I will repent, please. I will wait until the seven plagues are completed. I am chosen and faithful. I saw a railway bridge ahead. There was a path which left the road and climbed parallel with the railway line along an old broken-down fence. Now another scruffy bank of grass. It was quiet, I had left the crowds behind. The ground fell away and there was a little stream. I found a hidden place under a bridge over the stream. I crawled in behind the bushes and lay on the ground and hugged my rucksack and drank the water.

The trains came and went. I am not riding the red beast. I banish the demons, I am not the queen, I do not deserve to be tormented, I took the money to survive and live, I do not want to die. I do not deserve to burn. Do not hurl the stones at me, there is too much blood in me, it is spilling out and filling the bowls of wrath. I am writing on the books of life, the book will be opened and my name will be found on the scroll of the living, and I will see the One who sits on the great white throne.

It was dry and quiet and there was the soft sound of the running water and I watched the little weeds trailing in it and playing over its surface. And he said to me, 'Write this down for these words are trustworthy and true. Indeed they are already fulfilled…. And the city had no need of sun or moon to shine upon it; for the glory of God gave it light, and its lamp was the Lamb. By its light shall the nations walk, and the Kings of the earth shall bring into it all their splendour.' My name is written on the scroll of the Lamb. He is coming soon. He is coming soon. Do not come and find me, let me be. The beast rode me, he trampled me and broke me. Leave me …

There was a gap here and some words crossed out and Jonathan read on.

… I slept and woke to see daylight. The trains came and went. Slanting sunlight hit me from the side and I sat up and reached out for the rucksack. It was gone.

I crawled out of the little shelter under the bridge over the stream behind the bushes. There it was. Scattered over the scruffy grass were my notebooks and bits and pieces, my comb, the bottle of water, some tissues, some crumpled clothes. I gathered everything up, counting the notebooks as I went. And then I realised that the money was gone.

I will die here now God if that is what You want. Is there the mark of the beast on me? Is my name on the scroll of the living? Are You going to take it off and let me die? You know all my sins, You have always known

*my sins, and You know when I lied about my sins, and You know when
I didn't learn the words you told to Jesus. You know when I let myself get
in a muddle about the seven beasts and the creatures with eyes inside and
out and the angels and the plagues. I let myself get in a muddle because I
questioned Your words and thought I would never understand. I am a
thief and I came away in the night, I crept away and I can never go back.
Oh let me die, but save me from the torture. There is no blood here, this
stream is pure cool water and the sun is warm. Why do you make Your
world so beautiful if You are so angry with me?*

*I will wait to die but my soul will have nowhere to go. There is no one who
wants me. What does the mark of the beast look like? Why can't I see
it? Is it because I lied? I am not a chosen one, I know that now. I lied to
myself, I thought You had put my name on the scroll in the sky. I thought
You wrote my name. Even the creature has left me now, it has abandoned
me. It watched me because I had been lying but now there is no hope for
me and it has gone away.*

This took Jonathan's breath away and he held the little
notebook to his heart. There were seven notebooks, all full of
horror. But this is the one Belinda wanted him to read. She
must have been on the run in London before someone found
her and just before he managed to find her in the hospital. It
was summer. It was astonishing how he had managed to find
her. Now he glanced through some of the other notebooks –
she described the incessant, insane questioning she had
suffered about the dark and powerful images in the Book of
Revelation, and there were little bits of information about her
time alone in that house, and a terrifying night when she hid
under a blanket, hearing heavy footsteps on the stairs. Her
solitary fears, her imaginings. The man she often thought was
following her, well who was he? Someone in her mind.

This was truly and utterly astonishing. *Pamela knew
Belinda wanted him to read this - because Belinda told her - and Belinda
is dead.* Pam was doing what she had to do. She had sent him a
letter which he would receive safely, not an email which would
get buried under many others or a text message which might
vanish into the air – he put the little notebook back in the

rucksack and fastened the zip and laid it on a chair. What was
to be done with it? There is no court of justice where it can be
examined, there is no newspaper who would print it and make
appropriate compassionate comments – there are no
appropriate compassionate comments. There is no one who
will believe it and no one who will understand it.

Jonathan stands up. He hasn't eaten for hours. He moves
wearily to the bedroom door and walks along the corridor and
down the wide staircase. It's as though he's been in another
world and the Manor House is still waiting …

He goes into the small office off the hall and finds the
box with the old files. He carries them outside and make a pile
on the grass. *Tell Your Psychiatrist Everything, Go Back and Tell
Mummy, Tie Up Your Partner and Tell Them the Truth.* He couldn't
tell Pam the truth, he couldn't even tell it to himself, fragments
of it blow through his mind and are gone before he can look
at them properly. Though it's true that she doesn't understand.
She is already tied up, they both are, their arms and legs are
strapped to the chairs, they are both prisoners in their own
minds.

Did he really doubt what she said she had seen about those
boys imprisoned in that house? Perhaps he should have been
more careful what he said, and then they could have hung on
to the fragile threads that linked them, and their love would
have been transformed into something stronger again. There
must have been other things in her mind that day, too much
overwhelming her. Had she seen events that were happening
in the Manor House and were still going to happen? *And was
she seeing them in those moments while they were talking?* He tries to
remember, when did the trouble begin? Was it when she saw
he wanted the Manor House. But how could things have been
different?

He goes back into the house and runs up the back stairs
and along to the storeroom, he shuts off anything he might feel

or hear and moves to the window and struggles with the catch which is rusty. He gets it open and takes hold of anything he can, boxes, magazines, tables, drawers ... he hurls it all out of the window and hears things fall on the grass below. Wood falls on wood and cracks.

He runs downstairs and takes a box of matches from the window-sill in the kitchen. Outside he pushes everything together into a great untidy pile, the old Games files spill out and he kicks them under a broken drawer. He sets it all alight. The ground is sodden, but the flames leap up. Through the days and weeks the truth has become more and more complex and more and more mysterious, the clarity he craves retreats and dances before his eyes and slips through his fingers. But now ... something new and very beautiful is creeping into that space, gentle as the air.

But disturbed thoughts persist. What would Pam have said if *she* had been in the storeroom and heard those sounds. She would surely know something he didn't. He watches the flames take hold. He tries to quieten his mind, but he remembers how Hugo pushed past him as he came out of the door with that look of fear on his face. *And was whatever it was still there now?*

How much of this did Pam see, it must have been terribly frightening for her. Though she has an inner strength, a courage that comes from somewhere he doesn't understand. Jonathan's thoughts have a life of their own as he throws the last file on top of the others, *Unmix the Messages, a Fun Game for Couples.* Fun? George had struggled and struggled to write this Game but then Lawrence had taken it over and it had moved away from what the Games were about. There was nothing more effective than a kind, listening ear when people were in trouble.

Hugo was always more than George could handle. But in Jonathan's mind Hugo is now locked in a room and the key has been thrown away. He is the last person to whom that key will ever be given. When he thinks back Jonathan wonders yet again ...*who was the man who said he was Peter Ennistone?*

It is twilight, neither day nor night. He sees paper and broken wood falling away and adds it to the fire. Then he rushes back into the Manor House and along to the kitchen and lifts the pile of books from the table. As he runs down the corridor one falls but he lets it go. He drops them on the ground and then picks them up one by one and reads the titles in the flickering orange light. One by one they go into the flames. He watches his bible burn. How much of it is lies pretending to be the truth?

A brisk wind has started up and he moves away from the smoke and pokes at the embers, there is no sound except the crackling. The sky darkens and a dull glow in the distance fades and the huge cedar trees bend towards him. And then there is a flash and the rumble of thunder coming from a far-off hillside, almost inaudible, then coming again as if to confirm itself. He stands and breathes and thinks of the angel of the air who is always there. There is a brighter flash and he see a figure illuminated, standing the other side of the bonfire. For a short moment an angel of vengeance has come to punish him. But then he sees who it is. The thunder breaks and roars and the rain begins, softly pattering, then louder and stronger and the trees shake harder...

She is watching and waiting. He walks around the broken fragments and the smouldering blackened wood.

'Are you alright Jonathan?' she says, 'I saw the flames and I wondered. You can see them from miles away.'

'Are *you* alright Jan?'

'Not really. But I wanted to come, I wanted to see you and I was worried.'

'I'm ... clearing things – burning rubbish.'

'Yes.'

'Did you hear the thunder? Coming nearer.'

'Yes, it's louder now.'

'Can you come inside out of the rain? Have you got time?'

'Well, um ... maybe I could for a minute. I've left Andy

with my friend. We're sharing a house.' She follows him in through the side door and along the corridor to the kitchen. He nearly trips on a book on the floor and bends down to pick it up. *Another Look at an Extraordinary Story.* 'It's the one that got away.' he says.

'You mean …'

'I threw the others on the fire. But this one … I need to read it.' He places it on the window-sill.

'And for you … a cup of tea or a glass of wine?' She is standing nervously by the table.

'Well …'

He finds a bottle of red in a cupboard. 'This one's been maturing nicely. Sit down a minute Jan, it's lovely to see you.'

They sip the wine. 'You been on your own?' she says, 'Since we all left.'

'Yes …but not really, it's like I've been with many people, including one who has died. And I've been reading and thinking and finding things out.'

'Sounds busy.'

'It feels like several years. I could try and tell you about it sometime if you had the patience.'

'Yes.'

'And you?'

'Well, being here really helped, it was so lovely, such a beautiful old house and a complete change from what was happening to me before … I could tell you about it sometime if you had the patience.'

They look at each other. Then they freeze. A terrible heart-rending cry can be heard from somewhere upstairs. There are some words there, you can just make them out.

'Ahhhrrrr! Oh. Ahhhhh. Help me. Please … Ahhhhhhhh! '

'Oh Jan – I can't explain now, but please. Can you help, can you come with me. There's something – I know this sounds mad, there's *something* in a storeroom, I don't know what, it's been there a while and I ignored it, but now ….' The barely human cry comes again and there are faint banging sounds.

'What Jonathan? Who is it? Is it dangerous? Do you think we should call …?'

'No – I need to do this. It's been taunting me, I need to …. I think I know what to do. Please!'

He takes her hand and reluctantly she comes with him, and they hurry along the corridors and up the back stairs. They can hear the desperate cries which get louder as they approach the storeroom. Jan pulls at his hand but he glances at her, 'I need to do this Jan, you must help me, you must. *Please.*'

'Ohhhhhhh… ' Now in the storeroom the cries seem close by - 'Ahhhhhh ….' Then tapping sounds, then a crash.

'Sounds like someone's trapped but behind the wall. Is there a room there?'

'But no. That's the outside wall.' *But this sounds like a human being who is trapped. Someone in trouble. But how?'*

'You could speak to them,' she says, 'You could ask them, tell them we'll help. There's someone there.'

Someone! A human being?' Jonathan stands paralyzed. How can there be a person there? It's impossible …

Jan moves to the wall and knocks and then calls out. '*Is there anyone there? Do you need help?'*

The shouting and banging stops. She calls again, the same words, she adds more, reassuring, normal human questions. And then …

'Yes! Please help me! I'm trapped.'

'So …' she says, 'It's someone. A person.' She watches Jonathan's face.

'Where are you?' she shouts, 'Tell us so we can help.'

'I'm in a room, a secret room. The door has jammed and I'm trapped. Thank God you're here!' The voice though muffled sounds familiar.

'It's Keith. Is Jonathan there? He knows me. I can explain if you can get me out, I can tell you where the door is and you can knock it down or something. Can you do that?'

'Yes, we can do that, just explain it.'

Jonathan is looking out of the window and sobbing quietly. 'Yes he's here,' she shouts, 'He's a bit confused. Now tell us what to do.'

'The door to this secret room is outside in the corridor,' says the voice, 'Try pressing a small panel near the floor to the right of the storeroom door. That might work from the outside.'

She walks over and has a look. She bends down and presses a panel in the wall. There's a click.

There's no need to pray, there's no need to be tested, there's no need to fail, there is no evil spirit …

Just a narrow door to a secret room. It has opened, Keith is behind it and steps over the threshold and comes into the storeroom. He looks dusty and thin and is carrying what looks like a handwritten letter and moves towards the broken chair, sitting down heavily. 'Thank you, thank you, I thought I would die in there. The secret door to the secret room, we played here as children. It never jammed before. But I found it, I've found it.' He looks up at them, 'I found my father's letter. It explains it. Read it. Please.' He hands it to Jan and his shoulders are shaking.

Jan looks at Jonathan who turns back and wipes his face. She holds the letter up where they can both read it. Old fashioned writing on old fashioned notepaper.

My Dear Dear Boy
I so wish I could speak to you again before I die. And I so much regret what happened when you left. It was your mother who couldn't live with it, only her. And when she died I knew I should get in touch. But I didn't know where to start. I am so sorry.
I hope this letter finds you with the help of the Post Office. At the moment I am uncertain of your address but several people are trying to help me find it. I must tell you at once that everything has changed because your brother's bad behaviour

has now reached a point where I must act despite my former reservations.

I will be changing the will very soon but John must not know. He is talking about going off to do some project or other. Everything will come to you, the house and what's left of everything else. Dora is my lovely daughter but she is not worldly wise and I realise now it won't be sensible to continue with the plan of putting this responsibility onto her shoulders. So you see how important it is that this letter finds you. Please write back immediately but post it to the PO Box 4027 where Sandra frequently collects other mail for me. She brings it back discreetly so your brother knows nothing about it. It is vital that he doesn't know as his behaviour is unpredictable and often very cruel. Now I am a helpless invalid it has got worse. Sandra does everything and is a great help and I can trust her. Without her I would be without anyone to rely on and this is an alarming prospect.

Keith I am glad you have made a life for yourself and your work is rewarding. The human psyche is endlessly fascinating isn't it. I can see all that now and wish you well. Yes, I was angry and disappointed before, but that has changed.

I will change the will and the Manor House will be yours. John doesn't know I changed it in favour of Dora and he mustn't know of this new plan. So when I die – and that may not be far away, I am getting very weak which is very strange after being so strong all my life - you must cherish it. What a beautiful house it is. Fill it with love and happiness. It has witnessed terrible hatred and bitterness but that must change.

With the greatest love and sorrow and I hope not for the last time,

Your father

Major John Henry Green

Keith looks up and wipes his face. He sees that they have read it and are waiting for him to speak. He stands up and holds onto the back of the chair. 'I'm sorry,' he says, 'I sneaked into the house when the boiler men came and I've been staying in the secret room. I sometimes crept down to the kitchen at night and took some food. Some of the women saw me but I said I was fixing some things in the house and they seemed to believe that, there've have been people about recently. I've been searching and searching for this letter or something to help me understand. You see it was our family home, I lived here as a child with my family, my parents and John and Dora, I was the younger brother by ten years. But then I … I'm sorry it's painful to talk about … I told them I was gay and my mother went mad. Everyone else was ok, and John and Dora were coming and going and busy with their lives, so I hardly saw them anyway. Though I think John preferred to cut all contact after that. But I had to leave, she was never going to change. My father was shocked but …well, you can see from this letter … And for a while he was disappointed I didn't follow him into the Army …After I'd left home for years I knew things were bad, I had lost touch. Then stories reached me about my brother, and I wasn't sure what to believe. Then I heard my mother died. Then there were several years …' he pauses and wipes his face again with a shaking hand… 'when I kept thinking I should try and make contact. Time passes and we grow older and things that made us angry don't seem important anymore. Then … I heard news of my father's death. I moved nearer and heard more stories. It sounds like he never made the new will. Of course I didn't know about it then. Or maybe it was lost, or not signed or witnessed. John had gone off somewhere and made a lot of money. Dora was alone now and she couldn't cope, she let the place down. And then it was sold to George and Millicent. Something about paying for Dora's nursing home fees. It should never have been sold. I don't know if Dora thought of me. I never really knew what she thought about … any of it. But I had changed my name, I hadn't wanted anything more to do with my family.'

Jan gives him back the letter. 'I needed to find this, I thought there must be *something* - it looks like it was never posted, and it was lying between two old books. I was searching through bits and pieces that were being tidied away in the psychiatrist's office and other things that had been left lying around when the house was sold to George. Perhaps the person who was supposed to post it decided she shouldn't post it, who knows? I didn't know any of that, I didn't know about Sandra, but I hoped I might find something ... I did a bit of searching when I worked here when the Games were happening but had to be discreet of course. I thought the Games were wonderful - at the beginning. For me it was like I was at home but no one knew who I was and the house was being used to help people. But then of course Lawrence came along and the Guests seemed to change, there were some unpleasant and pretentious people ... And George began to find it all too much ... and I tried to persuade him to carry on but I got too emotional, of course he didn't know the full story. I did talk about the way mental illness is treated and my own fears and worries, but I couldn't tell him what was really on my mind. And I ...' Keith pauses and looks at them apprehensively. 'I think you'll understand this Jonathan, you always were the kindest man. I love him. I love George.'

Jan is very quiet and glances at Jonathan. Then she goes over and puts a reassuring hand on Keith's shoulder. 'You've been through a lot,' she says.

'Thank you. For listening to this ... recently ... I simply had to get into the house and search. I just couldn't live with not knowing. It seemed like everything had stopped, no Guests, no Games. It was like the house needed me, and I needed things to be resolved in my mind, that's all. I couldn't explain, Jonathan, there seemed to be other things going on and I couldn't ask you if I could come and work here again, though I thought about it and offering my services in some way, but there never seemed to be the right moment.'

Jonathan moves forward and take Keith's hand. 'I am so sorry ... And I am so very glad you've found it.'

'What's happening with the Manor House, does it still belong to George? Will he be coming back?'

'Yes, it still does, but he wants to give it to me, but it's a long process and we're going to have to spend quite some time with the solicitor. George has been busy packing and organising things and moving to a little house in town ...'

Jonathan is still holding his hand. Keith looks confused and worried.

'But Keith ...' Jonathan says, 'The Manor House is *yours*. Obviously. I'm very sure of this and we'll work it out with George. I'm sure he'll agree. It's *yours*. Now you look a bit the worse for wear, come down to the kitchen and I'll put the kettle on.'

They make their way slowly down the great old staircase. Keith is shaky and has gone rather quiet and takes Jonathan's arm as they walk down the corridor to the kitchen.

'Thank you, Jonathan.'

EPILOGUE

William turned the car into the short drive where uneven shrubs straggled over worn bumpy gravel and patches of brown grass and parked in front of his mother's house. Ugly, old fashioned and run down, he couldn't wait to get rid of it. Now finally he needed to get on with sorting it out, he must sell it as soon as possible ...

He had wasted a few months working in far off places. It made a change ... and he had been pleased he had managed it at all, but women had left or turned miserable, he had been robbed twice, he had narrowly missed being involved in an accident. Now it would be a relief to just stay put for a while and get on with the house. In the back of his mind was the thought - would Susan be back? Yesterday after their latest nasty and bitter conversation she had left, the bed was stripped and untidy sheets on the floor were tangled up with the crumpled duvet cover. Bitch!

He had been to the DIY store and started unloading the car, grabbing hold of flat packed furniture and decorating tools and walking to and fro to the front door. He put the key in the lock and stood in the porch and saw that the inner door was open and a radio was on in the kitchen. By the bookcase in the hall there were two bags of groceries and a coat and bag had been flung across the banisters.

'Susan!'

'William!'

'What are you doing back? I thought you said ...'

'Well, we both said a lot of things ...'

'I'm expecting my friend Jake any minute and it's important, we don't want to be interrupted.'

'Well, I'll be going out in a min. Got to see a man about a dog.

William went out again and began bringing in packages

and tins of paint and rolls of wallpaper and piling them up in the hall. He glanced at Susan who stood watching. 'Okay,' he said, 'But I'll phone you when we're through. Okay? Don't come back before.'

'Okay. I'll go now, I'll leave you to put the food away.' She walked past him, grabbed her coat and bag and went out, slamming the front door.

He was tidying everything away in one corner when the bell rang, one of those sugary sweet little sounds, his mother had had it put in. Just like her really. Soothing and empty of anything that anyone would want to remember, selfish and unreliable. No wonder my Dad left when I was so little, he did the right thing. I don't know why he was so violent and what sort of life he created for himself but it sure was better than the one he would've had with *her*. He made no attempt to support me or take any interest but that was *his* mistake! And *she* never tried to explain anything about him and just faded away in the nursing home without ever showing any interest in my life. God knows there had been plenty for her to have taken an interest in! Whichever way you looked at it.

'Come in Jake.'

'Hello William. Shall we go to the pub?'

'No. I've got a lot to say, it needs to be discussed in private. I'll make you a cup of tea, count yourself lucky to get that.'

Jake followed William into the kitchen and put his briefcase on the floor and stood watching while William arranged the tea bags in the mugs. They went into the living room where the paper manuscript of *'Jonathan's Mistakes, a gripping love story'* - William had insisted on paper – lay on the coffee table.

'You've read it then.'

'I've read it. *Of course I've fucking read it Jake,* that's why I asked you over!'

'It was quite a long way to drive, we could have Skyped or Zoomed. I'm very busy.'

'I needed to see you in person. There's so much wrong with it including the title. Sit down Jake and shut up. For once in your life listen to what I've got to say!'

Jake took his cup of tea from the tray and sat down on the threadbare armchair. Had William been drinking already? But this was the reception he had expected after some recent rather bizarre phone calls and emails. 'You're doing a great job stripping that wallpaper.'

'Don't change the subject. We both know why you're here.'

'Well, if there are things you don't like I'm sure we can talk about them calmly! But it doesn't actually matter whether you like it or not does it! Basically we met in the pub that day and you talked to me, rather a lot had been happening in your life and I was looking for an idea, and you agreed I could use your story but disguise everything and everyone. That was all it was.'

'Hmm.' William took a sip of tea and then picked up the manuscript and started looking through the pages. 'I've read it all and I've made notes, now where did I put them? You've made me into a real muddler, an incompetent fool. I wouldn't have started things up just like that without more planning, or wasted time interviewing every idiot that came along.'

'Well … it's not *you* who's the incompetent fool, … it's Jonathan.'

'You're going to have to hear me out. Please don't keep interrupting.'

'I'm sorry William. You're missing the point. It would help to discuss each thing as we go along. I don't need one of your speeches.'

'You see! You don't hesitate to mock me! Now, another thing, you left the blackmail question unclarified. Maxwell explained his experience to Anthea, that was fine, it was quite sugary sweet really how he said it made him a better person, but so-called Ruby never even mentioned what happened with her.'

'No, that's because I, we agreed to …'

'And you've made her into rather a nice person. Kind! Sad! Give me strength.'

Jake had opened the briefcase and was placing some papers on the coffee table, 'Here's everything, the summary I wrote of the story you told me, list of biblical quotations, list of blackmail victims with their background, plan of the village … other name changes … and … Everything I used to start from scratch …'

'I told you Joanna turned me down at the beginning, she was a cold fish. That was when I first came to the village with Annabelle. We were sleeping in separate rooms by then so naturally I was looking around. Joanna lived nearby in that tiny cottage, she didn't go to church, she kept away from what she called - *that sad little crowd* - but she kept talking about her work and she never showed any interest in *me*, not real interest. Everything was a bit of a joke to her, especially the church. Now why did you make her into this Ruby … a lonely, sad, desperate type … who wanted to help Belinda?'

Jake hesitated. This was worse than he had feared and how long was it going to take? 'Look William, you seem to be forgetting, it all needed to be changed so no one would recognise the village and various people who'd been in the newspapers, and you yourself of course. So I made it that you were the one turning *her* down. So what, does it matter? *She* loved *you.* Like all the other women chasing after you and fancying you like mad. As Jonathan in the Manor House you were an enigmatic sexy man!'

'But you've gone so far from the real story. Real life is much more interesting than your version.'

'Just a minute William. You're not listening to me. The novel is finished. I've worked hard, I thought you'd love it! But it doesn't matter if you *don't* love it. The publishers are ready to go. Then we split the profits and everybody's happy.'

William put his mug on the floor. 'I'm *not* happy. You should have let me read it first, you need to slow down.'

Jake paused. 'Well, could you perhaps make a note of

things you …'

'No Jake! There's too much, far too much! We need to *talk about it properly*. You've made me into a bumbling idiot who hasn't got a clue. Who thinks you can just house a bunch of disturbed women and everything will be rosy. Who thinks just talking to an abused teenager will sort her out. And there's the question of why did I become a priest in the first place, hmm? You never explained that. I told you all about it, how I had this imaginary friend, from a young age I seriously believed in Him and He helped me through a very lonely childhood while my mother carried on with her nephew right in front of my nose, though I was too young to know what was really going on.'

'Well, I did mention the imaginary friend, but I put that in a conversation with Ruby.'

'Yes, well I've just said, Joanna and I never talked like that, she never listened to me. She was worried about something she'd done, she hinted at it a few times, and then I found out. She wouldn't have understood or been sympathetic about why I desperately needed that friend, and then when …'

'But it doesn't matter! William, you're in a muddle, it doesn't matter! The book is fiction. *It didn't happen.* You were kind enough to agree I could use elements of your story, that's all it is. I know it must be a big adjustment for you to read the finished manuscript. Of course. A huge adjustment. But you did say you wanted to see it.'

'Of course I wanted to see it. But there's so much good stuff you've lost in the process!'

'Don't shout William! If you're going to shout we can't get anywhere. Let's talk calmly about this and read some of this again.' Jake waved the papers.

'But there's too much, there's just too much.' William held out his hands in a theatrical gesture of helplessness. He drank his tea.

'There's a lot to unravel,' said Jake, relieved that moment had passed. 'Let's take it a step at a time. I'll make notes. Perhaps a few things can be modified or altered so you're okay with them. He picked up a notebook and a biro. 'Could we sit at the table, perhaps in the kitchen? And by the way I'm starving, I only had a coffee at the motorway service station. You made it sound so urgent.'

'You're just not listening Jake.'

'Shall I go out and get a take-away? I need to eat William, *you* need to eat.'

'Okay I need to look at what we agreed,' said William, 'Let me see those lists. You go out if you want to, there's a fish and chips shop, go out of the drive, turn right, second left and it's at the end near the office building. You can usually park.'

'Alright. I'll go. But first Ruby. You now want me to make her more like Joanna really was. But why? And anyway won't Joanna guess it was her then? I wouldn't like to meet her in a dark alley if she knew we'd revealed what really happened and what she did. It could all get into the papers all over again! With respect William I don't think you've thought this through.'

'Well write these things down Jake. When you get back. One thing at a time. Ruby – Joanna – well you see I think the real Joanna is actually more interesting, wicked selfish people are more interesting than kind ones who don't have a clue what they are doing.'

'Is that what this is all about?' Jake gave William one list and was putting everything else back in his briefcase. 'Who wrote something to do with - 'goodness made interesting' was it about Tess of the d'Urbervilles?'

'Keep to the point!'

'If I make Joanna as she really was she'll guess and she'll sue us. In the book she's madly in love with Jonathan and a sad case who likes a bit of philosophy to help her get through the day. And she was taken in by the ghastly landlord.'

'Well yes, he was okay, he was pleasantly devious. And pleasantly repulsive. But that whole thing of her creating a new identity was a bit far-fetched.'

'She was shit scared of getting into trouble.'

'What Ruby was you mean. Joanna would never have

been so incompetent or naïve.'

'Look, Joanna had to be completely disguised. And of course, you *yourself* had to be completely disguised. Is there *anything* about Ruby you approve of?' Jake was standing by the sofa.

'Well …'

'I was pleased with the scenes in the hotel and Belinda losing her memory and all that, and imagining Tim was some sort of evil entity.'

'Yes … well. Your imagination certainly went to town with Belinda's imaginings.'

'I really got into the whole thing,' said Jake, 'The Book of Revelation is absolutely disgusting! I read it from beginning to end, I just couldn't believe it. So it set my mind working and one thing led to another.' As he spoke Jake watched William anxiously, there was no knowing what he would say next.

'Yes,' William said eventually. 'I see what you mean.'

'Obviously we never intended that I should write anything that could be recognised. I invented the petty criminals and Belinda getting locked out of the house.'

'Yes. That bit's okay, Jake.'

'And the psychiatric ward. I've got a friend who was in one, that helped, she was willing to tell me everything she remembered. They let her out before she was any better, in fact she was worse.'

'Yes … okay.'

'And cocaine addiction. Sadly I've got another friend who's in a bad way. His life's ruined. I'm surprised he's still alive.'

'Mmm.'

'Now we're getting somewhere,' said Jake. 'I'll go now. Then we can sit down and talk this through. Take one character at a time and sort it out.'

'So why was Jonathan so frantic to find Belinda?' William asked. They were now sitting at the kitchen table with another cup of tea and the remains of the fish and chips had been cleared away. Jake opened a bottle of wine he had bought and poured a glass and put it beside William who sat with the manuscript and several of Jake's lists in front of him.

'Well … because he cared. *Obviously*. Because he feared he shouldn't have brought her to meet strangers, uprooted her from his house and routine, all that kind of thing.'

'Looks like he'd been up to something and was terrified of the authorities.'

'No … it doesn't! Look William, you've got nothing to worry about here. Belinda *doesn't exist*, remember? I invented her. And her ridiculous father. And a lot of other things. We couldn't have all the real people you told me about, interesting though they were. And mostly criminals. You were spending time with some extraordinary people! But in the beginning the things you told me got my mind working. You must remember. I'd just come out uni, I'd read a lot of books but my life was very limited, I needed to get experiences to write about, and then I met you and as you know it's an unusual story. *Very* unusual.'

'Yes … well there's another thing …   the search in London, not very convincing.'

'You could say that, but these things happen.'

'He should have got help with her, she was discharged from the psychiatric ward too soon, she was obviously nowhere near able to cope.'

'Yes. But that's the reality of how things are, overcrowded wards, overworked staff. *Come on*! That gave possibilities for how it would develop. And Belinda *seemed* ok – most of the time. She learnt to behave as if she was coping.'

'And Susan's so-called predictions. Who is going to believe all that?'

'Look William, Susan is well disguised as Pamela. Have *you* ever known a psychic?'

'No. Load of rubbish. Convoluted stories.'

'Well one of my best friends is a psychic, and believe me that kind of thing does happen, and they do talk like that.

It was based on real life. Look we need to go back and work through this list, there are so many things you're unhappy with and we could be here for hours getting nowhere.' Jake drank his tea and watched William who was now drinking wine and leafing through the pages of the manuscript. What was this *really* about? A cry for help? Guilt? Loneliness and desperation?

'I did like George,' said William after a pause, 'He reminded me of someone I used to know. When I was seeing the Bishop and being interviewed by the Ecclesiastical Court and trying to explain my doubts and worries – which was of course a complete waste of time - I bumped into someone in town near the village, I used to know him as a child and it was remarkable that he'd moved down there. He was just like George, it was uncanny. Kind and supportive, he didn't judge me. I even thought maybe I would try and explain why everything had gone so wrong for me, there were good reasons for all of it. By the way I didn't *keep* the money, I gave it to people who needed it. No one discovered the blackmail and it was only the one time, and some people paid up and they often went on to make better decisions as a result. I posted money through people's doors in the middle of the night carefully wrapped in strong envelopes so the dogs wouldn't chew it up. People I knew who were desperate including Hugo's family. I mean Garth's family. Well it was only him and his sister by then in that shabby house. You mentioned a bit of that but it wasn't explained. That was annoying.'

'No, well …Let's start with the first person on the blackmail list. Can I see it, or will you read it out?'

William peered at the list and looked confused. Then he began to read. 'Michael Blane the surgeon. Had affair with Martina the widow living in the Old Vicarage. William learnt about it at dinner party at Manor House when Phillip and Maggie won the lottery.'

'Yes. Now stop there a minute. I did get Martina – now Annie and a TV presenter – to refer to the awful event when Michael was murdered by her ex's brother. Except that Michael became Augustus White, the surgeon who was murdered by a TV cameraman. Changed the details but left it vague but it added intensity to the scene when Pam and Natasha were searching for Belinda.'

'Mmm. Well next comes Joanna Smythe. Told me, that's me, William she'd given information to someone and she wasn't sure who it was – and then she was prosecuted and it all blew up. I blackmailed her before the press got hold of it, that was clever. Just quietened her down a bit for a while and gave some of her money to people who needed it. She didn't know it was me of course, no one ever knew. Had a bit of fun with some emails with her though, she told me things later on she wouldn't have done in real life ...'

'Yes. Well obviously I couldn't repeat that part of the story, so I made a decision that Ruby had a story about her niece drowning and she'd been blamed. That was completely different. Actually Jonathan encouraged her to get it straightened out at the beginning and it all got mixed up with her sad, jealous side ...'

'Mmm.'

'Who's next on the list?'

'Thomas Smith. Disguised as Maxwell the wealthy, womanising neighbour. Thomas was having affair with local MP he met at dinner party – it was obvious to anyone there what was going on. I blackmailed him successfully. Thomas dumped MP and started taking better care of his sick daughter. Well in your version Maxwell stopped seeing Phillipa and took better care of his sick wife.'

'Yes. I made those changes.'

'Maxwell was similar to Thomas. But Thomas would never have made porn moves, so that probably did the job. That was a nice touch. I was ok with Maxwell, he was suitably unpleasant and domineering.'

'Who's next William, we're making progress.'

William drained the glass and poured out more wine. Some for you Jake?'

'I won't, driving later.'

'Well, let's see … There's Gilbert Westlake here on the list, but you've not written anything about him. A feeble twit with a nasty wife, I remember. And – what happened was, he got all wound up and thought the blackmailer was a van driver he'd been bribed by to keep quiet about an accident when an old woman on a bicycle got killed. He paid though, and no one knew. But you haven't given him another name and he never appeared in your version.'

'No but I had to make these decisions. The story was getting too complicated and really all that was ancient history when the narrative began.'

William drank some more wine.

'In any case …' Jake began nervously.

'What?'

'Well it's a lot for people to swallow.'

'*What is!*'

'Well. *You're* a lot for people to swallow. The real you. I had to … create Jonathan. He was a bit scatty, a bit disorganised, unstable. Fundamentally unreliable. But … look can we leave the list of blackmail victims for the moment? There's another list here, all the biblical quotes, how did you feel about all that? I had to be selective, I had to choose my moments.'

'Yes, well …I suppose there were times when I almost felt Jonathan *was* myself and I was raging along with him. Yes. We could go through each scene.'

'But that would take *hours*. And what would it achieve?'

'Let me find something …' William was turning the pages, 'Now where was it … oh yes, when he was reading about Saint Paul. It was a bit long winded all that.'

'Well, you could make a list of what bothers you, that would be the most helpful thing. Can you do that and email me? But to be honest I also thought it was all very shocking, I've never really read the bible like that or gone to church much, so that was quite an education for me. And surely these things must haunt people!'

'Well ... they certainly haunt me! Though of course I was breaking the rules of the Church by questioning the bible. Seems incredible in this day and age doesn't it. Now going back to the story you told of Jonathan as a little boy ...'

'Well, it was like you told me, I just changed some details. I didn't put in that you remember your father raging and striking your mother, I said he left when you were a baby.'

'Yes, now you could have made that clearer, the effect it had and how I had to have the imaginary friend as I had no one ... I mean no one knows about that, just you and me really so there would have been no danger in including it as it was. I was a withdrawn, lonely child, and my mother didn't do much right, but she did take me to church and I met a kind woman who taught the Sunday school and I became fascinated by the stories ...'

Jake stopped writing and sat back. Maybe there was another bottle of wine somewhere? It would probably help William just to talk, he was obviously in a bad way.

'Jesus was so wonderful. So magical. Can you imagine what it was like to be there?'

'Mmm.'

'To just follow and listen. Even if you didn't understand all the parables. To see the healings. To hear His voice. I imagined I was there, I made up stories about things He said to me, my imaginary Friend, He was like a Father and I was special to Him. And then of course He was like a friend and teacher and magician and guide. He was everything. You couldn't explain Him, He didn't really explain himself very clearly, that was part of the problem later. As I got older I tried to get my head around the whole Jewish prophecy thing, but it's hard for a modern mind to do that. Perhaps I'll have another go when I've got this bloody house under control. And the whole Roman thing, the cruelty, the *unbelievable* cruelty, the fear ...'

Jake drank his cold tea and waited. William had occasionally spoken like this, usually when he was drunk.

But now he had gone a bit quiet and seemed to be thinking.
'And what happened?' said Jake, 'With you. Can you understand what happened? Where it all went wrong? I didn't know everything you see, so I had to make it up, and yes, there wasn't time to explain it all that evening, you're right. And I didn't think I should ask you more about it, I was going to have to re-create so much anyway.'

'Well, I grew up. I realised a lot of it was in my mind because I needed it to be, the father thing, the guide thing. But though I distanced myself from that part of it, I had already started along what you could call a safe path, a protected path, I needed that and people around I could rely on, I was too insecure and pathetic to branch out and do anything else - I needed to study *something*, I liked history and theology, it was interesting and I was with people who were – boring, predictable and caring in their own little way … one thing led to another and in the end I was ordained.'

'And what was it … *really* like?'

'You mean …'

'Being ordained?'

William drank some more wine. 'It was very sacred. Very holy. It's like God was there.'

'So … sorry I just don't understand. What happened to all that?'

'Well, that was one thing. Like when Annabelle and I went to Assisi before we were married. The Church of St Catherine. You walked into the dark interior and something overwhelmingly loving and wonderful hit you, it was in the air and the fabric of the building, or perhaps it was coming from all those devout people, it was tangible.'

Jake sat very still and thought about Pamela's dream, he didn't want to disturb what William might say next. But again the silence lengthened.

'So … that feeling, that presence … what happened. Wasn't it always there?'

'Well, these things can be interpreted in different ways.

We can deceive ourselves. All religions and faiths have these elements, this devotion and the search for transcendence. It doesn't *prove* anything. Other things got in the way, I told you. Once you start to distrust what you're reading in the bible you can't go back, that coloured everything.'

'Did you feel you were a chosen one?'

'Maybe for a while. But don't we all think we're chosen ones? My life was empty of anything else then. It was before I questioned ideas and found them repulsive and cruel and unfair and incomprehensible.' William got up shakily and went to open a cupboard and selected another bottle of wine. 'This won't be chilled but never mind. A glass for you?'

'No, I won't thanks, driving later.'

'I mean I could have persevered with it, I did try for a while. Hung onto that, whatever it was, believed in it to the exclusion of everything else. But alternatively I could have been an Indian holy man sitting in a cave for eighty years, or a Buddhist monk in Tibet ... why is *that* any different?'

And what was it like when ... well when you confessed to the Bishop?'

'Oh that... well confessing was easy. That I had doubts. I didn't feel *guilty* that I had doubts, but I was treated as guilty. Explaining and communicating was impossible. These people put up barriers around themselves to protect it, whatever *it* is ... There was no compassion, no attempt to see what might be behind it, I was a nuisance for the Ecclesiastical Court, an unusual case for them to deal with, they were confused and embarrassed ... eventually they were relieved to get rid of me. Lifetime Prohibition. Conduct Unbecoming and Inappropriate to the Office of a Clerk in Holy Orders.' William drank some wine.

'So – did you stop being a priest then? Was there a moment when that ended?'

'Well officially it was over. But not a moment, it was gradual and drawn out. I knew my own mind but *they* didn't, they wanted to be sure. They were so sad while I was ... relieved. I didn't *devalue* what I had experienced, I just couldn't believe it was what it seemed to be before. It will always be part of me. But I had to remove all the words and just let it be – whatever *it* was. The words that are used ... in creeds and so on, a load of incomprehensible nonsense.'

Jake glanced at his watch. It was getting dark outside.

'When I was first ordained I didn't feel close to anyone but I knew where I was with them, I knew how to behave and what to do. The people were calm, predictable, but you could relax with them, no pressure. I found public speaking easy. I enjoyed writing sermons. I found listening to people easy. You usually didn't have to say much at all. People had *their* idea of who I was. Once I was wearing the uniform. I went along with it, I'd already read some of the bad stuff but like everyone else I glossed over it and took what I wanted. But then when the training was finally over and I was more on my own I began to see so many people were living in misery and confusion and creating their own hell. And telling them about Jesus became impossible, farcical, who was I give them rules and expect them to be able to understand? Did I tell them they were almost certainly going to burn in hell for eternity? How absurd! And the creeds were a load of abstract ideas and concepts that none of us can possibly understand, mostly invented by the Emperor Constantine and his henchmen, and we know what *they* were like! So if I couldn't talk to *them* about it well what use was it to *anyone!* The ones who were already there with it, well they didn't need anything from me, they were inhabiting their own comfortable little worlds and they didn't want them disturbed. They knew they were alright, they were the *chosen ones* and they were safe. Never mind that they were selfish and judgemental and unkind and narrow minded. Never mind that the world outside was full of pain and anguish. What did they care? So I was just muddling along but all the time these odd sayings were preying on my mind and they wouldn't go away. I was bound to reach that point when I couldn't pretend to myself anymore, it was just a question of time.'

'You sound like Jonathan now,' said Jake.

'Well, yes, alright. And Jonathan sounds like me. *Some* of the time ...'

'Of course there's a lot I didn't know and all that ...'

'Well, yes. But ... obviously you had to improve me, I'm a dreadful human being. I broke the law and got away with it, I use women and don't care, I drink, I think bad thoughts and I'm lazy. Look at this house. I'm broke and unemployed. Well various people sort of employed me for a while when I was abroad, all quite casual of course, and actually I must admit, I stole some money during those weeks ... but it soon ran out ... I'm very bitter and angry about my childhood and old and ugly enough to be able to get some help and put it behind me. But I don't, I wallow in self-pity.'

'Mmm'

'But I've lost something ... huge, and I can't get it back.'

'Yes. Jonathan said that.'

They managed a smile and sat in silence. 'Thank goodness you're a hard worker,' said William, 'At least one of us is worth something.'

'We're all worth *something*,' said Jake.

'Now ... we've had a talk about it, are you feeling any better? Can I make some more tea?' Jake got up and went to fill the kettle and stood eating cold chips out of the paper wrappings.

'Well ...' William stood up, 'All that tea and wine has gone straight through,' he said and went out of the kitchen.

Jake acted swiftly. He retrieved a small packet of white powder from his jacket pocket. The wine glass was nearly empty and the bottle next to it was half full. He opened the packet and emptied the powder into the glass and watched it dissolve. He poured a little of the remaining wine into the glass and went back to the sink.

He was just bringing two cups of tea over when William came back. 'So can you make a list and email me? Put down your thoughts about some changes you want,' said Jake, putting the mugs on the table and sitting down.

'Well …'

'It'll help you clarify it after our discussion don't you think?'

'I suppose so.' William drained the glass. 'Shall I keep this list then?'

'Yes, you keep it.'

William's hand rested on the manuscript on the table.

Eventually Jake eased the list from under William's pale, motionless hand and stood holding it and looking down at the unconscious face. What *you're* worth is another matter. Someone lurking at a dinner party, waiting for his chance. Putting two and two together and making five. They're just names to you aren't they, Thomas Smith, a local MP and a sick daughter. Just names that you gave me permission to play with, you weren't particularly interested in my writing, you were absorbed in your own dramas, ours was just an evening in a pub like so many others. What you didn't know was that the MP was my big *sister,* my beautiful Isobel. Who had worked and worked to get selected as a candidate, competing with ex public schoolboys and rich women, and then worked and worked to get elected, tirelessly pounding the streets. My mother was ill but she made it to Isobel's celebrations after the by-election, she was so proud. I took her back home afterwards and she went downhill fast, but at least she never knew what happened after that.

Isobel had achieved so much but she had no connections whatsoever because she came from an ordinary family. So then she goes to a dinner party, her neighbours Phillip and Maggie have won the lottery and are so delighted they want to share their good fortune so they fill the Manor House with trestle tables and hire good caterers. They invite anyone they can think of. And my beautiful Isobel meets Thomas Smith, Mr Handsome Nice Guy. Never mind that he's married and his daughter urgently needs medical treatment. Isobel's bewitched by her Knight in Shining Armour, and now she has all the connections she could possibly want. Though I doubt the quality of *them* if they were friends of *his*.

And there you are, dog collar on or off, it doesn't make any difference. Listening and waiting. There's your chance. And then, little whispers to the press, money has been changing hands in sordid places, and then, bingo, the extra special titbit for the newshounds, Mr Criminal Vicar. *What a find eh!* Never mind that he gave money to the poor and needy, who would believe that silly little detail! Luckily for you the Church Authorities don't appear to have seen those articles. To them he was just a muddled fool who had sadly betrayed his calling.

And what happened to Isobel hmm! A local issue blew up, it would have been hard for an experienced MP to deal with, it was complex and there were no right answers and there were powerful individuals fighting on both sides. Press intrusion, lies, harassment. Reporters started camping outside her house. It went on for weeks. She had loved her Knight in Shining Armour and she didn't know why he had abandoned her, it didn't make sense. She tried to pick up the pieces, do her work, escape from the photographers. But nothing could repair the damage, she was weakened.

And how did I know all this hmm? Well, it was the moment in the pub when you started writing the list of blackmail victims … after we agreed about me writing some sort of story. I looked at the list and realised what lay behind what had happened with Isobel and her new lover. You probably didn't give her a thought, why should you, too busy being Robin Hood. When we met it was weeks after this had happened and her life had taken a tragic turn – after not being elected again she got ill and lost her strength. She sold her lovely house and bought a miserable little flat and then there was trouble with other residents who were a nightmare, and disputes about the building and who was going to pay for what, and it went on and on, I have tried to help. She's a shadow of her former self.

Now you might say that's hardly your fault, but it was

your thoughtless action that made her life go in a new direction. You were quite proud of blackmailing Thomas Smith, you thought he would go back to his wife and look after his daughter, and everything would be rosy. Well, he did of course. You didn't see Isobel as a victim, you didn't *see* her at all. You didn't know the events surrounding her were all going to blow up in the papers and she was so heartbroken, she couldn't cope.

Some of those articles were vague about who you were. But when I realised that night that you were behind it all I did wonder … should I really spend time with this writing project … I had to think long and hard about *that*. You didn't know that I knew all that, of course, I quietly took all the information away with me. But in the end it was too good a story, strange and unusual. *You* are strange and unusual. So I started work, I had no idea how things would develop. I turned Thomas into Maxwell, the wealthy neighbour, and of course I watered him down but Maxwell was a still nasty piece of work with a terrible jealousy problem.

And you, you're a nasty piece of work, y*ou're damaged* Mr Criminal Vicar, you've damaged yourself and others, you've done it and look at you now. Jonathan changed, I didn't know how that was going to turn out and he *was* like you in the beginning, he was just brooding about the bible and jumping into bed with Pam and in a muddle about helping Belinda, but then he came to life. He was kind. He was sad and vulnerable and he struggled. He adored Pam. He tried to help people. He really honestly didn't understand all that bible stuff and he really couldn't handle it. He's *real* …

Jake picked up the wine glass and mugs of tea and rinsed everything in the sink, got tissues out of his pocket and put the glass back on the table, half filling it from what was left in the bottle. He wiped everything he had touched, the mugs, the backs of chairs, the table, the door handles. He slid the list into his briefcase and found a plastic bag in a cupboard for the bulky paper manuscript and wiped the handles to the cupboard. He looked around one more time, and then went out to the bathroom and then wiped everything again before silently letting himself out of the house. He drove down the drive and turned into the road, no one noticed him in the dusk.

As he reached the motorway he took extra care because he knew how tired he was and several things occurred to him as he covered the miles – thank goodness they didn't get on to a discussion about Hugo! He had come alive too in a most unexpected way - one of life's utter tragedies. And what part did Marissa play in it all – she was a liar and a troublemaker. And there were so many other things … cocaine addiction? And William hadn't seemed to want to talk much about Belinda, perhaps it was all too much for him to take in while he was in such a depressed state of mind himself? It was almost too much for *him,* Jake, the author to take in – where did these people come from and why was it they all had a life of their own?

A better title had been in his mind for a while, it had a rather satisfying double meaning – A MAN WHO SEEMED REAL - a story of love, lies, fear and kindness

Publish and be damned.

ABOUT THE AUTHOR

Elizabeth Tebby Germaine has also written non-fiction books.

The books on history happened because she had some striking original documents and photos and was given more.

LIVES IN BURMA AND CHINA 1927-1951

STORIES OF SURVIVAL IN BURMA WW2

The book on piano playing is based on ideas used during years of piano teaching and playing.

PIANO PRACTISING – fresh and effective ways of working

The violin/viola duets are based on material she would carry around when teaching string instruments in schools and conducting beginners' orchestras. They contain finger charts, basic theory, arrangements of folk music and original compositions.

REALLY USEFUL VIOLIN DUETS! beginners to grade 3

REALLY USEFUL VIOLA DUETS!   beginners to grade 3

www.elizabethtebbygermaine.co.uk

Printed in Great Britain
by Amazon

53774550R00145